Reader Reviews

The Dreamer- the Beginning is a captivating tale, giving a convincing and passionate voice to a young man from humankind's early history. It is well researched and based on scientific study, lending additional credence to a very creative story involving a time in our history that is very much shrouded in mystery and conjecture.
~ N. I. Bourdeau

As an avid reader I am always excited to step out of the box and read something different, The Dreamer Series delivers! A delightful journey set during the last Ice Age brings to life a Neanderthal family; their lifestyle, daily struggles to survive, love and loss. The author delivers a story set in prehistoric times described so well, so vividly it leaves the reader wanting more! Write faster, we want more!
~ Donna R. Fox

Fascinating saga of the times and life amid a Neanderthal family as seen from the perspective of a man with a special gift and a love of his family. It's just like being there; you become involved with their trials and joys. The dreams give you a glimpse of future dangers and events, leading you through an engrossing journey.
~ C. H. Beusee

This is not the usual type of book that I read but I was fascinated and could not put it down. The author did so much research that it felt like I was reading a true story of a family and how they lived during that time! I wish the author could write faster so I could get my hands on those next ones...keep them coming! ~ L. B. Collins

This is a unique and interesting read. I couldn't put it down–almost missed my flight! ~ J . Simmons

Just like The Dreamer – The Beginning, once I started reading Dreamer II – The Gathering I could not put it down. It is so interesting with a great personal story line. And I love all the historical information. After reading the first two books of this series I cannot wait to get the third one! Keep it up! ~ Patti Stribling Lauer

I read this book and thoroughly enjoyed it...so exciting that you can't put it down. Kept me on the edge of my seat. Great writing. ~ J. Stuller

I've read the whole Clan of the Cave Bear series by Jean Auel, and I was bummed when it ended; you got the ancients going again in totally different happenings and people's! I will probably read all three again. Can't wait for book four! ~ John G. Smith

Books in this series:

The Dreamer ~ The Beginning (2016)

The Dreamer II ~ The Gathering (2017)

The Dreamer III ~ The People of the Wolves (2018)

The Dreamer IV ~ The Cave of Bones (2019)

The Dreamer V ~ The Blood-Red Skies (2020)

The Dreamer VI ~ The Outsiders (2021)

The Dreamer VII ~ The Challenge Circle (2022)

Coming in 2023! Final book in series!

The Dreamer VIII ~ The Talking Stones

The Dreamer VI

THE

CHALLENGE CIRCLE

The Dreamer Book Series

By E. A. Meigs

Dreamer Literary Productions, LLC

2022

For information regarding this novel or permissions

to reproduction selections from this work, please

visit

Dreamer Literary Productions at:

www.dreamerliteraryproductions.com

ISBN: 978-1-7350558-6-2

First Edition

Cover photo by my friend Paula Krugerud

www.PaulaKrugerudPhotography.com

I dedicate this book to my siblings.

I am so grateful to have you in my life.

 Fonts used in this novel 

Papyrus was created by Chris Costello in 1982.

Garamond was designed by Claude Garamond in the early 1530's.

The Dreamer VII

❧

THE
CHALLENGE
CIRCLE

The Dreamer VII ~ The Challenge Circle continues an ongoing saga that follows the life of a young Neanderthal man. The story takes place at a time in history when much of the world was experiencing brutal climatic changes and man's position within Nature's food chain was indeed perilous. The Dreamer VII is written as a stand-alone novel, meaning it is not necessary to have read the preceding volumes to understand the plot. An updated version of the original Introduction is included for those who are new to this time period.

Introduction

This tale takes place approximately 40,000 BCE (Before Common Era), when the last Ice Age was well underway. At the peak of the Great Glacial Maximum, nearly one-third of the Earth's surface was hidden beneath a thick layer of ice. A substantial percentage of the planet's moisture was frozen solid, causing the oceans to recede and coastlines to become greatly expanded.

At that time the Eurasian landscape consisted of vast, wind-scoured tundra and small pockets of woodland populated by at least three groups of people: the Neanderthal, Homo sapiens (in this case, the Cro-Magnon), and the Denisovan. These populations probably coexisted in parts of Eurasia for only a relatively short period of time, geologically speaking. It was likely that they lived a seasonally nomadic lifestyle. We can only guess at what their lives would have been like: their languages, their social behaviors, their spirituality. Due to the passage of time and the impermanent nature of most materials they would have used in their day-to-day lives, there is little to tell us about their existence besides the tantalizing clues left by their remains, their tools, their art, their burials, and . . . their refuse.

Analyses of fossilized Neanderthal skeletons show that the males averaged five feet, five inches to five feet, six inches in height. The tallest Neanderthal men found to date were five feet, nine inches. The females were five feet to five feet, one inch. Their bones were about one-third stouter than ours. They were heavily muscled and had tremendous upper-body strength. The Neanderthal had the largest brain size of any known humans. Initial DNA testing showed that they likely had fair coloring: red to auburn hair, green or hazel eyes, and pale, probably freckled skin. Later genetic research on Neanderthal individuals found in different parts of Eurasia revealed that some had brown hair, brown eyes, and dusky skin. It is now considered likely that the Neanderthal had the same variety of skin tones, hair and eye coloring as do modern Eurasian people.

The Neanderthal roamed the Earth for roughly 200,000 years (longer, if you include the proto-Neanderthal) before their trail went cold around 37,000 to 42,000 BCE. That said, the Neanderthal may have persisted to eke out a living for some time afterward. However, since most modern humans outside of sub-Saharan Africa share between one and four percent Neanderthal DNA, it would appear that the Neanderthal are still with us even now, albeit in diluted form.

Homo sapiens may have first appeared in the European fossil record as early as (approximately) 200,000 BCE, but more conservative estimates range from 40,000 to 65,000BCE. The previously mentioned Cro-Magnon have been dated to 42,000 to 47,000 BCE. They were named for the rock shelter in which they were discovered in the Dordogne Valley in France, in 1868. At one time, early anatomically modern humans in Europe were often referred to as Cro-Magnons, but that term has since fallen out of favor. However, since these novels take place almost entirely on the ancient lands we now know as France, my Homo sapiens characters actually are Cro-Magnons.

Over a period of tens of thousands of years the predecessors of the Cro-Magnon migrated out of Africa, gradually making their way into Eurasia. The men averaged about five feet, nine inches in height, but it is thought that some taller individuals may have been upwards of six and a half feet. Like the Neanderthal, their brains were also bigger than those of today's people. They are believed to have had dark coloring: brown to black hair, brown eyes, and shades of skin ranging from tan to brown. (Blond hair and blue eyes are a relatively new development in modern humans, having first appeared about 6,000 to 12,000 years ago, long after the pinnacle of the Ice Age, but possibly coinciding with the end of that last glacial period.)

This novel reintroduces the Denisovans to the series. Not much is known of these people at this time. What little information we have comes from a few teeth, a handful of bone fragments, a number of artifacts, and what can be gleaned from the study of their DNA. The physical characteristics of the bones suggest that the Denisovans were a sturdy people, perhaps with a build resembling that of the Neanderthals. Their teeth, on the other hand, were quite large, about one-third bigger than that of either the average modern human or Neanderthal. We might then surmise that they probably had a heavy jaw to accommodate those teeth. DNA from a finger bone disclosed that it was taken from someone with dark hair, brown eyes, and brown skin.

When we consider the artifacts that have been attributed to the Denisovans, it must be acknowledged that they were an intelligent, skilled folk. Their needles (dated to approximately 50,000 to 60,000 BCE) look much like our needles of today. A bracelet of green stone shows that they had sufficient technology to drill holes and to shape and polish stone. We can only hope that further discoveries bring us more data on these intriguing people.

* * *

It is my humble opinion that after so many years of existence in a world that often presented extreme challenges, these intelligent beings would have been at the top of their game in leveraging the available resources to ensure their own comfort and the continuation of their species. Some indications suggest that early man was potentially much more advanced than is generally credited, and it is my guess that we will continue to be surprised by what is revealed when ongoing and future anthropological studies peel back layers of time as we search for ourselves within the lives of our ancestors.

* * *

An animal index is presented at the end of this novel for the convenience of those unfamiliar with the animals of Ice Age Europe. It gives basic information about most of the creatures mentioned in this book. It might be useful to know, for example, that a wisent is a species of European bison, and that the animal North Americans refer as a moose is called an elk in Europe.

* * *

This is a work of fiction and it is not intended to hold up to scientific scrutiny. I merely seek to tell a story that is set amid this ancient backdrop. I have peopled it with those whose lives — when broken down to their most basic elements — would not have been so different from ours: sharing care and concern for loved ones, enduring all life's hardships, and reveling in serendipitous moments of love, beauty, and joy when they grace us with their presence.

 **Chapter One** 

I hear their calls. I turn back to stare into the icy blasts of wind-driven snow and get a glimpse of the group as they struggle to make headway against the raging blizzard. Just then they become bogged down in a deep drift, and all is obscured by a curtain of white.

It was a wet snow. I could feel each snowflake hit my face with a light splat.

"Puh-Puh! Puh-Puh!" A voice called. A child's voice; it was my daughter Pony. But Pony was not here. How did she come to be by my side? How had I not noticed her presence before this? I must bring her home – she should not be out in this weather!

"Wake up, Puh-Puh!" Pony's voice became more insistent. "See what I caught!"

Jarred from my Dream, I opened my eyes and I found myself face to face with the gaping mouth of a fish. I started, momentarily taken aback. The creature was still quite alive. Each frantic attempt to thrash itself free of Pony's secure grip sprayed droplets of water, making Pony squint against the liquid onslaught and liberally sprinkling me, as well.

"That is a trout," I said to Pony, wiping the sleep and droplets of trout-splashings from my face with one hand, while simultaneously wrapping an arm around her to pull her to my side with the other. "And a very nice one, at that."

I must have succumbed to a nap after consuming a heavy midday meal. The predawn waking for an early-morning hunt had meant a return just in time to process our kill before sitting down to partake in my share of a number of roasted rabbits, whose delicious aroma still permeated the air.

Pony grinned as she sat down beside me, and she turned the fish toward her to better view her prize.

"That is what Uncle Inlee said," Pony told me. "*A nice trout!* It has freckles, just like you, Puh-Puh! See?"

"Indeed," I said, smiling at her observation. "Do you want me to help you clean it?"

"Yes, Puh-Puh," Pony said with a nod, blinking at the shower of water the struggling fish again sent her way. "He is fighting very hard and my hands grow tired. Perhaps we could clean it right now?"

"Yes, my little one," I said, standing up and taking the trout from her.

Pony seemed relieved to relinquish the fish; she too rose to her feet.

"Uncle Inlee is helping Fox with his fish," Pony announced. "Fox caught four trout and one tiny fish he returned to the water. He said, *Go now and grow big! I will come back and catch you another time!*" Pony giggled at this, with her soft piping laugh.

Pony was my eldest daughter. At six winters old, she was a lithe sprig of a girl, but quite strong for a child of her size. Her older brother Fox was seven winters old. Of all my children, Fox was the only one who resembled me. He was a very large boy with red-gold hair, pale green eyes, and freckles. His three sisters, Pony, Raven, and Lily, took after their mother, my mate, Morning Star, sharing her daintiness, her lovely black hair, dark eyes, and dusky skin — all but Lily, who had fair skin and hazel eyes, and whose brown tresses showed glints of red.

The trout seemed to be losing some of its vigor as I carried it to the trunk of a fallen tree often used for cleaning various fish and fowl. The tree had been dead for many years, and most of its bark had come loose a long time ago. Its trunk had broken off at about hip-height, and the remaining upper branches acted as supports to keep the work surface nearly level to the ground. It still had a slight slant, however, I found that to be beneficial, as it served to let the blood and bodily fluids run off as I gutted the creature.

Pony tagged along, eager to watch.

I drew my knife from its sheath at my belt and made a slice along the fish's belly.

"We do not want to eat those parts," Pony said as I removed the fish's intestines and organs.

"Not me, anyway," I concurred.

"Fox found a really big spider down by the lake," Pony informed me. "He picked it up and looked at it. Then he chased Raven down the beach with it."

"Did he?" I responded mildly.

"Oh, yes," Pony answered. "But Uncle Inlee called him back and told Fox he must never do things like that. Uncle Inlee said to Fox that families must always take care of one another and we must not do things to tease or scare them."

"That is true," I agreed, pleased that Inlee had made this point to Fox, Pony, and Raven.

"Besides," Pony went on, "Uncle Inlee said what if you teased someone so often that when something dangerous really did come along and you tried to warn them – what if they did not believe you? And they were eaten by a – a bear or something. He made Fox promise not to frighten people anymore."

I nodded as I looked around for a branch I could use as a spit. Leaving the now-deceased fish on the tree trunk, I selected a slim branch on a bush and snapped it free. After I removed the extra twigs, leaves, and loose bark and sharpened one end, Pony queried, "Puh-Puh, may I put the fish on the stick?"

She had watched me do this countless times.

"How about if I help you?" I asked.

Pony grinned and nodded. I held the fish with one hand and provided the extra push to help her skewer the fish through its open mouth, until the stick had passed lengthwise through its body. Just then, my mate Morning Star approached, accompanied by our youngest daughter, Lily, and our dog, Raena. Morning Star smiled as she caught sight of us.

"I am happy to see you are refreshed from your nap, Tris," Morning Star said with just a hint of jest in her voice.

"Muh-Muh, look what I caught!" Pony proudly displayed the trout to her mother. "Fox has four more!"

"Such a lot of fish!" Morning Star marveled. "I am so pleased we will have fresh fish with our evening meal."

Raena seemed impressed as well. She sniffed the fish inquisitively, tongue darting out as though she might like to lick it. But Raena was a well-behaved dog, and she did not follow through with the impulse.

"Uncle Inlee told us it was because there were so many bugs on the water," Pony said. "The fish came into our special spot and we caught them in our nets!"

The *special spot* was a place where the lake's shoreline had been altered to make an inlet where we hoped fish could be more easily trapped with nets or a barrier made of twigs. These trappings had not worked well, since it was difficult to imprison the intended victims in the inlet quickly enough to prevent them from escaping. But when fish were enticed to the shallows by a recent insect hatch that was just too much to resist, the special spot did provide a place where fish might be scooped up by a net.

Fox and Uncle Inlee had created a large circular net with rocks secured to the edges that could be thrown over unsuspecting fish, allowing them to potentially catch multiple fish with one cast. The trick was to fling it just right so that it opened as it spun through the air before descending into the water. Pony, on the other hand, preferred to use a net that was stitched to an old snowshoe frame. It made a big splash when she thrust it into the water, but sometimes she did manage to snag a fish, even if it was all she could do to hold onto some of the bigger ones.

* * *

The past few years had brought about many changes to our lives. At Uncle Inlee's invitation we had left the familiar comfort of our clan's old compound to relocate our families to the vast woodlands to the north. Our former home had been occupied by generations of my kin for as far back as anyone could remember. At first, it was just my clan. Then, after Morning Star and I were paired, her family, who were of a tribe belonging to The People from the East, had set up housekeeping on our compound. Next, when my sister Ru was paired with Bror, a new home had been created for them. And the same for Morning Star's sister Petal and her mate, Fish Hawk, and my brother Ty and his mate, Aessa. Lastly, a group of men from The People of the Wolves clan had joined us for a short while, but they did not stay. They were adventuresome and restless to move on, in hopes of finding mates of their own. Even now that we had relocated some distance away, they stopped in to visit each time they were in the area. However, the remoteness of this place meant that we seldom saw anyone outside of our families.

We missed our old home; the small but cozy hillside dwellings, each chopped and clawed from the hillside, and enlarged as new family members were added; the cheerful stream of burbling water; and the protective summertime canopy of leaves overhead. But our new setting offered many benefits. Healthy populations of game animals and migrating herds of reindeer that passed nearby each spring and fall meant there was never any lack of meat. A lake and a river were within easy walking distance, so water was plentiful as well. And the forest, while it consisted primarily of conifers and birch, was comparatively untouched. The woodland surrounding our former home had been subject to firewood harvests for years untold, and worse, a wildfire had destroyed many of the standing trees that remained. This had left only the newly sprouted saplings and old trees large enough to withstand the fire but much too big to be felled by our axes.

Here, the gently sloping land did not provide enough depth to create the same hillside in-ground homes, thus we were forced to hack our way into the ground with red deer antler picks, giant deer antler shovels, and digging sticks. It was not just the heavily compacted soil, but also the thick tangles of roots that slowed our progress. Our springtime arrival had given us a window of warmer weather in which we could reside in hastily erected temporary homes while we worked on creating more permanent structures. The necessity of continual hunts, hewing of firewood, making and maintaining our weapons and tools, made for a busy season indeed.

We would soon begin our second summer here. We were still working on our homes, adding little touches and comforts that time had not previously permitted but that now could be completed. I especially enjoyed being near my uncles, who were older brothers to my late mother. My Muh's parents had cut all ties with her after she had defied them to become paired with Puh, so I had not met my uncles Inlee and Trae until recent years. I had found them to be intelligent, fine company, and skilled huntsmen, but it was not until they had become our neighbors that I was able to spend any amount of time with them.

Uncle Inlee was my Muh's oldest living brother. Despite his advanced age, having reached his fifty-first winter this past year, he was still a surprisingly strong and active man. Like many in my Muh's clan, he was tall. Uncle Trae was his younger brother. Trae was also taller than average, but somewhat shorter than Inlee. Trae, at forty-nine winters, had suffered several grievous injuries over the years. His back was bent, and a bad knee had left him with a painful limp. Both uncles had families, but most of their children had moved away and were now adults with families of their own.

Before our arrival, the residents at this site had dwindled to four adults and four children, of whom Inlee had been the only one still capable of hunting large-prey animals. We had stopped by as often as we could to help him bring down game. It was their need for assistance, coupled with the lack of resources at our former home that drove the necessity of making the long, tedious trips required to bring our families here. In spite of all the difficulties, I was glad we had come.

* * *

Puh and I had slipped away early this morning in hopes of bringing down fresh meat – perhaps a deer. Luck had been with us, and we had managed to bring in a young roebuck. He was small, but he would provide a good meal for our evening sup, which now would be supplemented with fresh fish. After the little buck had been bled out, he had been promptly butchered and his organs harvested so they could be cooked and immediately consumed. By now, his carcass had been roasting most of the day. This meal typified the kind of eating we had been treated to since our arrival. No more eking out a living on gamey old boars and whatever else we could find. Now we could be selective about our kills and take down only the choicest animals.

When Fox, Raven, Uncle Inlee, and Morning Star's father, Black Wolf, returned from the lake, Fox proudly showed off his gutted fish.

"Look, Puh-Puh," Fox said, holding the fish before me. "We threw the net many times and caught these fish."

"They are very nice," I told him, nodding with approval.

"Come, Fox," Uncle Inlee said, motioning to my son, "let us cut a few spits from the bush and place these beauties over the coals."

Fox nodded, grinning broadly, and followed Uncle Inlee, fish still in hand.

"I want to go, too!" Pony stated.

"Me, too!" Raven added, tagging along with them.

Black Wolf, Morning Star, and I watched them leave. Unlike his petite daughter – my mate, Morning Star – Black Wolf was an enormously tall man. He stood a head higher than Uncle Inlee and I. Black Wolf was also conspicuously hairy, covered in a thick coating of black body hair. At this moment, I noted that his preponderance of chest hair gave the appearance of a furry animal trying to escape from the neck opening of his tunic.

Black Wolf also had a deep voice that seemed to come all the way up from his toes. His head was adorned with a curious hairstyle, sometimes referred to as his "spider hat," as the numerous braids sprouting from the top of his head looked something like the legs of a huge spider. Black Wolf's coiffure sometimes raised the eyebrows of those not well acquainted with him, but his great size meant that it was seldom mentioned. That being said, he was my father's oldest and closest friend, and a good friend to the rest of our family as well.

Black Wolf scratched at his intricately braided beard thoughtfully, and then he gave a low chuckle.

"It is as though the children have three grandfathers!" Black Wolf mused. "But I am pleased. Inlee teaches them many things."

"I am pleased, too," I said. "I had never seen anyone net fish before. I had heard of it, of course, but never seen it done. The basket traps we used at the coast would not work well here."

"Yes, there are no tides here," Black Wolf agreed. "Now that we are too far away to make our annual trips to the shore, I miss eating shellfish and feeling the hot sand on my sore feet. The lake is a nice substitute, though; it provides plenty of fresh fish, water lily rhizomes, cattails, and bulrushes. I am even learning to throw the cast net. Inlee told me that the taller you are, the easier it is to throw the net. What with my height, I have certainly found that to be true."

Little Lily perked up at hearing water lilies mentioned.

"Water lilies?" She repeated. "Lily go in water?"

"Not today, my sweet little one," Black Wolf said, gently chucking her under the chin.

"Yes, not today," Morning Star confirmed. Then she went on, "I prefer the lake. It is much safer than the ocean. At first I found life at the coast to be enthralling; the sea was so beautiful, and there were so many foods to be harvested there. But after that terrible storm swept over us, I do not mind if we are unable to go to the coast anymore."

"Well, it is not only too far, but we will have no time to journey there," I said. "We still have too much work to do on our homes. Also, since we are overrun with young dogs, I foresee a journey to the mountains in the near-future."

Morning Star suddenly smiled broadly.

"I have not seen Cousin Gray Elk and his family in such a long while," she said. "Perhaps this time, the children and I might accompany those traveling to the mountains."

Black Wolf and I exchanged glances. Gray Elk was his cousin, a man who made his living breeding and trading dogs. My dog Raena had come from Gray Elk's collection of canines, and her pups regularly added to Gray Elk's stock. Last year's litter had consisted of six puppies, all of which mysteriously died while still quite small. I had never seen anything like it before, nor had I since. Most dogs seemed to thrive no matter what, but the experience was a sad reminder that life was uncertain.

This had been reinforced when Morning Star gave birth to our fifth child, a son, during late winter. We had named him Wren. By all outward appearances, he was perfectly formed. We were pleased to have a brother for Fox, but we could soon see something was not quite right. The infant did not have the hardiness of his siblings. This baby had the look of one already weary of the world. He did not cry. He had little interest in eating. Slowly, his life ebbed away.

It was a warm spring day when we laboriously excavated a small hole in the ground. After we hit the permafrost, it had been necessary to thaw the frozen earth with a large fire within the pit. By sundown, the various families who made up our clan had gathered around the patch of scorched soil and bits of wood ash that surrounded the hole.

Morning Star held the hide-wrapped bundle that enveloped our infant. Tears streamed down her cheeks, but when I took the baby from her to place him in the ground, she openly wept. I paused to comfort her, wrestling with my own grief, and then turned and knelt over the grave, cradling the nearly weightless child in one arm. Gently, I placed him on the still fire-warmed floor of the small trench. I then sat on my heels and scanned the gathering of people. Puh stepped forward and put a hand on my shoulder.

"I will help you," Puh said, indicating toward the pile of dirt by the grave.

I could only nod. At that moment, Pony came up to me and placed one of her toys, Horse, which she had created from a piece of deadwood that only vaguely resembled the animal, into my hand.

"Put Horse in, too, Puh-Puh," Pony requested. "For Wren."

I leaned into the hole one more time to set Horse next to the baby. As Puh and I filled the grave with earth, I heard Morning Star whisper, "Fly away, my little Wren. Fly away."

It was now the cusp of summer, and some of the sadness from that time had dissipated, but at moments such these, I blinked back tears at the memory of that day. I was also grateful to recall that we had four healthy children. My parents had buried three offspring – four if you counted the infant my mother miscarried at the time of her death. How they had endured such sorrow was difficult to comprehend.

Morning Star looked at me closely at my change of demeanor, and I smiled down at her to allay her concern.

"I think that is a fine idea, but let us discuss it at the evening meal," I answered her.

"I believe that Tor has spoken of bringing Ria and Mror," Black Wolf added, speaking of Puh's mate, Ria, and their six-winters-old son, Mror. "The snow has completely melted and the weather has been favorable. It would be good to see Gray Elk again."

"Indeed," Morning Star agreed. "I have not visited with our cousins since I was a girl. I remember Gray Elk's mate, Buttercup, as a tall, handsome woman. She and Gray Elk were so warm and welcoming. And of course, their children were older than I, but they were great fun to be with."

"With luck, we will see them soon enough," Black Wolf said.

"See who?" I heard my Puh's voice as he walked up from behind me.

"We were just talking about making the journey to take the puppies to Cousin Gray Elk," Morning Star told him.

Ria and Mror were with him.

"We had been speaking on that as well," Ria said. "Now that we have the spring hunts behind us and Tris and Tor have brought in a deer, it would be a good time to make the trek."

"And the weather is mild," Black Wolf added. "This would be an ideal opportunity to make a detour to the Fen of Falls, too."

We all nodded knowingly. Black Wolf and his mate, Little Fawn, had not been more than hostile housemates in many years. In fact, when they constructed their new home here, Black Wolf had fashioned his own quarters within the house so that he had at least one small space all to himself. Some years ago, however, Black Wolf had found love elsewhere with Willow Woman, the Head Elder of The People from the East's tribes. She and their son Black Oak would have moved to their summer home at the Fen of Falls by now.

But nothing more was said of the matter. My clan took the responsibilities of being paired very seriously and considered it to be a life-long commitment. I knew that outside of my clan monogamy was not always strictly practiced because of life's often tenuous nature. One never knew when it might be abruptly snuffed out, so there were some who took comfort wherever and whenever they could find it. But just the same, it was considered bad form to flaunt an illicit relationship while you were paired with someone else.

Just then my little half-brother Mror put his hand on my arm to get my attention.

"Tris, look at my bow," Mror said, holding out a small bow to me. "My Muh-Muh is teaching me how to shoot it."

I bent down to examine it. When Ria came to live with us, she had brought a weapon none of us had ever seen before. It consisted of a thin strap of wood with the two ends bent toward one another and held in shape by a length of twine, attached at each end. Ria used this device to launch tiny spears into the air. She had tried to teach many of us how to use a bow, with varying success. I could hit stationary targets fairly consistently, but my favored weapon was still a spear.

"That is well," I said to Mror. "If you learn to shoot as ably as your mother, you will be a great hunter."

Mror grinned broadly at this.

"And look at what Fox gave me!" Mror held out his other hand, in which he held the crumpled and desiccated shed skin that must have once covered a rather large arachnid.

"A skin of that size must have come from a very big spider," I commented.

"That is what Fox said," Mror responded.

"Fox chased poor Raven down the lakeside with it, until Inlee called to him to stop," Black Wolf said with a chuckle.

"So I heard," I told Black Wolf, "only Pony thought it was a live spider."

"When I admired it, Fox said I could have it," Mror said as he studied the object in his hand. "I did not know spiders could shed their skins. I thought only snakes did that."

"Well, the world is a curious place," Puh observed. "Filled with many curious creatures."

Chapter Two

We needed only a few days to plan and prepare for the journey. Most of our group would remain at home, where they could see to the endless tasks that must be accomplished to keep our families housed, warm, clothed, fed, and watered. And although Morning Star was eager to make the trek, most of our neighbors preferred to stay at the compound. The outing would not be without its perils, and when we reached the foothills of the mountain, the climb would be downright arduous. I marveled at my mate's pluck, but then again, even looking back at the days when we were children, Morning Star's spiritedness was one of the things I had always admired about her. After our pairing, she had settled into domestic life and caring for a rapidly growing family, but at times such as these, a hint of the young girl I had known still shined through.

Black Wolf's two sons, Swift River and Hawk, pleaded to join us as well. They were now young men, at seventeen and fifteen winters old. Most of their contemporaries would have become fairly seasoned hunters by now, but much to Black Wolf's consternation, his only sons with his mate Little Fawn had been slow to develop the level of maturity needed to hone these necessary skills. Now that they were on the verge of manhood, their training process would have to be stepped up. Little Fawn was very protective of her cherished boys and she was reluctant to expose them to anything that might bring them to harm. Black Wolf was no doubt quite aware that should one or both of the boys return home from this journey in any way injured, their mother would blame him for not looking after them.

In light of their advancing years, Swift River and Hawk would not only be included in large hunting parties, such as the spring and fall reindeer hunts, but they would also be involved in more social interactions. This was the first year they would be brought to The People's annual fall Gathering, over which the Head Elder would preside. They had not yet met their father's paramour, nor their young half-brother. They had previously expressed an interest in meeting their half-sibling, but the opportunity had not yet arisen. It was common knowledge that Black Wolf had a second family, but as this was not discussed in the proximity of Little Fawn, it made the planning of such a trip a bit tricky.

* * *

I was glad to be embarking on this excursion at a time of year when the foliage had not yet begun to proliferate and overtake the pathways. As of now, we could drag the sled without encountering too many obstructions, leaving my mind free to wander. The raging blizzard Dream had visited me again the previous night; it was so vivid that I felt as though we should be in the midst of winter, rather than enjoying today's early-summer weather.

Most dreams did not niggle at me. In fact, most dreams were forgotten as soon as I opened my eyes. But these Dreams, the ones that brought startling moments of insight, often presented more questions than answers. It was said that I had inherited the ability to see other times and places through my great-grandmother. Gran had often offered guidance, although even she professed that some Dreams were complete enigmas to her.

Gran had lived to an extraordinary old age, but she had passed several years ago. I sorely missed her and her words of wisdom. At odd moments I would hear her voice as she imparted some tidbit of knowledge, or I would recall her fondly telling me, as she often did, how much I resembled my father. Puh was much scarred by a lifetime of hard existence, and I was taller than Puh, but we both had the same color hair and eyes, and speckled skin. Gran had been well pleased that I also shared many of Puh's personal traits, although oftentimes felt I fell short of him. Puh was always quietly competent in everything he did; he was unflappable at all times, and always caring and considerate of his family and friends. I strove to be like Puh in all ways. Not only because I wished to be like him, but also to set a good example for my own son.

Puh and I were at the head of our group, pulling a travois sled. The sled was loaded with everything we would need on our journey, and it also provided a place for the younger children to rest when they tired of walking or needed a nap. We were accompanied by my dog, Raena, Puh's dog, Auchs, and Raena's five half-grown pups, which bounded up and down the trail all around us. After Puh and me came Ria and Mror, Morning Star and our children, and, finally, bringing up the rear and guarding the back of the procession, Black Wolf and his sons.

In spite of all Black Wolf's family complications, he seemed lighthearted as we hiked along the well-worn trail. He often sang in his deep bass when we traveled, *The Mighty Hunter* being one of his favored tunes, and this time was no exception.

The Mighty Hunter seldom misses his mark
Whether the sun is high or the sky is dark
The Might Hunter knows when prey is near
And he must step lightly so none can hear
The Mighty Hunter must feed his clan
When they see him, they say now there goes a man …

Black Wolf glanced over at Ria and laughed.

"Unless they are looking at you, Ria," Black Wolf said. "You and your little bow have taken down enough game to make anyone proud."

Ria laughed silently, as we Old Ones do.

"Many thanks, Black Wolf," she replied. "I am not a good cook, nor can I sew as well as some of the others, so I had better have something I can do to contribute to our welfare."

"You do plenty," Puh assured her.

Between the chattering children, panting dogs, Black Wolf's songs, occasional idle conversation, and the continual scraping of the sled, we were a noisy procession. But that was good. Most animals will avoid humans if they can, and I was sure that we were giving the local wildlife ample notice that our group was intruding on their territory.

* * *

We had been on the trail for two days; the sun was strong and the breeze had died down. The heat and arid conditions had dried up even Black Wolf's songs, and we all trudged along without speaking to preserve what little moisture was in our mouths. Despite the sled's harness chafing at our skin, Puh and I had removed our tunics early into the day's journey. The thick woodland offered some shade when the tree canopy provided cover over the trail, but when the trail cut through the lower brush, the sun was relentless. As we dragged the vehicle, I could feel the sweat on my brow and the sun's scorching rays on my naked torso. I knew that by the end of the day I would be well sunburned.

We found a stream around midday. Besides being grateful to slake our thirst and refill our water bags, many of us also chose to splash ourselves with the delightfully refreshing water. Even the dogs took advantage of the clear, running waters, and they cavorted at the stream's bank while the rest of us sank down in the cool shade beneath the trees, where we ate a quick meal of dried foods before hitting the trail once again.

We continued on in the merciless heat until suddenly Puh stopped and held up a hand to signal for everyone to halt. I was perplexed for a moment, and then I heard it – the low grunting-groan of a bear. Puh pointed ahead of us, well off the trail and through the trees, where I could just detect the movements of a large brown, furry body. The bear seemed to be deeply occupied with his task. Given his size, I guessed him to be a male, otherwise known as a boar bear. He was digging up huge chunks of soil; the clumps of earth were mostly held together by fine roots, and each swipe of his enormous paws flung the pieces of sod an impressive distance.

As we stood silently watching, I wondered if the bear was attempting to bury a kill. If so, this was not a good place to be. Bears were ferociously defensive of their food caches and were known to kill those who happened upon them. But then there was another noise – the vocalizations of another bear, but this one's voice was higher-pitched. It cried out in terror. As my ears strained to take in every sound, I also heard the muted mews and bleats of what could only be very young bear cubs. Had this boar bear attacked a sow with little ones? Our dogs were wild-eyed, and their hackles bristled. They were trained to respond to hand signals, and even the half-grown pups knew the sign to stay quiet. They panted anxiously and watched us carefully for further instruction. As I exchanged glances with those in our group, I could see that our families were scarcely less anxious. The children sidled closer to the adults; Raven and Lily clung to Morning Star, and Pony came to me, holding up her arms to be picked up.

I obligingly lifted Pony off the ground, even as I stood in the sled's harness. She promptly put her arms around my neck in a tight embrace. Fox and Mror were the only youngsters not to seek solace with a parent. They imagined themselves to be too grown up to need such comforts, but their visages bore traces of unease as we listened to the bears' furious battle.

Suddenly, the boar bear dove headfirst into his excavation, at least as far as the opening would allow, leaving his rump plainly in sight. The shrill cries continued to emanate from the sow, accompanied by the keening little ones. It was hard to tell from where I stood, but I thought I saw a smaller paw of the she-bear dart out from the hole and smack the boar on the side. The boar only renewed his attack, repeatedly thrusting his upper body into the cavity, his roaring muffled by the earth.

Puh motioned that we should back away. I thought it was a good plan to do so, while the bear was preoccupied. Bears have an acute sense of smell, therefore we would have to retreat some distance to remove ourselves from his range, and thus lose all the progress we had made that day. Without speaking, we made haste to a safer locale where we could discuss the situation.

At last, Puh and I pulled the sled off the trail by the cheerful stream where we had stopped earlier. Pony had ridden on my back throughout the return trip.

"Let us rest a bit," Puh said.

This was a pleasant, shady spot in which to consider our options. Our families knew that the bears presented a serious impediment to our travels. They looked at Puh, Black Wolf, and me questioningly.

"What will we do?" Morning Star asked. "We will never get past that bear undetected, even if he is very busy right now."

"That is true," Puh replied. "Not a big group like this with a number of dogs. But Tris and I might."

"Might what?" Black Wolf inquired dryly. "Rescue the sow from being ravaged and molested by an angry brute?"

"The bear is so distracted I think we can sneak up on him and kill him," Puh stated. "I believe that once the boar is dead, the sow, if she is still alive, will bolt with her cubs."

Black Wolf appeared to think on this for a moment. He motioned for Puh and me to withdraw a short way from the group before we spoke further.

"The trouble will be killing the bear fast enough so that he cannot come back at you," Black Wolf pointed out.

"I agree," Puh said. "I think we should each take several spears and hit the bear as often and as hard as we can, so that he will pass as quickly as possible. What say you, Tris?"

"He is not the biggest boar I have ever seen," I began. "I think we can bring him down."

"He is big enough," Black Wolf countered. "What about the dogs?"

"I would rather leave the dogs with you to help protect our families while Puh and I are gone," I said.

"That was my thought as well," Puh concurred. "I trust you, Black Wolf, and your boys and Ria to watch over the others."

Black Wolf nodded solemnly.

"Of course," he replied to Puh.

We returned to our families, who waited with apparent trepidation for us to make an announcement as to our decision.

"Tris and I will take down the bear," Puh stated. "We will not be gone long."

"Let me come, Puh-Puh," Fox pleaded. "I can help."

"Not this day," I said quietly, while removing a few extra spears from the sled's lashings. "But I do have a job for you. I would like you to make sure the dogs stay here and stay quiet. Can you do that for me?"

"Yes, Puh-Puh," Fox said with evident disappointment.

"I will help Fox," Pony piped up. "We will keep the dogs from barking."

"That is good," I said, smiling at them both. I then turned to face Morning Star. Her face betrayed a certain amount of worry, but she was calm. I wrapped my free arm around her and kissed her. "I will be back shortly."

Morning Star put her arms around my neck and pressed up tightly against me.

"I know you will take care," she said simply, but her dark eyes conveyed far more than her words.

"I will, indeed," I assured her. I then bent to quickly kiss my children and pat Raena on the head and motion for her to stay put while Puh was also taking his leave of his family.

After our farewells, we set off to retrace our steps down the trail, following the sled's furrows in the dirt. Puh and I proceeded cautiously, walking stealthily and pausing to listen every now and then. If the bear had abandoned his attack, we did not want to blunder into him. In that case, I had no doubt he would be agitated and in no mood to tolerate the intrusion of a couple of hapless humans.

But the path remained empty of all but ourselves, and the area seemed oddly devoid of life. Not a whisper of wind disturbed the air. There was only a faint hum and buzz that emanated from a multitude of insects to accompany us down the path. Puh and I kept to the side of the trail, where we could stay in the shadows of the trees' canopy, both for protection from the sun and to obscure our presence.

Finally, the still-furious grunts and roars reached our ears as we drew nearer our quarry. Puh and I took pains to approach from downwind, as silently as possible. I watched Puh carefully lest he signal some instruction to me, but he did not just yet.

The cries of the sow bear had grown weaker and more desperate in tone. The cubs, if they were still alive, made no sounds. As the boar came into view from between the trees and heavy forest undergrowth, I could see his muscles rippling and powerful shoulders working as he plunged his upper half into the hole again and again, each time grunting with effort as he seized huge chunks of earth and stone and pulled them forth. By now, the bruin was quite winded, and he panted for breath. He had lost much of his earlier vigor during our absence.

Puh did not waste any time. He motioned with a nod of his head that we would move forward immediately. It made sense not to linger and possibly give the bear an opportunity to sense our proximity.

I expected that we would conduct this hunt as we did almost any other, except that we would not lie in wait to ambush our intended victim. Instead, we would simply close the distance between us and the bear as quickly as possible, and then drive our spears into the boar, strategically hitting the places where we might hope to lance his lungs and heart. We proceeded cautiously over the haphazardly flung piles of loose dirt and stones, ready to engage the beast at any moment should he suddenly turn to see us.

Just as Puh and I were poised to strike, the bear ceased his digging, and except for the heaving of his sides as he fought to catch his breath, he went rigid. Now was the time to make our first hits. However, within an instant he had pulled his upper body from the excavation, and he spun to face us. For a large animal, he was impressively nimble.

Puh and I struck out with our spears as the boar raised himself on his hind legs. We hit the animal on his chest – lower than we would have preferred, but plunging the weapons deeply into his gut, just the same.

The bear lashed out with a paw, causing us to leap backward and to land awkwardly among the clumps of dirt and rocks that the beast had carved from the earth in his effort to reach the sow and her cubs. We managed to keep our footing, but just barely.

The boar now came at us, even as blood gushed from his belly. He stood on his hind legs once again and bellowed in rage, nostrils flaring and lips curling back from his teeth. Puh and I each still had two spears left.

"Tris, I'm going to feint to my left," Puh whispered, his eyes never leaving the bear. "When the boar moves to meet me, you hit him as hard as you can. Aim for his heart."

I nodded, "Yes, Puh."

Puh darted to his left, and as expected, the bear also turned to follow him. As Puh had instructed, I lunged forward and drove one of my spears into his chest. The boar cried out and dropped down on all fours, which actually forced the butt of shaft into the ground, driving the spearhead even farther into his body. Puh struck with one of his spears as well, impaling the creature in the side. The boar now sat back on his haunches, panting harder than ever. Suddenly, he rolled onto his side, tongue lolling and bleeding profusely from his wounds, and to a lesser extent, from his nose and his mouth.

Still clutching our remaining spears, we watched the boar breathe his last. When all was quiet, the sow peeped out from of the top of the hole. She looked thoroughly battered. One ear was torn from her head and the other hung in tatters from her skull. As she slowly raised herself higher, I could see that she sported bites and deep gashes to her face, chest, and shoulders. The sow looked at us, her eyes still wild with panic and fear. The cubs' squeaks now resumed.

"Go now, Mama," Puh said, speaking to her soothingly. "You have done your duty well and kept your babies safe. Go now."

As if responding to Puh, she pulled herself free of the excavation, her eyes looking anxiously around for the marauding boar. She seemed utterly exhausted, but her constant vigilance never wavered. The sow snapped her jaws nervously at us as Puh and I stood motionless. Bits of fur fell from her with every movement as she slowly and painfully limped away. The three cubs readily followed her. They were indeed tiny; they must have been born during late winter, probably inside that very den. Puh and I watched in silence as the little family toddled off and disappeared into the forest. It then occurred to me that this may have been the first time the cubs had left their home.

"I hope the sow survives," I said to Puh.

"I hope so, too," Puh agreed. "We will know if we come upon a sow with lots of scars and no ears. She was pretty worn out. With luck she can find a place to bed down with her cubs and can recover her strength before she meets with her next threat."

Just then I noticed blood on Puh's chest. I had been so fixed on the bears I had hardly looked at Puh until now.

"Puh, are you injured?" I asked with concern.

"I do not think so . . ." Puh peered down at himself, examining his arms and legs.

"Your chest," I pointed out. "Just below the old scars where that cave bear . . ."

"I must have gotten caught on the boar's claws when he swung at me," Puh answered quietly, but quickly cutting me off in midsentence. "I do not believe the wound is serious. Let us return to the others."

Puh seemed eager to dismiss the topic of the cave bear attack. It had killed his older brother Mror, for whom his youngest son was named. I gazed at Puh sympathetically as a rivulet of blood ran down his lean stomach. Just then, the silver strands in his pale red hair were highlighted by the sun and the lines in his face seemed deeper. I was suddenly struck by the notion that Puh was aging. Perhaps the effect was temporarily heightened by his grief, but there was no denying that he was nearing forty winters old.

Puh seemed to sense my momentary scrutiny, and a look of wonder entered his gaze. I smiled in an effort to lighten Puh's mood.

"Yes," I agreed, "they will be worried."

* * *

After finding our group where we had left them by the stream, Puh and I stooped over the running water to cleanse Puh's injury and the splatterings of the bear's blood from our bodies. Our companions clamored around us to hear what had happened. They appeared greatly relieved at our return but eager to know what had transpired. Puh and I assured them that nothing untoward had occurred and we were quite safe. Glances to the slash across Puh's chest did not exactly inspire confidence in our story, but no one questioned our tale. Puh's mate, Ria, pasted a salve over the injury to aid its healing. We then rested a short while, sipping water and consuming a few handfuls of dried foods, before once again slipping into the sled's harness so we could continue our journey.

We went just as far as the bear's carcass and stopped to harvest some of the choicer cuts from it. It would be good to have fresh meat for our evening sup, and also to feed to the dogs. Our canines appeared to be rather suspicious of the bear. Their hackles stiffened, and they growled at the dead creature as they sniffed it fearfully. My dog Raena did not like the children to be near it; she kept trying to insert herself between them and the boar's body and push them away. All the same, the children were quite interested. They did not have many opportunities to view such a fearsome animal up close, and I hoped future viewings would be under similar circumstances. A bear is a powerful beast, not one to be taken on lightly. Had this boar not been so absorbed with his pursuit of the sow, Puh and I would not have chosen to tackle him by ourselves. As it was, we were pleased to be able to retrieve the spears we had left behind and gain a little meat — as least as much as we could easily transport.

As Puh and I butchered the bear, Black Wolf stepped carefully around the crater the boar had excavated in his attempt to reach the sow's den and peered into the opening.

"The sow was fortunate to have such a deep lair," Black Wolf said. "I see a lot of fur and blood. But you say she was able to lead her cubs away?"

"Yes," I answered. "But she did look thoroughly mauled, poor thing."

"She must have been able to withdraw to the very back and use her body to shield her cubs," Puh speculated.

"Lucky for the cubs," Black Wolf mused.

When we recommenced our trek, the sun was more than halfway through its descent. It was frustrating to lose so much travel time this day, but there was no avoiding such delays. We had traveled some distance and the sun was nearing the horizon when we smelled smoke.

"Someone is up ahead," Black Wolf stated. "If they are amicable, perhaps we will have company this evening."

"We have plenty of food to share," Puh said.

"I hope they do not mind the dogs," Morning Star added.

"I hope the dogs do not mind them," I responded, knowing how protective Puh's dog Auchs and my Raena could be.

We made no effort to disguise our presence, to give those up ahead warning that we were in the vicinity. In fact, now that the air had cooled with the arrival of early evening, Black Wolf began to sing once again.

The Mighty Hunter has journeyed a long way
His stomach is empty and his feet cause him dismay

The Mighty Hunter looks forward to the end of the trail
Where he can rest by the fire and enjoy roast quail
The Mighty Hunter is not a picky eater
He will gobble down deer, bear, or beaver
He will consume almost anything so long as it is not a
hyena . . . .

Just then a voice called out "*Ho!*"

It sounded familiar. I was pleased to see our old friend Bewok, from The People of the Wolves clan, come into view.

"Black Wolf!" Bewok exclaimed. "I thought that sounded like you!"

"Yes, it is I," Black said with a hearty laugh. "Is your camp far from here?"

"No, it is just a little way up the path," Bewok replied. "We heard an approaching sound and we debated for quite some while what it could be, but then as it grew louder, I was convinced it must be you. And I must say, I had hoped that you would be accompanied by some of the others from your combined families. How glad I am to see you all."

Bewok grinned at us happily and greeted everyone by name. We had last seen him and his fellow Wolfmen about six or seven moons ago, when they had stopped by our compound during the previous fall. We exchanged brief bits of news as Bewok guided us to their camp. When their fire came into view, we knew we had reached our destination.

Karno, the leader of the Wolfmen, rose to his feet, smiling broadly as he saw us walking toward him. Karno, like all his comrades, was in his mid-twenties.

They were swarthy in appearance and well known for their prolific and highly stylized animal tattoos. The Wolfmen were the only people we had ever seen to wear their hair shorn just a few finger-widths in length from their scalp. Their wolfskin cloaks often covered this oddity, and those not acquainted with Wolfmen were frequently surprised when the cloaks came off. The cropped hair left their heads looking strangely naked. But we had known the Wolfmen for some years now, and we were used to them. We knew these men to be true friends and merry companions.

"Karno hear that voice and he know *Back Woof* is coming," Karno said, by way of greeting. "No other man have voice like *Back Woof.*"

Karno never could pronounce Black Wolf's name, but his observation was quite astute. I had never heard another voice that even remotely shared the same timbre.

"Join us," Bewok invited, "We will help you set up your shelters for the night while we wait for our nightly sup to be ready."

"Thank you, Bewok," Puh replied. "It would be pleasant to spend time together and catch up on what has transpired since our last visit. We have a considerable amount of fresh bear meat we can contribute to the meal."

By now the other Wolfmen were on their feet, too. I was pleased to see that they all seemed well, and I looked forward to hearing how they had passed the long winter moons. After our lean-tos were erected, the Wolfmen bade us to join them around the fire.

Darkness gradually enveloped our campsite. A sliver of moon rose higher and higher amongst a field of brilliant stars as we gratefully settled down to eat. The dogs were as eager to be fed as were we. Raena and Auchs, both familiar with the Wolfmen, sat next to them, knowing that they were very partial to dogs and would feed them nearly as much as they fed themselves. The pups soon caught on, and they were eager to sit with the Wolfmen, too.

My son Fox was seated next to Bewok. I noticed that Fox was observing his seatmate carefully.

"Bewok," Fox finally spoke up. "Why do you wear animals on your skin?"

Bewok grinned as he considered his reply.

"Our people have always done this," Bewok began. "Do you see this deer? It represents the deer I killed when I became a man. This boar came next. But it was only small, so it is a small tattoo. Then came this elk; he was small, too – no antlers, see? But we needed the meat. We add each beast we make a kill, or at least make the first strike on. That is why our bodies are decorated with so many animals."

"It good when tattoo tough skin," Karno added, "but once that covered, then we tattoo other skin," Karno motioned to his neck, under his arms, the backs of his knees, "and then . . . *gah*! Very sore!"

Bewok cast a glance toward Black Wolf and looked him up and down.

"Your tattoos match those of the Head Elder, Willow Woman," Bewok noted. "Will you cover yourself with the markings, the same as she?"

Willow Woman was the first person I had ever seen bedecked in tattoos, and so far as I could guess, all but the center of her face, the palms of her hands, and the soles of her feet were completely decorated with horizontal parallel lines, sometimes connected by diagonal lines, and interspersed with various markings. Black Wolf, presumably as a demonstration of his devotion to her, had had the same patterns tattooed on his forearms and lower legs, one limb at a time.

"No," Black Wolf said, shaking his head. "I am content with what I have."

"Good plan," Karno said, nodding with approval.

"Where did all this bear meat come from?" Bewok asked us. "It seems very fresh. Did you meet this bear on the way here?"

"Yes," Puh replied. "He was just off the trail, attacking a sow bear in her lair. It was unsafe for us to continue, so we withdrew our families a ways, and then Tris and I went back to dispatch him while he was distracted."

The Wolfmen nodded knowingly. Bears were highly respected by all.

"Bear not have good day," Karno surmised. "But it good for us! Good friends! Good meat!"

"Where are you headed?" I asked Karno. I wondered that they had not settled down somewhere yet. I would have thought that they would have been eager to start families of their own.

"We go to clan where we stay some moons, few year ago," Karno told us. "See if any change. Good women there."

A conflicted look crossed Bewok's face and his mouth opened for a moment, but then he quickly closed it.

"Do you not want to go?" I inquired of Bewok.

"Not very much," Bewok responded. "It is far from here. I know Karno would like to set himself up as Great Man there, or convince some of the clan to join us and establish a new clan elsewhere, but I am not optimistic of our chances. And as I said, it is too far away."

"Too far away from where?" Black Wolf interjected, having overheard the last of Bewok's words.

"Here," Bewok said, "I do not want to go so far."

"Do your old injuries still pain you?" I asked.

"I should not be surprised if that is so," Black Wolf said to Bewok. "That cave lion was nearly the end of you. You are lucky to have survived."

"Yes, I am," Bewok concurred. "Sometimes my chest and shoulder ache, but I have noticed that it is only when the weather changes." Bewok grinned. "Now I can foretell when we will get rain or have a storm. The lion's bite gave me an unexpected gift."

"I do not know as I would call it a gift," Black Wolf started, "but it is a more pleasant way of looking at it."

"Where do you go?" Bewok asked us. "I see you are accompanied by many young dogs. Do you go to Gray Elk?"

"That is exactly where we are going," I answered. "That is why we bring our families on the trip; so that they may visit with Gray Elk and his kin."

The rest of the evening was spent exchanging news, but before the fire died down, the Wolfmen treated us to several of their chanting songs. We listened, spellbound, and then we all retreated to our little shelters for a night's rest.

 **Chapter Three** 

An air of unease fills the dimly lighted chamber. Hazy smoke from torches burns my eyes, as its acrid smell mingles with the odors emanating from of the multitude of humans filling the space. Willow Woman is seated near me, evidently presiding over the large assembly. She turns to me and speaks in a hushed voice. "Tris, you must do this for me." Her tone is desperate.

We recommenced our journey the next morning, happy to have the Wolfmen accompanying us for at least the early part of the day. Bewok walked by Puh and me as we dragged our sled along the trail, chatting with us pleasantly. All the same, my mind wandered. I thought on the Dream that had visited me last night. It appeared to be taking place at The People's annual fall Gathering, but what did I have to do with it? Why was Willow Woman so anxious, and what did she want me to do?

I again mused that if Great Gran were still living, I could tell her of the Dream and ask for her interpretation. Gran might not have had an exact answer for me, but generally she could steer me toward at least a few possible scenarios.

Now, Dreams were my only means of seeing her. Sometimes they were ordinary dreams, in which Gran came and went, going about mundane tasks, just as she had in life. But sometimes they had a stark clarity, and it was as though Gran were really with me once again.

A moon or so ago Gran had been with me in a Dream, and I told her about Morning Star's beauty. This Dream was a vision from the past. I was perhaps twelve winters old, and Morning Star and I would not be paired for another five years. But even at that young age, I had already been in love with her for some time. Morning Star was like none other; she was vivacious, petite, and lithesome. Her black hair was long and glossy, and she had dark eyes that lit up when she smiled or flashed when her anger was piqued.

Gran had grinned and patted my knee.

"Tris, Morning Star is a pretty girl. She will attract many admirers by the time she becomes a woman," Gran said gently. "I understand why you dote on her."

"I want to be paired with Morning Star," I said firmly. "She is the most beautiful girl I have ever seen."

I had heard that Old Ones and The People were not likely to become joined as mates; however, I had cherished the naïve belief that my love was strong enough to overcome anything that might stand in our way. Somehow, I would make Morning Star love me. Then her parents would be so charmed and inspired by our love that they would allow the pairing. Other people would also be so swept away by our apparent happiness that they too would overlook the unconventional union and share our joy.

I could see that Gran looked troubled. She did not respond at first.

"If you win Morning Star, that will be up to her," Gran had said decisively. "She has a strong heart and a strong mind. And that is more important than her outward appearance."

I was puzzled at this.

"You must look for beauty the eyes cannot see," Gran went on. "For the qualities that will last beyond youth and will provide a lifetime of love and care; that will raise your children, keep your home. That is what is important."

All these years later, I realized that Gran had been right.

My eyes sought out Morning Star. She was with our daughters, walking ahead of Puh, Bewok, and me, where she was herding our girls along as best she could. Our daughters, like most small children, were easily distracted by the novelties we happened upon on the trail. Often they wanted to stop to pick up a feather, point out an animal, or look at a butterfly. As Pony stooped to collect a pebble that had caught her fancy, Morning Star paused to look back at me. When our eyes met, she smiled. I returned her smile with what was probably a dopey grin, but now, as always, my heart leapt. We exchanged not a word, but that one glance and loving smile brought to mind that I was exceedingly fortunate to have a mate who was not only outwardly beautiful, but who also owned a beauty the eyes could not see.

I felt grieved not to have had more time with Gran, but then, she had lived a very long life; how much more could I have expected? I wished I had not wasted our conversations with talk about my own Dreams, instead of allowing her to tell me more, and thus soak up more of her knowledge.

I was vaguely aware that Bewok had left Puh and me to rejoin his comrades. Our paths would soon part. We would continue to head east while they would veer off to the north.

"The Wolfmen will leave us soon," I remarked to Puh.

Puh nodded in response.

"Most of them will, anyway," Puh said.

"Most of them?" I repeated.

"Bewok has not said anything definite to me, but I have a hunch he will ask to stay with us," Puh explained.

"I remember that he had asked to live with us many years ago," I recalled. "But that was a long time ago. I liked the idea of him staying with us, but then after Ru and Karno's brief love affair, and then Ru's rejecting him, he could not add to Karno's grief by leaving his old friend, so Bewok did not stay. I was disappointed, but I understood and I admired his loyalty."

"Yes, I was sorry to lose Bewok as well," Puh agreed.

"What makes you think he will ask again?" I inquired.

Puh shrugged, a small smile playing about his lips.

"It is just a feeling," Puh said. "I do not want to speculate further."

I knew better than to press Puh, so I was silent and concentrated on pulling the sled.

It was nearing midday when the Wolfmen requested we halt our journey. They had selected a place where a number of tall pines shaded the trail, providing a pine needle carpet on which we could rest and take nourishment.

As always, the Wolfmen lavished attention on the dogs, but just now, perhaps even more so, as they were about to take their leave of us. They revered canines above all other animals, and I guessed they were as sorry to leave the dogs behind as they were us.

"Karno, why do you not have dogs of your own?" Black Wolf asked him.

"We live no life for dog," Karno said. "Dog need home. When Karno find home, then Karno have dog. Maybe many dog."

I thought Karno was somewhat subdued manner. Even considering his broken sentences, he normally spoke in a decisive and authoritative way. Was he sad not to have a home? Sad not to have a dog? Or both? Karno was stroking one of the pups as it panted and wagged its tail happily.

"Perhaps a home is not too far in the offing," Black Wolf stated hopefully, as though to encourage the downcast Wolfman.

"*Perhap*," Karno said. "Karno think he be Great Man of clan we stay with year ago. They Great Man not look good when we leave. He say go, but I think we wait and come back later." Karno smiled. "Now, *Back Woof*, we come back."

"I wish you well," Black Wolf responded.

"Maybe someday you sing song about Karno," Karno suggested. "*Mighty Karno* instead of *Mighty Hunter.*"

"I will think on that," Black Wolf answered noncommittally. "It has been pleasant to see you and your fellow Wolfmen again, but we must continue our journey soon. We hope to arrive at my cousin Gray Elk's home on the day after tomorrow and we still have a long ways to go."

By now, we were all rising to our feet to say our farewells. Puh and I returned to the sled and slipped into the harnesses. Morning Star brought our youngest daughter, Lily, to me.

"Tris, Lily is tired. She would like to ride on the sled – maybe she will nap for a while," Morning Star said.

"Yes, of course, my sweet," I replied, taking Lily into my arms and snuggling the small child. "You are sleepy, are you not? Here, lie down on the sled. It is a bit lumpy, but I will lay my tunic down and you can use it as a blanket."

Puh and I had removed our tunics at some point during the morning as the heat of day warmed us, and now these garments served to pad Lily from the many objects stowed on the sled, and to cover her as she dozed. As I again took up the harness, Bewok approached.

"Tor," Bewok began, speaking to Puh, "I once asked if I might be part of your clan. You were kind enough to grant permission, but then I could not stay. I ask again, now, if I may be part of your group."

Bewok seemed nervous, as though he did not know what to expect. Puh smiled at Bewok warmly, setting him at ease.

"My answer has not changed," Puh responded. "You are always welcome to stay with us, whether today, next year, or ten years from now."

Bewok's face beamed with pleasure.

"I had hoped you would accept me," he said. "My friends are leaving; I will say goodbye and then I will be ready to go with you."

Puh nodded and Bewok swiftly returned to the other Wolfmen, speaking rapidly in their native tongue and then he embraced each one of them. It was a short farewell, and it seemed to me that none of his companions gave any indication of being surprised at Bewok's sudden departure, although they did seem saddened to lose him.

* * *

By the end of the following day we had reached the foot of the mountains. These lands were sparsely treed, and puddles of snow still clung to the shadows of the undergrowth and rock formations. It was distinctly cooler here, and when we began our trek the next morning we found that a light frost had settled over the earth during the previous night. However, the rising sun was strong enough to make the fragile white crust evaporate into rising wisps of mist.

"It is still spring here, Puh-Puh," Pony noted.

"Summer will soon arrive," I assured her. "But it will be a very short season."

"The dogs have run ahead," Fox abruptly pointed out.

I, too, had seen Raena bolt up the trail, with the other dogs quickly running in pursuit.

"Do you think Raena can smell her old home from here?" I asked Puh.

After all, Raena had been born at Gray Elk's dwelling. We were still some distance away, but I knew dogs had keener senses than we.

"We will not reach Gray Elk's until past midday," Puh said, appearing to mull over the question. "But she definitely is on to something."

"I hear voices!" I said, now alert, my ears straining to catch more of the sounds. They were faint, but there was something familiar about them.

"I hear them as well," Puh replied.

Raena and the other dogs soon rejoined us, only moments before a small hunting party came into view. They, too, were encumbered by sleds.

"Halloo!" One of them hailed us.

It was my cousin Dor. I had not seen him in some years – perhaps three or more? Then I saw that he was accompanied by his brother Lor. Both men had been skinny, rather puny youths, but they had filled out into robust men. Dor and Lor greeted us with wide grins.

"Tris! Tor!" Dor called out. "How good to see you!"

The cousins continued to drag their sled nearer, and we proceeded forward until we closed the distance between us. They were accompanied by a few friends. After the introductions, we took advantage of this serendipitous meeting. We settled down by the trail, breaking out our water bags and various foodstuffs.

"You have been hunting," Black Wolf stated.

"Yes," Lor said with a nod. "We wanted to take down a few more reindeer before the spring migrations end."

"We managed to take three more. Young bulls." Dor added. "But they were thin. And the flies were so bad it is a wonder we and they were not bled dry by the biting swarms. Ugh. I am glad to be out of that valley, even if it means working our way through these rough and rocky foothills to get back home."

"How is your family?" Puh queried. "Your mother? Sere?"

"Muh is well," Dor answered, "And so is Sere. I have been paired since we last met, to a young woman from a northern clan. We have a fine son now."

"That is great news," I said, happy for Dor.

"I am paired now, too," Lor piped up. "We are expecting a child this summer. My mate is from the same clan. It would seem the clan had lost several hunters and it was struggling to keep everyone fed and clothed. So some of the clan, including these women, were eager to find new homes. We took in their parents and a few siblings, as well. Our home is large enough to accommodate all these and more, and we were pleased to have them."

"How is Bror?" Dor asked about this eldest brother. Bror was paired with my sister Ru and had lived with our clan for many years now.

"You will be glad to know that Bror and Ru are doing very well and raising three very pretty little girls," I told him. "Bror will be disappointed to have missed this meeting. He has often spoken of a longing to see his family."

"Has Twie been paired yet?" Lor asked, referring to one of my sisters. "I suppose she is next. She must be – what – fifteen winters old by now?"

"She is not paired," Puh responded. "But yes, she is fifteen winters old, and she is of age. She has not mentioned an interest in any particular mate yet."

"That day will come soon enough," Black Wolf chuckled. "It seems one moment they are just tots and you are carrying them around in your arms, and the next, they are grown and you are carrying their little ones."

"That is so," Puh agreed.

Our reunion was brief. If we hoped to reach Gray Elk's lodgings by sunset, we must push on. Dor and Lor gave us a package of smoked reindeer meat to take with us in parting, and we gave them a slab of bear fat. Lastly, they asked us to give their regards to their brother Bror.

This part of the trip would be the most demanding. As the trail passed through the last of the foothills, we came to another path. This one was steep, and it constantly zigzagged as it skirted rocky crags and a few stunted and gnarled pines.

No one complained, but this was difficult terrain for a people used to relatively flat lands. Bewok insisted on hitching himself to the travois sled to help Puh and me pull the sled over the uneven ground. At times it was necessary to lift the sled over an obstacle, requiring the assistance of Black Wolf, as well. It was not long before our leg muscles were burning with effort. Even the dogs panted, their tongues lolling out of their mouths.

"Da, how much farther?" Black Wolf's oldest son, Swift River, asked. "We must be getting close by now."

"Just a bit more," Black Wolf informed him. "You have not been here since you were quite small. You were probably carried most of the way. Your brother Hawk certainly was."

"I still remember," Morning Star joined in. "The climb seemed to go on forever. But I will never forget Cousin Gray Elk's amazing home. I have never seen a cave so large! And so many dogs! But we had so much fun with our cousins! I am glad to endure a little hike just to visit with them again."

"*A little hike!*" Hawk repeated. "That is like calling this mountain *just a little hill!*"

We stopped to rest several times, taking the opportunity to knead our sore leg muscles, and to eat and drink before resuming our climb. The sun was edging toward the horizon by the time we heard distant barking.

Raena and the other dogs barked in return. Raena's nose twitched inquisitively. Her eyes were bright, as though the sights and sounds had rekindled some hazy memory of her old home. By the time we reached the entryway to Gray Elk's cavernous abode, the noisy barking echoing off the stone walls from our combined canines was deafening.

Gray Elk stood inside the cave's opening, smiling broadly and waiting to greet us.

"So, it is spring and another litter of pups arrives," Gray Elk said jovially. "When we did not see you last year, we wondered if all was well."

"We had no pups to bring last year," I answered. "But, as you can see, we have a litter of half-grown pups, and I had hoped that once again you would be willing to take them."

"Of course!" Gray Elk replied. "The demand for dogs is greater than ever lately. More and more people drop by looking for dogs. I do not know where they come from or how they find me."

"You are famous," Black Wolf said lightly as Gray Elk embraced him in greeting.

"Ha!" Gray Elk laughed shortly. "Perhaps my dogs are famous. I am just the person who houses and feeds them." He paused as he looked Black Wolf up and down, "How well you look! Life in the North Country with Inlee and his clan must be agreeing with you!" Then Gray Elk stopped short when he saw Morning Star.

"Oh! This could only be Morning Star!" Gray Elk exclaimed. "And look at these lovely little ones! I see you have been busy!"

"Hallo, Cousin Gray Elk," Morning Star said as she hugged him. "We have a boy and three girls, and yes, they do keep us quite busy."

When Gray Elk came to welcome me, I was pleased to see that he looked well fed, but the passing of time had left him with thinning hair and sagging, deeply creased skin. He must be well over fifty winters old by now. After greeting me, and then Puh, he stopped abruptly in front of Bewok.

I then realized that Bewok, whose tunic was tied around his hips by the sleeves and was clad only from the waist down, presented a startling sight. Bewok was smiling gently, but his appearance was a stark departure from that of Gray Elk's typical visitors, what with his full-body covering of tattoos, vivid scar on his chest and shoulder from the lion attack, and a head-full of thick black hair that was chopped so short that it stuck out from his skull at all angles. But Bewok continued to gaze congenially at Gray Elk, who hesitantly returned his smile.

"Hallo, friend," Gray Elk said to Bewok, a trifle unsurely. "I am Gray Elk. Welcome to my home. Come and meet my family, if you can make your way through all these dogs."

"Gray Elk, I am Bewok," Bewok responded. "Thank you for inviting me to meet your people. It will be my honor to be among them."

At that, we were ushered through the resident throng of large furry bodies, each one ecstatic at the arrival of guests who would, no doubt, be apt to want to pet and spoil them. It was a challenge to bring the sled into the cave without doing an injury to the many dogs, but eventually we succeeded in dragging it through the entryway. Only our own dogs continued to follow us down the long passageway to the living quarters. Gray Elk's dogs preferred the cooler air near the cave opening to the warmth of the inner chambers.

The corridor was sparsely illuminated by lamps that were placed on high rock ledges and interspersed amongst numerous deer and elk skulls. The giant deer skulls, complete with vast spreads of antler, never failed to impress me each time I visited. The elk and red deer skulls and antlers were grand, but they were nothing compared with the incredible size of those belonging to the giant deer. I always had a sense that the spirit of the animals still resided within the empty craniums, and that they watched us as we passed below them from their lofty perches overhead.

No one spoke as we traversed the enormous passageway, the sounds of our footfalls and the scraping of the sled resounding off the tall stone walls. Even in the dim light I could see that children's heads constantly swiveled as they took in the sights. They silently pointed out to each other particularly large skulls and antlers as we walked past the most impressive specimens.

When we reached the cave's main chamber, the warmth from the fire at the center of the room was immediately evident. Here, Puh, Bewok, and I placed the sled just to the side of the opening. I was relieved to finally step out of the sled's harness. I was so accustomed to dragging its ponderous weight that it felt strange to move about without it. I was grateful to take a seat by the hearth, where we all settled ourselves while Gray Elk momentarily left us to collect his family from their various locations within the cave.

Excited chatter signaled their approach as it emanated from the other rooms. The cave's stone walls provided eerie acoustics, causing the voices to bounce off the rock surfaces in such a way that it was sometimes difficult to determine where the sound was coming from. Soon we were joined by Gray Elk's mate Buttercup, his daughters, the mates of his sons, and a number of children.

"Where are your young men?" Black Wolf inquired. "Did they go out for reindeer?"

"That they did," Gray Elk replied. "They have been away almost half a moon."

"We can give you a taste of what is to come," Puh offered. "We met up with the youngest and middle sons of my late brother Mror as they were coming down the foothills. They gifted us with some of their harvest. And we bring a bit of bear fat, as well."

"That would be most welcome!" Buttercup exclaimed. She was a spare but tall woman. She was seated next to Morning Star, who was nearly a head shorter than Buttercup, but they were gabbing with great animation, busily taking the opportunity to get caught up on news. They had not seen one another in many years, and neither could tell when or if they might have a chance to visit again.

Puh retrieved the packages and held them out to Buttercup, who thanked him warmly.

"Thank you, Tor. I can already smell the reindeer meat's smoky aroma." Buttercup rose to her feet. "I will add this to our evening meal," she said, motioning toward the foodstuffs roasting over a pile of coals that occupied one end of the fireplace. "Our evening sup was not going to be very inspiring, but now it will include a real treat."

My stomach growled hungrily at the mention of food. As if on cue, one of Gray Elk's older granddaughters brought out a birch bark tray laden with roasted nuts and thin slivers of dried salmon. I took a small handful of items from the tray.

"Many thanks," I said to her. The girl nodded shyly in return and moved on to Morning Star, who sat at my side.

It was remarkably pleasant to sit and converse companionably, trading stories and eating and drinking our fill. The grandchildren of Gray Elk and Buttercup frolicked with utter delight now that they had visitors their own ages with whom to play. It was not often that other youngsters came to this remote location, so our children were treated as cherished guests. When the fire burned low, it was time to retire for the night.

Morning Star and I unpacked a number of pelts and hides from our sled to use as bedding. Away from the heat of the fire, it was quite cool, and I reflected that we would need those pelts and hides to stay warm.

My family was shown to a large room that we would have all to ourselves. Gray Elk led the way with a lamp, which he set on a rock shelf.

"There are a few sleeping platforms," Gray Elk said, indicating the piles of springy twigs padded with dried grasses and then covered with layers of hides. "I think there are enough for you all to sleep on."

"Many thanks, Gray Elk," I said to him. "I am very grateful to you for your hospitality."

Gray Elk smiled thoughtfully.

"I am grateful to you for all you and your Puh have done for my family over the years." Gray Elk paused for a moment. "But is that not what we are here for, to help each other?"

"Indeed," Morning Star agreed, shifting the weight of Lily, who was already sound asleep in her arms. "This little one is getting heavy. I will go and lay her down. Come, children, it is time to settle into bed." Morning Star began to usher them to one of the sleeping platforms.

"Not yet, Muh-Muh. What is this?" Fox inquired. He had been investigating the chamber. Fox pointed at a portion of a wall where I could see faint marks, despite the deep shadows.

"Oh, you have found the Talking Stones," Gray Elk said as he picked up the lamp and walked toward Fox. "This cave is very old. Older than anyone knows. A very long time ago, someone scratched pictures into the wall that tell a tale."

Morning Star still carrying Lily, joined us as we gathered around Fox and Gray Elk. We looked in amazement at the pictures. I had never seen anything like it. Someone had made a fire in the room and later used a sharp rock or stick to etch images into the soot-blackened stone. Some scratches appeared to depict reindeer as they ran from other animals, possibly wolves. There were also several woolly mammoths, including two bulls, battling head-to-head.

"This looks like a fox!" Fox cried out with delight. "It is chasing a rabbit! And here are two bull mammoths locked in battle! The pictures do tell stories!"

"Are they not a thing of wonder?" Gray Elk said with a laugh. "We almost never use this room; sometimes I forget these drawings are here."

"They remind me of Bewok's tattoos," Fox noted as he examined the images.

Pony took a stick from one of the sleeping platforms and began to scratch a line into the blackened surface.

"Pony," I said gently as I pulled her back, "this is not our wall. We cannot make marks without first asking permission."

Pony looked up at Gray Elk, her eyes wide with apprehension, but he smiled down at her kindly.

"Do not worry, Pony," Gray Elk said softly. "Just so long as you don't disturb the original drawings, I do not mind if you add your own."

"Thank you, Cousin Gray Elk," she said. "I will take care not to make marks near the pictures."

Pony carefully scratched a creature that looked vaguely like a bird.

"What is it?" Fox asked his little sister. "It has big wings . . . is it an eagle?"

"I have drawn Kaw," Pony replied. "Your crow friend. I was sorry when we had to leave Kaw behind when we moved to be near Uncle Inlee. Kaw must have a very large family by now. I wonder if she still remembers us."

Fox became solemn. He had raised Kaw from the time she was a fledgling.

"I miss Kaw, too," he said. "I hope to see her again when next we travel back toward our old home." Fox seemed to think for a moment, and then he added, "I would like to borrow the stick you are using."

Pony passed the stick to Fox, and he too began to etch lines into the blackened wall. I was amused to see that it was a crude figure of a human – a boy, perhaps – next to the crow.

"That is me," Fox stated. "Now Kaw and I will have our story on the wall, too."

"Come now, it is very late," Morning Star said, again attempting to herd the children to a sleeping platform.

Morning Star laid Lily down gently and covered the tot with a soft pelt. Lily was soon joined by her siblings as they climbed onto the platform and snuggled into the furry blankets.

Gray Elk gazed down at the children fondly.

"You have such delightful little ones," he told Morning Star and me. "Well, *little* all except for Fox. The top of his head nearly reaches my shoulder! I predict he is going to be a large man."

"Considering that Black Wolf is his grandfather, it would not be a surprise if Fox continues to be tall for his age," I concurred.

"And you for a father!" Morning Star said lightly, looking up at me.

"Yes," Gray Elk acknowledged with a chuckle. "Fox most definitely bears an uncanny resemblance to you, Tris."

"But that is good," Morning Star stated. "Every mother wishes for her son to grow to be big and strong. And wise."

"I can contribute size," I said to Morning Star, "but you contribute the wisdom."

"Can we leave the lamp by the Talking Stones?" Fox interrupted. "I want to look at the pictures as I fall asleep."

"I think that would be fine," I answered.

"I want to dream about Kaw and the other animals," Fox said, craning his neck from his place in bed so he could see the drawings.

His eyelids drooped as though this dream would not be too long in coming.

Chapter Four

A gusting wind rustles the field of dry, yellowed grasses and rattles the naked branches of leafless brush. This area had once been a forest. Now the lifeless lea is studded with innumerable splintered tree trunks. The desolate scene fills me with a deep sense of foreboding.

I awoke from the Dream feeling chilled, but it was not just from the coolness of the cave. Something about that field pricked at my consciousness; it was as though an ominous cloud hung over it, threatening doom. I tried to purge the thought from my mind. But the mental image of the field niggled at me. What was its significance, and why was I there?

The lamp had burned out, leaving behind only blackness. I snuggled closer to Morning Star in an effort to dispel my unease. She stirred slightly in response.

"What is it, Tris?" she whispered.

"Just a Dream," I said softly, nuzzling her neck and then kissing it.

I felt Morning Star slip her arms around me and pull me closer, effectively vanquishing the unsettling Dream.

"Did the Dream tell you to kiss me?" she inquired lightly.

"No, that was my idea," I told her.

"I believe I have an idea to kiss you, too," Morning Star replied.

She kissed me long and deeply. I did not know how long we had before dawn, but we seldom missed an opportunity to share our love when time and privacy permitted. The children were sound asleep on the far side of the room, but I heard Raena awaken briefly; the scuffling of her feet indicated she had changed position and then settled back down again.

* * *

Our stay with Gray Elk was to be brief. We spent the night and then departed the following day to begin the next leg of our journey, which would take us to the Fen of Falls. This was where the Head Elder, Willow Woman, spent the warm weather months. The cascading falls and the shade cast by the tall pines made for an enticingly cool area, even if the turbulent waters were deafening when you ventured too close.

We had gifted some of our supplies to Gray Elk and his family, so the sled was much lighter as we made our way down the mountainside. This was a relief, because a heavy sled sometimes wants to descend a slope faster than those dragging it, causing Puh and me to brace against its weight, lest the sled careen over us.

I was saddened to leave Gray Elk and Buttercup so soon, but I was also eager to visit with Willow Woman and the other members of her household. After the many years of our acquaintance, they had become as close to me as members of my own clan. I had not been to the Fen of Falls in some time – not since her original home at that location had been burned to the ground by a group of exiles deemed Outsiders. They had come back to wreak revenge on her for banishing them from our lands – a punishment reserved for only those who engaged in most heinous behaviors. By now the miscreants had paid for their many crimes with their lives. We hoped this meant we could enjoy a period of relative quiet, at last free from the threat of being harassed, robbed, and hunted by the Outsiders.

Black Wolf refrained from singing as we navigated the mountain trail; the path required much concentration as we carefully trod the uneven rocky terrain, ever watchful of our surroundings. Snow leopards were stealthy predators, and this was one of their favored areas to stalk. They preferred ibex and the like, but an unwary human would suffice.

"Why not attach a rope to the back of sled," Black Wolf suggested. "Then I can hang onto it, to keep the sled from suddenly charging you every time it has a notion to slide forward on its own."

"That is a good plan," Puh said. "If we are to bring a sled up to Gray Elk's home again, I think it would be worthwhile to make a special vehicle for the trip. It would be more like the one my nephews Dor and Lor were using: narrower, and with long handrails that can be gripped, instead of using harnesses as we do."

I thought this a practical solution. Our wider travois sled constantly snagged on rocky outcrops, and the rope and leather harnesses allowed the sled to yaw from side to side. It also slid forward and backward as we either ascended or descended inclines. This was the first time we had attempted to bring a sled up and down the mountainside, and it was clear if we were to do this again we would need to make some adjustments.

We brought our procession to a halt. While Puh quickly added a length of rope to the rear of the sled, each of us took advantage of the break to quickly consume a bit of food and water and rest our already-taxed muscles.

"I hope I am heavy enough to stop the sled before it mows you down," Black Wolf said as he gave the rope an experimental tug.

I hoped so, too. If there was anything worse than being run over by your own sled, it was being run over by your sled and the very large man attached to it.

"I have faith that you will be able to sufficiently anchor the sled," Puh said simply.

"If you would like to run a second rope," Bewok began, "perhaps I could tie up to Black Wolf and stop him from being pulled forward if the sled starts to slide."

Bewok had been walking at the front of our group, providing protection for those between the two of us pulling the sled and Black Wolf, who brought up the rear.

"That is good of you, but I doubt you are heavy enough to hold me back," Black Wolf spoke with a laugh.

"Many thanks for your offer, just the same," Puh said.

Bewok merely smiled and nodded in reply, and then returned to the front of the line.

When our break was over, we resumed our trek down the mountainside. Hawk and Swift River joined Bewok at the lead, soon joined by Fox and Mror, as well. They seemed to be enjoying the journey and one another's company. Morning Star, too, gave every indication of being delighted to be on the trail, even though she carried a pack and often toted Lily. Our older girls dutifully followed their mother, sometimes catching up with her and taking her free hand or showing her something they had found. I was glad that the trip was not yet wearing them down. I knew all too well that long expeditions could become quite tiresome. This time, however, the good weather had held out and we were well supplied. With luck, in four or five days we would reach the Fen of Falls.

Other than a spell of rain that caused us to abandon the trail early one afternoon and quickly set up huts in the steadily increasing downpour and rumbling thunder, the journey progressed smoothly. Black Wolf was particularly eager to arrive at our destination, where he would be at long last reunited with Willow Woman and their son, Oak. He fretted at the rain delay, but he was otherwise cheerful and scarcely complained at all about his sore feet, or the heat and humidity left behind by the rainstorm.

At last we entered the piney forest that signaled our proximity to the Fen of Falls. This woodland was comprised almost entirely of huge pines that rose majestically from the mossy and pine-needle-carpeted ground. Brush dotted the forest, but there was little else to snag our sled, and we made good progress through the fragrant landscape. It was cooler here, where scant direct sunlight filtered down from the tall trees. It was not long before we heard the faint rush of the cascading waters. The farther we ventured down the trail, the more the roar of the falls filled our ears and a pervading dampness filled the air.

When Willow Woman's lodge came into view, I was relieved to see it standing once more. The last time I had visited, it was nothing but a charred and smoldering hulk. The new structure looked remarkably like the old one, although it was slightly larger and obviously constructed of fresh materials.

Puh whistled loudly to announce our impending arrival, but Black Wolf had already sprinted ahead. This no doubt rendered Puh's warning moot, as Black Wolf's sudden appearance on the compound was bound to alert the residents that guests were about to descend upon them.

Willow Woman exited the lodge, shrieking with glee at the sight of her beloved. The sound resonated in my ears like the fervent bugling of a giant deer buck during the rut. Black Wolf continued his headlong dash toward Willow Woman, and upon reaching her, he swept her into his arms and off her feet, swinging her around as though she were but a child. There was a time when this act would have required great strength, but Willow Woman, who was taller and more robust than many men, had diminished significantly in girth in recent years. While still a large person, she looked to be half her former self. Her tattooed skin, once gloriously plump, now hung in loose folds. Willow Woman and Black Wolf were still engaged in a joyous reunion as the rest of us entered the compound, but when she saw us she broke away from his amorous greeting and stepped forward to graciously receive us.

Willow Woman's year-round attire consisted of what we would consider a woman's summer garb. This style of garment was made of cured deerskins, usually taken from several small deer whose thinner hides could be made especially soft and pliable. The hides were sewn together to form a long rectangle with an opening cut at its center through which one poked one's head. Then, with the long flaps of hide draping front and back, it was belted securely at the waist. This protected one from many things, including sparks that tended to pop out unexpectedly from cooking fires and sunburns, particularly on the back and shoulders. But for Willow Woman, who was not required to cook or spend much time outdoors, I guessed it was strictly a matter of modesty and the fact that her copious natural insulation did not seem to require her to wear as much to cover herself, even in cold weather. Now, I saw that she also wore a short cloak of lynx fur draped around her, although after Black Wolf's greeting, it hung rather lopsidedly to one side.

"Tris! Tor!" Willow Woman threw her arms simultaneously around Puh and me and hugged us with great enthusiasm. She may have lessened in size, but she still had remarkable strength. "How good to see you both!"

Puh and I barely had time to gasp at her crushing embrace and utter a brief acknowledgment before she released us and moved on to the others in our party, gushing with happiness and greeting each individual with loudly brayed words of affection. Upon witnessing this, Swift River and Hawk backed away, seemingly unsure of what to make of our hostess.

Black Wolf, still grinning from ear to ear, came to join them, ushering his eldest sons forward to meet Willow Woman. He unceremoniously shoved the two boys toward her.

"Willow, my love, I have brought Hawk and Swift River to meet you and Oak," he told her. "Where is Oak?" Black Wolf looked around, as though expecting to see Oak suddenly appear.

"Such charming young men," Willow Woman exclaimed, embracing the boys as they squirmed, their eyes widened with alarm. "I am so glad you have come! I have waited a long time to meet you!" At this, Swift River and Hawk smiled shyly. Then she answered, "Oak has gone out with Gray Owl and Slow Bear; they are gathering herbs for Gray Owl's remedies. They should soon return."

As we milled about exchanging news, others from the lodge came out and quietly began to build up the fire in the outdoor hearth and set down mats to be used as seating. Willow Woman's staff were, as always, unobtrusively efficient and no doubt were anticipating that the new arrivals would appreciate a hearty evening sup after many days on the trail. One of the men, White Cloud, I remembered from previous visits. White Cloud handled most of the meal preparations, and he now approached bearing a large birch bark tray laden with various foodstuffs.

"Thank you, White Cloud," Willow Woman said to him. And then to us, "Do sit, if it should please you, and take sustenance." Reaching out to Black Wolf, she pulled him nearer to her, and they found a comfortable place to be seated. "You boys come and sit by me, too," she instructed Hawk and Swift River, who promptly obeyed. Willow Woman was as kind and generous a person as one could ever hope to meet, but her tone commanded respect, and there was no dithering nor arguing with her when she spoke.

Before settling down with the others, Puh and I moved the sled out of the way and stepped out of the sled's harness. Morning Star wanted to retrieve some things from the sled, so she placed our napping toddler in my arms as she untied some of the lashings and began to search through the various articles stowed on it. Fox was busy with the other boys, eagerly awaiting Oak's arrival, but Pony and Raven stood by their mother, apparently wanting items off the sled, as well.

Morning Star gave each child the playthings they sought, and then she found the bundle she was searching for. Fox, Oak, and Mror were very close friends, despite not being able to see one another very often, and Fox had pleaded with me to help him make a special gift for Oak.

Fox had always harbored a fascination with animals, but more so with birds than any other creature. When two eagles had battled it out on the lakeside near our home for possession of the fish one had caught, one of the eagles had been fatally wounded and subsequently perished on the damp shoreline. Fox brought the deceased raptor home so that he might study the bird more closely, and he finally decided that its claws would make a fine necklace for Oak. I agreed to assist, but only when necessary. Fox had arranged the claws so the halluces, the two longest ones, were placed at the center, and the six remaining shorter claws were tied more or less evenly spaced onto a leather throng. This was then knotted so it could be worn around the neck.

Morning Star knew that Fox was eager to give Oak this present, but she also had a gift to impart. Morning Star had devoted much time into curing a large otter's pelt, which she then had sewn into a pair of mittens. She wished to give these to Willow Woman as a token of her esteem, even though it would not be cold enough to use the mittens for many moons to come.

Morning Star and I now joined the gathering around Willow Woman and Black Wolf. The children, somehow not tired out by the long trip, still had sufficient energy to play, but we adults and our two dogs were happy to settle down on matting and rest. Even Lily, awakened by all the noise and activity, toddled around after the older children, doing her best to emulate their actions and join in their games.

Willow Woman skillfully managed to be attentive to Black Wolf without neglecting any of her guests. She engaged one and all in conversation, making sure that none of us were left out. Her genuine warmth and sincerity seemed to dispel Swift River and Hawks initial reservations about their father's paramour. I had to admit that when I first had met Willow Woman, I was startled by her as well. There was no getting around the fact that she was outwardly unusual, but upon coming to know her, I had found she was a woman of great intellectual and personal depth.

"The lines," Hawk whispered, nudging his brother. "She wears lines instead of animals."

Swift River looked to Hawk.

"*Lines?*" Swift River repeated.

"On her skin," Hawk said, still speaking quietly. "Lines like Da's markings, only she has a lot more of them."

Willow Woman must have overheard.

"Do you like tattoos?" She asked the boys. "I was about your age when I was first tattooed. It is the rite of passage all those in line to be Head Elder must endure, until we are covered, from head to toe . . . well, almost from head to toe."

"I like the Wolfmen's animal tattoos," Hawk told her. "Bewok said that each beast represents a kill."

Bewok nodded in agreement.

"For most hunters, it means that we also are covered from head to toe," Bewok said.

"A very old hunter might run out of skin before he can record all his prey," Willow Woman said with a laugh. "Our lines indicate our status. I have chosen to share my status with Black Wolf, and thus he is marked on his forearms and lower legs, but he has declined to submit to more tattoos."

"I am honored to share any part of your life and your role, but they are difficult to discern, anyway," Black Wolf said sheepishly, holding out a hairy forearm. "If I am going to go through all that discomfort, I would prefer to have something to show for it."

"So Oak will have tattoos one day?" Swift River asked. "Tattoos all over?"

"Yes," Willow Woman answered. "Ah, here he is now!"

"Look who is here!" Oak cried out as he and his companions, Slow Bear and Gray Owl, entered the compound. He left the two older men behind and ran toward the other children.

I had not seen Oak in several years. He was quite tall and well built for a boy his age. Fox himself was a large child, but even though Oak was a year younger, they were about the same size. There the similarities ended. In contrast to Fox's freckled skin, light green eyes, and bushy red-gold hair, Oak had his parents' dusky skin, dark brown eyes, and shiny black hair. The two boys had their heads together, talking with great animation. Then Fox motioned for Oak to follow him.

"Muh-Muh," Fox began, "do you have the present?"

"Yes," Morning Star replied, reaching into the bag she had retrieved from the sled. She placed an item into Fox's waiting hand. Fox grinned broadly, passing it to Oak.

"I made this for you," Fox said. "Well, Puh-Puh helped me a little. He showed me how to make grooves around each claw so it could be tied onto the thong."

Oak held the necklace before him, his mouth agape with awe as he examined it closely.

"Thank you! This . . . this is wonderful!" Oak immediately placed the necklace over his head. "Mother, Father, see what Fox has given me!"

Oak moved to stand before his parents, displaying the gift happily.

"That is very fine," Willow Woman said appreciatively. "Fox, you were very thoughtful to make such a special present for Oak."

Fox just smiled in response, but he glowed with pleasure at the reception his gift had garnered.

"And we have something for you, Willow," Morning Star announced as she produced the mittens from the sack. "These are for you." Morning Star gave them to Willow Woman, who seemed earnestly surprised.

"Why, thank you! Oh, they are lovely!" Willow Woman said, passing her fingers over the finely sewn seams of the otter's well-tanned leather, and then inserting her hands into the mitten's luxuriously soft and furry interiors. "They fit so well! And they will be so useful when the weather turns cool. I must be feeling my age; I feel the cold so much more in recent years."

"I am so pleased you like them," Morning Star replied, but she briefly exchanged glances with me. I could see the momentary concern on Morning Star's face. There was no doubt that Willow Woman, who surely must have been over forty winters old at this time, was showing her years. Not only had she lost some of her size, but the lines in her face had deepened and the gray strands in her hair were more numerous. But then Morning Star remembered herself and her sunny smile returned, and Oak and Fox left us to resume their play.

"The new lodge appears larger than its predecessor," I said to Willow Woman, changing the subject. "Does it suit as well as the old one?"

"Yes, it is a bit bigger," Willow Woman concurred. "The other was built before Oak was born, and his bedchamber was very small. He has much more room now."

"And you have more space for guests," Black Wolf pointed out. "I hope we have not arrived at an inconvenient time."

"It is never an inconvenience to have you here," Willow Woman assured us. "You missed Karno and his fellow Wolfmen by only a matter of days. Karno told us that he thought you might be coming this way soon.

He said you were going to Gray Elk's home. How is Gray Elk?"

"Like all of us, Gray Elk is getting older," Black Wolf said with a regretful smile. "He was happy to see us. He spoke of his sons' possibly attending this fall's Gathering if they complete the autumn hunts early enough."

Willow Woman sighed thoughtfully.

"Yes, autumn will be here before we know it," she said. "Karno expressed an interest in attending the Gathering, too."

The annual Gathering was held by The People from the East. Other peoples were not typically invited, although many years ago Black Wolf had brought some of us Old Ones so that we could be presented to the Head Elder to give testimony. However, we had not been entirely welcome, and, actually, it had caused quite a ruckus. We had not gone to a Gathering since that time. The Wolfmen had never been invited nor attended.

Willow Woman turned to Black Wolf and met his gaze.

"This is something we have spoken of for several years," she said.

"It is something that will come to pass, eventually," Black Wolf began. "It is not just that Karno will want to have a seat at the Gathering, but that we should include others, too."

"Do you mean everyone?" Swift River asked.

Slow Bear spoke up.

"The Gathering Hall, as big as it is, would not hold everyone who resides in our territory," he said. He was Willow Woman's most trusted advisor, after Black Wolf, and much like a grandfather to Oak.

"That is true," Willow Woman admitted. "But most clans send only their elders, or a small group to represent them."

Slow Bear shook his head.

"I understand what you want to accomplish," he said. "Times have been hard. Each passing winter seems worse than the one before. We would be better off to work in cooperation with one another, instead of trying to outcompete one another. But I think there are many who will be reluctant accept that notion."

I tended to think that Slow Bear was right. The one Gathering I had attended had been a novel experience for me. Of course, as one who dwelt deep in the forest and seldom saw anyone outside my own clan, it was a shock to see hundreds of people assembled in one place. I had not known there were so many of The People from the East on these lands. It had been a volatile assembly, which often seemed on the verge of breaking into an out-and-out melee. It was only the strength of Willow Woman's character and respect for her as Head Elder that had kept order. The reaction to the news that all peoples would be allowed to take part in the Gathering was bound to be mixed, at best.

"Whether they like it or not, I foresee that one day we may not have a choice," Willow Woman stated.

"Our survival may depend on it. Maybe not this year, or in the next few years, but eventually."

"Some of The People are building their homes around the Hall," Slow Bear said with a wry grin. "They plan to make a living by trading with those who attend the Gatherings. Perhaps they will put aside any ill will they might be harboring for the sake of trade."

"I have heard about that, as well," Black Wolf responded. "It would seem a new village is sprouting up by the Hall. The old village where many of them formerly lived is now deserted."

"There is plentiful water and game there," I noted.

"Yes," Willow Woman said, "their problem will be firewood. So many trees were harvested when we built the new Hall."

I did not envy them the chore of procuring so much wood. But then my mind wandered back to my recent Dream, with its field of hewn trees, the splintered trunks amongst the dead grasses. If it had been the grounds surrounding the Gathering Hall, no wonder I had felt unease. This was not a place of tranquility.

"Tris." Gray Owl had appeared at my side, and he whispered my name to get my attention without interrupting the conversation. Gray Owl was Willow Woman's healer – a small man who was dwarfed by his Head Elder, but whose skills and wisdom were highly valued by all.

"Yes, Gray Owl?" I answered.

"Your ear, it does not pain you?" Gray Owl inquired.

"No." I shook my head and pushed my hair away to show him the ear that had been partially shorn off some time ago. Gray Owl had treated the cropped ear, but I had left their company before it had fully healed. "My ear, or what is left of it, is well. Morning Star made sure that it did not become infected."

Gray Owl nodded.

"That is good," he said.

We listened to the ongoing talk about who else might attend the Gathering, but I noticed that Swift River and Hawk were distracted by the younger children as they cavorted around us. They could have opted to play, as well, but as young men, they doubtless considered themselves too grown up. I wondered if they missed the carefree days of their younger years, or if they were simply curious about their half-brother. Oak, like his mother, had an air of authority about him, even though he was now just a boy. He often directed the others in their games or worked with Fox and Mror to devise new strategies. Even though Oak was obviously in control, he nevertheless took care to make sure the smaller children were not injured or left out.

"I am so pleased Oak has other little ones with whom to associate," Gray Owl said. "He so seldom has other children for company. Just his mother and a group of older men."

"Fox and Mror have been so looking forward to visiting," I told him. "They have spoken of coming here for some moons. They think much of Oak."

"Their friendship may be what finally joins our peoples," Gray Owl responded. "If a harmonious relationship between the various peoples does not happen in our time, it will be much more likely to happen in theirs."

I thought this an interesting concept.

"But my clan and Black Wolf's kin have been friends for generations," I pointed out, "Is that not much the same?"

"It is," Willow Woman said, hearing our exchange, "but the mixing of our peoples has been very limited up until now. Additionally, Karno is on his way to Auchnic Village, where they have suffered great calamity over the last year. He hopes to become their Elder, or Great Man, as he calls it. If he and his men are successful, that may help our cause. The more we can normalize the acceptance of others, the better our chances. Like Gray Owl, I believe each succeeding generation will have an easier time of it."

"Tor, you have been silent during this discussion," Black Wolf observed.

"I am inclined to think — or hope — Willow is right," Puh replied.

"You sound hesitant about that," Black Wolf said to Puh.

"*Hope* is the operative word," Puh answered. "Often, people do not want to be dissuaded from their long-held beliefs. It may be better if there is no mention in advance that some attendees will be Old Ones or Wolfmen. There are those who would argue against it until their dying day. But we can make a case for the advantages of cooperation, such as being able to bring down more game — and larger animals at that —

and having more stores to put away for winter. That may hold sway."

"More pairings between peoples would surely help the cause as well," Bewok said with a grin.

Willow Woman laughed at this.

"I believe that is Karno's plan," she said. "Although, perhaps not with the goal of furthering harmonious relationships. If all Wolfmen had your charm, Bewok, they would have no shortage of mates."

Bewok smiled bashfully at this praise.

"You are very kind, Great Lady," he said to Willow Woman.

* * *

At day's end and after the consumption of a prodigious evening sup, we were shown to rooms within the new lodge. Morning Star and I were pleased to find our room was partitioned into two smaller rooms, each one boasting a small opening in the exterior wall that could be closed off or left agape to allow fresh air to circulate. Sleeping platforms and bedding were already set up, and I was eager to try one of them out. Oak had invited Fox and Mror to join him in his bedchamber, so it would just be Morning Star, our daughters, Raena, and me.

The girls gladly collapsed onto one of the beds and were soon sound asleep. Raena, who was also tired from our long journey, curled up by the entryway, her gentle snores filling the room. Morning Star looked up at me, hands on her hips.

"Well, the children and the dog are practically unconscious; they must be exhausted," she said.

Her words were punctuated by a few thumps and bumps and muted exclamations from a nearby chamber. I recognized Fox's voice amongst them.

"The boys are certainly enjoying their time together," I mused. "They are so excited – I wonder if they will get any sleep."

"If not, Fox will be cranky tomorrow," Morning Star predicted. "There is such a thing as too much fun."

"Not so far as I am concerned," I said, smiling and pulling her closer to me.

* * *

Our visit was to last a half-moon before we would return home. It was a wonderful respite from our typical daily existence. Puh, Black Wolf, his sons, Bewok, and I occasionally assisted with the hunts and work around the lodge, while Morning Star, Ria, and our collective children stayed around the lodge with Willow Woman, although sometimes they went to the quieter pools downstream from the falls, where they endeavored to tempt fish to bite their hooks.

I had not tried to fish this way; we had used fish traps in the ocean and nets in rivers or lakes, but Willow Woman had taught them to tie a small bone hook to a fine line woven of long strands of hair. From what I understood of it, she added tiny bits of feather or fur to disguise the hook, making it look as though an insect had alighted on the water, and then when a fish bit, she tugged the line sharply. It took great patience to bring in a fish this way, but it was remarkably effective. I very much wanted to learn more about this method, so Willow Woman promised me that one morning we would go down to a pool by ourselves, and there she would teach me.

It was a soft summer morning when Willow Woman and I set out for the lesson, and although I carried a spear, as usual, we also carried a few items of fishing gear. Raena accompanied us, trotting dutifully at my side as we walked down the trail, her eyes and ears alert.

"I enjoy fishing," Willow Woman told me. "It is one of the few things I like to do where I can just relax and let my mind go where it may. I miss it when winter comes and the water freezes, when even the great falls go silent."

"You would be at your winter lodgings by then, would you not?" I asked.

"Yes," Willow Woman answered, puffing a bit as she walked.

"Perhaps I should walk slower?" I offered.

I was used to marching steadily down a trail, often pulling a sled or carrying a heavy pack or game animal, so when walking unencumbered I was accustomed to striding along to cover as much distance as possible in the shortest amount of time. I doubted Willow Woman had ever so much as walked briskly in recent years.

"Thank you, Tris," Willow Woman replied, wiping her brow. After a few moments, she went on: "Do you know, I think that these past few days have been some of the happiest of my life. I am so pleased that you all have stopped over. Not only because I am able to be with my dear Black Wolf, and Oak can be with his father, but because it is so wonderful for all of us to have this time together. Hawk and Swift River are able to get to know their brother, the children can frolic, and we adults can enjoy one another's company."

"It has been memorable for me, as well," I agreed. "Many thanks for hosting all of us. Especially right after hosting the Wolfmen. You exchanged one crowd of people for another."

Willow Woman laughed at this.

"That is true," she said. "But I do not mind. Karno can be rather full of himself at times, but as I get to know him, I find there is more to him than meets the eye. Sometimes I believe he plays dumb so that people will underestimate him."

I was perplexed at this.

"*Plays dumb*?" I echoed her words. I had not heard this turn of phrase before.

"Yes," Willow Woman said. "You know, how he seems to struggle to speak our language, even after all these years and after all the other Wolfmen have become fluent. It is true that he is not a brilliant intellect, but he is canny. It is my guess that he could speak at least marginally better if he so chose – and he realizes that if others do not credit him with much mental vigor, they will not give him much notice."

This was a foreign concept to me. I was still unsure of her point.

"You mean that he may not want to draw their attention?" I questioned.

"Sometimes there is a benefit to that," Willow Woman said. "To live like a mole that spends much of its life underground, so no one will spare it much thought. And if they do, they do not think you are much of a threat. Also, you are not likely to incur their wrath or their envy for what you possess; nor will they object to your presence."

"That may be," I said with a shrug. "I do not really understand the reasoning behind it. But it seems to me that Karno was always eager to be well thought of."

"Amongst his friends, that is true," Willow Woman conceded. "And I might be completely wrong. This is just a notion that came to mind while they were here. He was uncharacteristically quiet during the visit. He appeared to be unusually thoughtful."

"He may have been concerned about what might take place after they arrive at the village," I speculated.

"A lot will depend on how they are received," Willow Woman said with a nod. "He is a mature man now, and he is eager to establish a clan and start a family."

"Yes," I responded simply. Willow Woman had become winded again, so I hoped a pause in conversation would allow her to catch her breath again. I slowed my pace once more.

Now the falls were a thunderous presence, but we did not approach them and instead headed downstream, following the raging river until we came to a spot where a small inlet created a pool of calmer water. This gave the fish somewhere to escape to from the roiling rapids, and a place to rest.

Willow Woman pointed toward a smooth boulder near the river's bank and indicated that we should sit there. Once we were comfortably ensconced on the large rock, she reached toward me.

"The sack, please, Tris," she requested.

I passed the satchel I had toted for her and she promptly opened it, producing several coils of line, each outfitted with a delicate hook and decorated with the tiny tufts of fur. Raena leaned closer, her nose twitching curiously.

"I know you smell the scents of past catches," I said to the dog, "but you do not want to become hooked." I gently shoved her back, lest she become our biggest catch of the day.

"Uncoil your line," Willow Woman instructed, holding one of the coils toward me.

I did as I was told, marveling at the long, continuous black string, which seemed to be made up of four strands of hair woven together and attached at one end to a small stick.

"We toss the hook onto the water?" I guessed.

"Yes," Willow Woman replied. "You will be able to see the tips of the fur on the water's surface. Jiggle the line just slightly. If you see the line take a sudden dip, pull it sharply; that will set the hook in the fish's jaw."

I threw my line out over the water, keeping hold of the stick in my left hand. Willow Woman also tossed her line, just downstream of mine. When our hooks began to sink, Willow Woman spoke.

"Pull in your line now, and try again. We will do this many times, and hopefully, we will have a few fish to show for our efforts by the time the morning is through." Willow Woman grinned at me. "You know, my mother taught me how to fish when I was a girl. I have such fond memories of those days. We used to sit right here, on this very rock."

"She left you with lasting gifts, then," I responded. "That is the best we can hope for, for our children. To give them the gift of knowledge and memories of happy days."

"That she did." Willow Woman became somber. "She died giving birth to my younger brother when I was nine winters old. I still miss her terribly."

"I am sorry for your sadness," I said. I placed my hand over hers and gave it a slight squeeze, at the same time feeling a pang of grief that sometimes assailed me since the death of my own mother. Even after so many years, the pain could still be sharp.

"Throughout much of my childhood, it was just my father and me," Willow Woman said with a sigh. "At least until he became Head Elder, but I was nearly grown by then. However, I am not complaining. My father was a loving parent, and I adored him. I suppose he would have liked to have had a son to one day take his place as leader of The People. He did eventually become paired with another woman, but they had no children." Willow Woman then glanced at me hastily. "I suppose that you, too, would like more sons."

"I would like more children," I admitted. "Whether boy or girl does not matter. Fox has expressed an interest in having a little brother, but by now, any little brothers would be too young for him to play with. He does enjoy playing with Mror, and he is very excited anytime we are coming to see you and Oak." I hesitated a moment before going on about the son Morning Star and I had lost, not knowing if I could trust myself to maintain my composure. Not because I was reluctant to show emotion in Willow Woman's presence, but because I did not want to feel the anguish just now. It was too fresh. But I blurted out the words before I could stop myself. "Morning Star gave birth to a boy during late winter. He did not live."

Willow Woman drew in her breath sharply. My hand was still over hers, but she now looked at me with sympathy and embraced me with her free arm.

"I am sorry, Tris," she said softly. "So that you know how much I understand, I will tell you something I have not told anyone, not even Black Wolf. I know I can trust you not to repeat this. I, too, have lost babies. I have had several miscarriages. I do not want Black Wolf to know, because I do not want to worry or upset him. Sometimes he is perplexed as to why we have not conceived more children, but I let him believe that it is just that we are too old. Fortunately, Black Wolf does not question it. I do not like to deceive him, but I do not see any point in divulging these losses since it would only distress him. We have Oak, and for that I am endlessly grateful."

Just then, Raena perked up and uttered a sharp woof. We had become distracted with our conversation and not yet tossed our lines back into the water, so we stood to see who was approaching.

"Halloo!" Black Wolf called out.

Fox, Mror, and Oak, followed by Puh and Black Wolf, emerged from the head of the path. The boys carried coiled fishing lines, while Black Wolf and Puh toted spears. Raena's tail wagged as she recognized our companions. Black Wolf greeted Willow Woman tenderly and sat down on her other side, while Puh ushered the boys a little way farther down the bank, where the boys could cast their lines without becoming entangled.

The heavy mood between Willow Woman and me instantly lightened. While I was grateful Willow Woman had sufficient trust in me to share her secret, I was relieved to have this cheerful company to lift our spirits. And now, perhaps I knew the reason behind the mysterious ailments that Willow Woman had suffered over the years.

 **Chapter Five** 

A black orb creeps across an ominous sky, threatening to blot out the sun. I have never seen anything like it. What is this thing that attacks the sun? Will we be left in permanent darkness?

I woke up with a start, feeling my heart pounding within my chest. In the past I had Dreamt of marauding beasts and frightening storms, but this Dream shook me to my core. Never could I have imagined that the sun's daytime presence, even if obscured by clouds, might not always remain constant. Like the earth beneath my feet, it was something I had always taken for granted. As I looked about, no light met my eyes. Had the darkness descended already?

We had returned home a few days earlier, and my full bladder told me that I had been asleep for quite some time. I felt for the edge of the blanket that covered Morning Star and me and pushed it back. I then rose to a sitting position and rubbed the sleep from my eyes before finally standing up and making my way into the main room of our home.

On the way to the dwelling's entrance I stepped on something that snapped, and the broken pieces poked into the sole of my foot. I stifled a groan of pain and then stumbled over another obstacle. Raena lay sleeping by the doorway, but she heard my approach and got to her feet as I unlashed the hide that covered the entryway. Together we went outdoors, where I stopped at a nearby tree to relieve my bladder.

The night air was balmy and the sky was still black, but the stars shone brightly. A sliver of moon hung low over the horizon. Morning was not far off. I stared to the east, but I could see no sign of a rising sun. My heart again began to thump with alarm. Raena, sensing my disquiet, stared at me and whined softly.

"Raena, what if there is no more sun?" I whispered to her. "What if the nighttime never ends?"

* * *

I seldom spoke of my Dreams to anyone. Morning Star often discerned when I was preoccupied with the potential portents of a Dream, but I did not wish to burden her with my fears unless pressed. The sun had risen after all, but the anxiety from the nightmare still gnawed at me. I soothed myself with the idea that it was preposterous; there was no such evil force that could snuff out its brilliance.

* * *

The height of summer was soon upon us. We labored intensely as we continued to work on our homes and build up stocks that would see us through the coming winter. Bewok settled in as though he had always been a part of our clan. Indeed, we had known him long enough that many of our children had known him for most if not all of their lives.

Bewok seemed determined to truly become one of us. His hair was still far shorter than ours, but he was letting it grow out. And while he still owned a wolfskin cloak, as did all his fellow Wolfmen, he no longer wore it. I thought it a shame that he was letting go of his old clan's culture, as there was much I admired about the Wolfmen. But that was for him to decide.

We were helping Bewok make a dwelling for himself, but in the meantime he was living with Puh, Ria, and their combined children. One morning I found Puh building a frame from which he planned to work an elk hide, under the watchful eyes of his dog, Auchs. I could see the large, wet hide rolled up on the ground nearby. The hide had spent the past three or more moons in the lake. There, it lay underwater among similar hides, rolled up in a loose bundle and weighted down with rocks, in order that the skin might soften and the hair would become loosened.

"Pleasant day to you, Puh," I said as I approached.

"Yes, it is," Puh agreed as he tied the timbers together.

"That is quite a large hide," I said. "Is it from the elk we took last spring?"

"Yes," Puh affirmed. "I thought we could use it to make a door flap for Bewok's house."

"I am sure he would welcome it," I mused, steadying a timber for Puh as he lashed another one to it. "The hides he has collected are all much smaller than this one."

Puh just nodded in reply. I knew the wet hide would be unwieldy, so I stayed to help Puh finish the frame and stitch the hide in place. Once this had been accomplished, the whole assembly was ready to be stood upright. I handled one side while Puh took charge of the other.

"We will position it between those two trees," Puh said, pointing to a pair of nearby trees.

"Yes, Puh." I responded.

We carried the frame to the spot, where the upright sides of the frame were then lashed to the tree trunks. We looked up at the top edge of the hide, which was higher than I was tall, even though we had set it up so that the longest length ran horizontal to the ground. Sometimes we would actually stake the hides to the ground itself, especially if they were smaller, but this one was too wide. If we had used that method we would only be able to clean the edges. Standing it up allowed the entire hide to be accessed, although it was necessary to turn the frame from time to time.

Just then, Puh's dog Auchs rose to his feet and stretched, yawning and wagging his tail as he noted that my three youngest sisters were coming to join us. Twie, Saree, and Mi were talking softly amongst themselves as they walked, completely absorbed in their conversation. I smiled to note that they were growing into young women. Twie and Mi had inherited my Muh's dark red hair and her height, but Saree was comparatively petite, with the red-gold hair that came from Puh's side of the family. In fact, eight-winters-old Mi was already taller than ten-winters-old Saree. Twie, now fifteen winters old, was almost the same height as Puh.

"We have come to help," Twie said when she saw they had caught our attention.

"Yes, we have," Saree replied. "We have brought scrapers. Bewok's house will soon be ready for him to move in, and he must have a door covering."

"Your offer of assistance is most timely," Puh told them. "I am sure Bewok will be quite pleased that you are looking out for his welfare."

Twie blushed at this and her sisters giggled soundlessly, in the silent way of our people. Puh exchanged a knowing glance with me, but he said nothing. Since Bewok had come to stay with us, it had become apparent that he was determined to court Twie. Bewok was never overt in his attempt, but just the same, it was plain in the way he was always attentive to Twie that he hoped to win her affections.

Twie did not let on whether she would accept him, but neither did she discourage him. I wondered if she recalled Karno's clumsy wooing of her older sister, Ru. The memory of it made me shake my head. Karno had been as reckless in his romantic forays as he seemed to be in all other aspects of his life. Bewok, on the other hand, presented a stark contrast to his friend and his people's leader. Bewok was a reliable hand during a hunt, but he had no need to perform heroic feats, or, should they occur, to brag about them afterward. In his leisure moments, he could be seen teaching Fox how to carve animals from bits of deadwood or create a tool from hollow section of bone that could be used to make bird calls. I thought that Twie would do well to accept Bewok — that is, if she did not think him too old for her. He was in his prime of life at twenty-five winters of age, but that was a great deal older than she.

The only other potential problem was the Wolfmen's steadfast aversion to kissing. I had been shocked to hear that they considered it to be extremely unclean and a repulsive act. We Old Ones and those from The People from the East were all devoted to the practice, and I, for one, seldom missed an opportunity to kiss my beloved mate or my children. I could not speak for Twie, but I could only imagine that she might feel put out to be paired with a man who would not kiss her. However, that was none of my concern. Twie was a sensible young woman, and I felt she was quite capable of handling her own affairs.

* * *

It was another pairing that caught us by surprise when Karno and a few followers strode onto our compound one day. Puh and I had joined Bror, the mate of my eldest sister, on a hunt earlier in the day and had come home with a young bull elk. There seemed to be a lot of young elks wandering around, possibly run off by their mothers after they had given birth to new calves, or simply seeking their place in the world. This young bull sported a rather modest set of velvet-clad antlers, but he was well fed. After attaching a rope to his hind legs and slinging the end of the rope over a sturdy tree branch, we three hunters, assisted by a number of helpers, grunted with effort as we hoisted the carcass into the air. Much of the elk's blood had already left his veins, but this would facilitate the final bleeding out and make it easier to skin the beast.

We had just finished tying off the rope when the various resident dogs began to bark. They were not barks of alarm but of greeting. We smiled at one another in anticipation of these apparently friendly visitors and then went to investigate the identity of the new arrivals.

A crowd had already gathered at the center of the compound, and there we found Black Wolf, Uncle Inlee, and Bewok speaking animatedly to Karno and his companions. They were accompanied by a woman. She was small, with thick brown hair that fell in waves. She seemed tired and a bit disheveled, but I thought her pretty. She was loaded with a pack and she carried a small child on her hip.

"This is Jura," Karno said, introducing her. "Jura with me, now."

Jura stared at us from behind strands of hair that hung over her dark eyes.

Morning Star stepped forward, toting Lily. "Hallo, Jura," she said. "I am glad you have come to visit with us."

Jura only nodded in response.

"What a lovely little one," Morning Star said, trying again to engage her in conversation. "Is it a boy or a girl? And what is your child's name?"

"He is Mino," Jura finally spoke. Her words were understandable, but strangely accented. Like Puh's mate, Ria, she had come from a distant clan, and although we used the same language, our words were pronounced with slight variation.

I thought I noticed a distinct sadness in her bearing. But the toddler's head perked up at his name and he repeated it.

"Mino," the child said brightly.

"Mino . . . just like . . ." Bewok began, but he quickly broke off.

Bewok looked to Karno as if for confirmation. Mino had been the name of their friend. Karno, Bewok, and Mino had been inseparable since childhood, until a few years ago when Mino was killed during a hunt. In fact, Mino was buried just a short distance from where we now stood.

"Jura was Mino's woman when we stay at her village two year ago," Karno said. "Now Jura Karno's mate. Karno take her. Karno take little Mino. Karno take care of family."

As I listened to Karno's broken sentences, I thought back on Willow Woman's recent observations about Karno – her speculation that he might purposely want people to underestimate him. This was an interesting idea, especially considering that I had always thought him to be a rather brash man who was exceedingly proud of his accomplishments and his social standing as a son of a Great Man, or Head Elder, as we called them. However, I was not inclined to dwell on this, as Karno grinned when he saw me and pushed his way toward me.

"Karno so happy to see you, Tris," Karno said, grasping me by my blood-stained forearms. "Ah, look at Tris; you make kill this day!"

I was liberally splattered with blood and grime from head to toe. I returned his grin.

"I am happy to see you as well," I replied, "and I am sorry to greet you and meet Jura while looking this way."

Karno waved my remark aside.

"What is such matter among friend?" Karno responded. "Karno very eager to bring Jura to see friend. We go to Jura village and find many people gone. Most men gone. They tell us go away two year ago, but now they want us stay. Karno be their Great Man. Take Jura as mate."

"I am sure Mino would be gratified to know that you are taking care of his family," Black Wolf stated. "I had not heard that Mino was paired."

"He was not," Bewok chimed in. "He would have liked to stay and be paired with Jura, but then we were unceremoniously invited to leave, so it was not to be. Just the same, Mino would have been pleased to know he had sired a child, and that his woman and son were being cared for."

"Village Great Man afraid of Karno," Karno said heatedly. "He die of sickness last winter. Big sickness kill many. Maybe it good he send us away, or we die, too."

"Come with me," Morning Star said to Jura, taking her by the elbow to lead her away. "Come and sit. You must be so tired, thirsty, and hungry."

But Jura stood rooted to her spot by Karno's side. Karno turned toward her and gave her a little push toward Morning Star.

"It all right. You go with Morning Star," Karno said to her gently. "She good woman."

Jura did not seem very comforted by these words, but she did as instructed.

"Shy woman," Karno said, shaking his head as he watched Morning Star lead Jura away.

"We are strange to her," Puh spoke up. "It might be harrowing to meet so many new people at once."

"And it would seem she has been through a lot of turmoil already," Ria added. "Give her time to get used to all the changes."

I thought it probable that she may also need time to get used to Karno. If she had been romantically attached to Mino, one might guess that she preferred a man with Mino's traits. Thus it was a possibility that she found life with Karno to be something that required a bit of adjustment. Mino was more like Bewok, in that both were quiet, modest, cheerfully good-natured, and industrious. Karno, on the other hand, was not known for being quiet or modest, but on the plus side, he was generally inclined toward optimism. He was fearless in a hunt and a ferocious opponent in battle. But most importantly, I was sure Karno would take good care of Jura and her son.

As the flies buzzed around me, attracted to the blood I was wearing, I was reminded that the elk still needed to be skinned.

"Karno," I began, "we must finish work on the elk before we wash up. Perhaps you and your friends will rest from the journey and take refreshment while we work."

"Yes," Black Wolf agreed. "Come, we will get food and drink, and you all" – he indicated Puh, Bror, and me – "can join us when you are ready."

Karno shook his head and inched closer to us.

"We come with you to clean beast," he said in a hushed voice. "Want to talk while we work. Have something to tell."

I was somewhat surprised at this, but Puh did not so much as blink at this revelation.

"Follow us," Puh said simply.

The entourage included every adult male on the compound, plus several younger ones.

"That fine bull," Karno remarked, studying the animal. "He had good summer until he meet you. He eat well. He has much flesh. Much fat."

"He is heavy," Black Wolf concurred. "Look how the tree branch bends under his weight, even though he is not entirely up off the ground yet."

As Black Wolf had said, the elk's front limbs and head still rested on the ground. The upper part of the suspended elk, that is, his hind legs, needed to be skinned first, and then he would be hoisted higher into the tree as we worked our way down his body.

"Karno come here because he want talk to you," Karno said, changing the subject. "Speak on many thing. But on way to talk to you, we see two mammoth bulls fighting. Tusk tangle – like this," Karno demonstrated by entwining his fingers as though his two hands were locked together. "Bull stuck, push back and forth. Stuck. And Karno think this good time to take them."

Karno scanned our faces eagerly, awaiting our reaction.

"How far from here?" Uncle Inlee asked.

"Walk all day," Karno answered. "Then we find them."

"Assuming they have not freed themselves," Puh pointed out.

"That sounds just like those two mammoths pictured on the wall of Cousin Gray Elk's Talking Stones," Fox said excitedly. "May I go, too?"

"Me, too," Mror piped up.

"And us!" Swift River and Hawk chimed in.

We worked as we conversed, but I paused a moment to look at Fox. His eyes were alight and his cheeks were flushed. I hated to squelch his enthusiasm, but he and Mror were still so young. Even if I did not think he was too young, surely Morning Star would not allow him to go. I then noted that Puh also was gazing at Mror.

"I will speak to your mother about accompanying us," Puh said to Mror. "If she is amenable to the idea and she will go, too, to keep you in her care, then it is all right with me."

I brightened at the thought. That might be the perfect solution. The younger boys could observe from a safe distance, under Ria's supervision. And likely Hawk and Swift River's too, if their mother Little Fawn would allow them to go.

"Karno not want Jura to know," he said anxiously. "Jura be afraid. She know mammoth kill Mino. Karno think we leave to slay mammoth, but tell Jura we go for bear. No worry."

"She likes bears better than she likes mammoths?" Black Wolf asked, looking down at Karno skeptically from his great height.

"Jura think bear taste fine," Karno responded. "She be happy to eat bear."

"Ah, well," Black Wolf said with a shrug. "A bear it is, then."

"I just hope she is not disappointed if we come back with mammoth meat," Bewok said with a grin. "Because if we do bring down these mammoths, we will be eating them for a long time to come."

 **Chapter Six** 

The next morning Karno and his three companions, Bewok, Black Wolf and his sons, Puh, Ria, and Mror, Uncle Inlee, Bror, Fish Hawk, who was the mate of Black Wolf's daughter Petal, and Fox and I began our "Bear Hunt". Everyone in our party was privy to our actual mission, but most of those left at home would not learn about the mammoths until after our return. I did tell Morning Star about our real plan, but I also told her not to be concerned. After all, the bull mammoths might well have freed themselves and left the vicinity before we found them. In that case, there was a chance we could track one of the beasts, especially if it was injured, but it was more likely we would come home empty-handed. Or perhaps we might find a bear for Jura.

The day started out cool and misty, but when the morning haze burned off, a blanket of heat settled over the landscape. Much of the trail traversed open countryside, so there was little shade to protect us from the sun's glare. Summer might soon be on the wane, but I knew that we Old Ones would be sporting red skin by the end of the day.

Based on Karno's description of where he had last seen the mammoths, we thought it improbable we would find the beasts that day, but if we hiked swiftly we might find them on the morrow. There was little else to distract the eye on these grasslands, so they should be easy to spot from a long way off.

Any place where a tree or a brook offered respite from our hot trek we stopped for a spell to cool off and slake our thirst. Fox and Mror, as the youngest members of our party, did not complain, but they were obviously exhausted by the end of the day. As the sun neared the horizon, we selected a small grove of trees in the distance and decided we would make that our destination. If it seemed an appropriate place to spend the night, we would set up camp there.

The trees proved to be handy for tying off our lean-tos. Despite the soaring daytime temperatures, nights could still be quite cold, and the lean-tos would help to keep us warm – not only to retain our collective body heat, but to entrap the warmth from the fire and shelter us from the wind.

It was a cooperative effort to erect a number of lean-tos and clear a spot to build a fire. It would not do to have stray embers ignite the nearby leaf litter and then spread to the dry grasses, where it could potentially cause a wildfire. Puh and I used fallen branches to rake away the dead leaves and then chopped at the ground with improvised digging sticks to excavate a shallow depression in the earth. As we worked, some of our companions deposited armloads of deadwood next to the new fire pit.

Mosquitoes hummed around us, biting and causing us to frequently slap ourselves as we sought relief from our tormentors. Smoke from the fire would help to drive away these pests, thus we needed to get the fire going as quickly as possible.

By the time a blaze was alight, the sky was nearly dark and a chorus of cricket song filled the air. We were grateful to find places by the fire and sit down, giving our tired feet a much-needed rest. Fox sat next to me, leaning heavily against my side. I felt him shiver.

"Puh-Puh, I am so cold," Fox told me.

"Here," I said, reaching for my cloak to unroll it and place it around his shoulders. "This may help. Just hold it loosely around your body; your sunburned skin will hurt where anything touches it."

"Many thanks, Puh-Puh," Fox said with a grin. "Ooh, my face hurts when I smile!"

Fox then grimaced.

"Your face is red," Black Wolf stated, looking at Fox. "It matches your red hair."

"It does not, Grandpa." Fox grinned again at his grandfather's jest, but quickly touched his face with the palms of his hands. "My cheeks feel hot."

"I am cold, too, Muh-Muh," Mror said to Ria.

Puh was prepared; he had already unfurled his cloak. He pulled Mror onto his lap and wrapped the cloak around himself, Ria, and Mror as they sat on the ground.

"This will keep us all warm while we have our evening sup," Puh said to Mror.

"Is my face red, too, Puh-Puh?" Mror asked Puh.

"Yes, indeed it is," Puh answered. "We can rub salve into our skin before we go to sleep. It should help." Puh paused and looked at me. His face was red, too, as I was sure mine was, as well. "I hope," Puh finally added.

Uncle Inlee laughed silently, as we Old Ones do.

"I hope so, too," Uncle Inlee said, passing a leather sack of dried elk meat to Bror, who was seated next to him. "If luck is with us, maybe tomorrow will be overcast and spare us from the brunt of the sun's rays."

"You funny people," Karno observed. "Karno never see another clan that change color in sun like tree change color in the time of rut."

"Thank you for noticing," Bror said dryly.

Bror's wry sense of humor was lost on Karno, but it made me smile, and my sunburned cheeks were suddenly stricken with a sharp pain as my skin creased.

"Much welcome," Karno replied. "Karno notice all things. We see sign of mammoth battle tomorrow. Ground churned up, grass very flat."

Just then, we heard a series of long whoops and several high-pitched cries.

"Hyenas," Black Wolf said, standing up to get a better view of the area around us.

"They will not like the fire," Puh stated. "But we will have to take turns keeping watch and maintaining the fire all night."

"Hyenas worry me less than a visit by lions," Bewok joined in.

I could not blame him one bit for having that notion. Bewok had already survived one near-fatal lion attack. A hyena's maniacal laughter rent the air.

"Not an amusing thought," Black Wolf agreed with Bewok. "Well, there are enough of us to fend off any unwelcome visitors if need be. And enough that if we all take turns keeping watch, no one should have to miss much sleep."

I felt Fox stir in his seat beside me. He was almost completely enveloped in the cloak, leaving only his face and one hand exposed as he ate. I worried that the talk of hyenas and lions might frighten him, but although he was wide-eyed, he appeared calm.

"We can sing to keep away the hyenas," Bewok said lightheartedly.

"Good idea," Karno concurred, nodding. "Eat first, then sing."

There was little talk as our meal of dried foods was quickly consumed. I was still hungry afterward, but I knew we would need to ration our stores. We had brought enough food to feed us for only two days, and I thought there was a good chance we would be out longer than that. Of course, even if we did not succeed in killing at least one of the mammoths, there was plenty of game available on these lands; we would not go hungry for long.

A cool breeze shook the tree limbs overhead, making the flames within the fire pit dance and causing puffs of smoke to occasionally blow into our faces. The shifting wind made it impossible to find a spot that was consistently upwind, but it did chase away the few mosquitoes that had not been discouraged by the smoke. We huddled under our cloaks, blinking our smoke-stung eyes and picking bits of dried meat from our teeth with long slivers of wood.

Karno coughed and cleared his throat.

"This smoke make sing hard," Karno stated.

"Even the hyenas have left us alone," Black Wolf noted. "I am ready for sleep. I will lay myself down. Wake me when it is time for me to stand watch."

"I would not mind taking the first watch," I said.

Fox had already fallen asleep, leaning against me as we now shared my cloak. He was comfortable and I could carry him into the lean-to later when it was my turn to rest.

"I will share the watch with you," Puh offered.

"We will share it with you," Ria agreed. Like Fox, Mror was cuddled up with his parents, sound asleep.

"Wake me when you go to lie down," Bewok said as he rose to retire to one of the lean-tos. "I will take the next watch."

"Wake me, too," Bror followed. "I will be more chipper after I have a bit of a nap."

"And me as well," Fish Hawk joined in. "If three of us stand watch at a time, we can be sure we are well protected from any creatures who may want to carry off one of our group."

"I will take watch with Da," announced Black Wolf's son Swift River.

"Me, too," his other son Hawk chimed in.

We all agreed that this was a good plan for the first half of the night. The others could be awakened as the night went on. They left us to find a place to lie down, and soon it was just Puh, Ria, and me and our boys by the fire. Puh emerged from under his cloak and stood up to rearrange the wood within the fire pit. He used long sticks to carefully form the burning wood into a tripod, gradually stacking up more wood against it. This structure was built to lean away from us. Now that one side of the fire pit was not surrounded by either people or lean-tos, we could attempt to direct the smoke away from us. The center of the now multilegged tripod glowed bright red as the heat collected there, and the lengths of wood created a chimney of sorts that funneled the smoke in the chosen direction.

Satisfied with his work, Puh resumed his seat with his mate and youngest son. It seemed very quiet now that all the others had gone to bed. The only sounds were the soft whispers of the wind as it rustled dry summer leaves, the crackling of the fire, and the hum and chirp of insects. But it was not long before loud snores met our ears.

"I hope our companions managed to get to sleep before Black Wolf," Ria said.

"Indeed," Puh agreed. "His snores would give pause to any beast that might be on the prowl. They would assume that a larger, more ferocious creature was already present."

It was well known that the same legendary volume Black Wolf could achieve when in full-throated song was also evident while he slept. Puh seemed thoughtful.

"I never know whether or not to erect our lean-to as close to his as possible for the potentially protective effect of his vociferous rumbles and snorts, or as far away as possible to escape the noise," Puh mused.

"Even if we built our lean-tos across the camp, I think the sound would easily follow us the distance," I observed.

"That is true," Puh said, nodding. "But as much as Black Wolf may have to endure a bit of teasing about his habit, I take comfort from the sound, as I know it means my friend is nearby. There are many times when it is good to know that you are not alone should help be needed."

* * *

The next morning brought the return of the mosquitoes, and biting gnats, as well. The wind and the fire had both died down, so the insects resumed feasting on our flesh. It occurred to me that those of us with sunburns now offered parcooked skin for their sampling pleasure.

We did not tarry; we quickly collapsed and packed our lean-tos, covered the fire pit with dirt to discourage the rekindling of any remaining embers, and then left the grove. We walked swiftly, hoping to leave the mosquitoes and gnats behind. Now that we were out in the open again, a slight breeze stirred the knee-high grasses, helping to keep the insects at bay.

It was chilly; we could see our breath on the air. The rising wind began to break up the last of the early-morning mists, causing the grasses to ripple like waves on the water. As we trekked along, we startled a large herd of red deer that bounded off as soon as they caught sight of us. I watched them with interest as they departed. They were sleek and vigorous animals; this boded well for the autumn hunting season.

"The deer have had a good summer," Fish Hawk said. "With luck, that will mean we will have a good winter."

"*Gah!* Deer too small," Karno said, waving his remark aside. "We get big kill. One, maybe two mammoth today. Not waste time with deer."

"Some of those deer looked quite large," Fish Hawk persisted. "Their buck still eyes us from over there." Fish Hawk pointed at the distant animal as it peered warily at us from his position at the edge of the herd. "Look at the size of him."

Fish Hawk was right. The buck was huge and his massive spread of antlers was half-cleaned of the now-rotting summer velvet, leaving his rack semi-festooned with the remaining strings of the putrid stuff. Another buck, one not so impressive, tentatively approached the herd while the guardian of the harem was distracted by our presence. The big buck's head suddenly swung around as he sensed the newcomer. The first buck wasted no time with bugled warnings or feigning a charge. He dashed at the interloper, who beat a hasty retreat.

The rutting season would not begin in earnest for several moons yet, but it was not unusual to see this behavior at the end of summer. The does were not yet ready to breed, but some of the stags might try their luck challenging another buck that already had a harem, or take part in a little sparring. The bucks were bulked up after a summer of good grazing, and they had plenty of energy. By late fall they would be thin and quite exhausted from the rigors of the season. Successful bucks would manage to maintain their harems and sire a good many fawns. The rest might have an opportunity to breed a stray doe but most likely would just have to wait it out until the next rut, hoping to have gained enough size and strength by then to win their own herd.

Fox and Mror walked side by side, carrying small spears they had made especially for this trip. They, too, watched the deer.

"One day we will hunt deer like these," Fox said to Mror.

"We will," Mror agreed. "We will go on many hunts." Mror turned to Puh. "Will we not, Puh-Puh? How old will we have to be before we can hunt deer?"

"That depends on you," Puh answered. "You must practice using your spears; you must be big and strong, and you must be able to sit or stand without moving, in absolute silence, for a long time. That is what it takes to kill a deer."

"What if I use a bow like Muh-Muh?" Mror asked.

Puh smiled at this.

"Then you must practice with that, as well," Puh told him.

Fox and Mror continued to chatter about how they would learn the skills needed to become hunters. I still had vivid memories of being a boy, so eager to accompany my father on hunting forays. I was impatient. The outings where I was simply an observer and not a pursuer of prey seemed to go on year after year. Sometimes it seemed as though my first kill would never happen. I had learned to snare rabbits and other small creatures, but such animals did not sustain our clan. We needed to bring in large prey on a regular basis in order to survive. Little did I know that what seemed like an exciting and gratifying activity would become just another chore, often carried out under less-than-ideal conditions. Whether it was hot, cold, windy, or wet, the family still needed to eat, wear clothing, and make tools. I kept my thoughts to myself. I did not want to spoil their excitement. With luck, Fox and Mror would grow up to become proficient hunters and they would learn the dreary realities of adulthood soon enough.

The sun was still rising and the day had become warm when we first came across an expanse of lea where large patches of grass and brush had been laid flat. Interspersed were clumps of earth, still bound together by roots and topped with withered flora. I imagined that the bulls, caught up in the heat of battle, had pushed up chunks of sod while in the midst of shoving one another back and forth. Or possibly a tusk had caught itself in the ground and plowed a furrow. Either way, it was evident that this was the beginning of the bulls' trail.

We paused to take stock of the damage. It looked as though it had occurred several days before. The bulls were nowhere in sight, so there was nothing we could do but follow their progress through the scarred field and hope we would eventually find the mammoths.

The sun bore down on us as we proceeded. I knew that for many of us, by nightfall our skin would be scorched worse than ever, but there was nothing to be done about it. The tree cover was almost nonexistent here, but as before, we broke from our journey each time we came across a bit of shade.

At last we arrived at a tall tree where we could break for a midday meal. As always, we scanned the tree's branches in case an unexpected surprise in the form of a lion or lynx was lounging there. Our only discovery was a number of birds. We were all hot and thirsty, so we smiled as we settled down on the cool earth beneath the tree.

"A real tree!" Fox said happily as he chewed a strip of dried meat. "A real big tree!" Fox looked up at tree's crown. "May I climb it, Puh-Puh?"

"Me, too!" Mror piped up. "I want to climb, too."

"Yes, you may," I told Fox. "Mror, you must ask your own parents if you may climb."

Mror secured permission from Puh and Ria, and as soon as they had gobbled down a few handfuls of dried stores and gulped a bit of water, they began to ascend the tree.

I watched them carefully. The boys were strong climbers and quite nimble, and they were light enough to scale the tree without worry of breaking off a branch. Within moments, their bravery had outmatched my sense of caution.

"That is high enough," I called to them.

"Oh, Puh-Puh," Fox said, his voice tinged with disappointment. But he obeyed.

Fox and Mror found comfortable seats amongst the tree branches; they seemed content to wait for our trek to recommence from their perches.

Ria came to stand next to me and looked up at them as well.

"They are like a couple of squirrels," she said. "They seem quite happy up there."

I nodded to Ria, but before I could respond, Mror stood up on his branch and pointed.

"Muh-Muh! Puh-Puh!" Mror cried out. "I see a big dark lump way over by a river! There are no other trees or anything – do you think it might be the mammoths?"

I now wanted to climb the tree myself to confirm Mror's sighting, but I had little doubt that Mror was correct. As he said, there was not much else out here that could explain the presence of a mysterious *big dark lump*.

"I think you may be right," Puh answered Mror. "Why do you not come down now? We are almost ready to leave."

"I see it too," Fox called down to us. "But the lump does not move. Does that mean they are dead?"

"It might," I replied. "There is no knowing unless we go look."

The boys quickly descended the tree.

"Look out, lump! Here we come!" Fox said cheerfully, picking up his little spear.

Black Wolf grinned at his grandson.

"Here we come, indeed," Black Wolf said.

"Puh-Puh, what if they are dead?" Fox asked me.

"Well, then they will be easy to catch," I responded.

The *big dark lump* was still some distance away. We would have to cross the open countryside, in full view of any creature that might be looking, including our intended prey. As we approached, our eyes sought any detail that might betray the identity of the lump; suppose it was just a huge boulder? Or a mound of discolored earth?

"There are vultures and a few ravens," Puh said, motioning toward the sky overhead. "I think we have found our mammoths. If they were dead, the scavengers would already be on them. They must be alive – at least alive enough to keep them away."

Karno had seemed glum at the prospect of coming all this way just to find two rancid corpses, but his spirits revived at this news.

"Good!" Karno exclaimed. "Good! Good! Mammoth not dead but mammoth be too tired to put up big fight!"

"One can only hope," Black Wolf replied.

I tended to agree with Black Wolf. Animals can greet humans with surprising vigor, even when it would seem as though they should be very tired after being lanced, and subsequently bolted to run pell-mell through endless forest.

There was no point in being coy about our approach, so we marched up to the mammoths. When we came to a slight knoll, we paused to take stock of the situation.

"They look pitiful," I said, feeling for their plight.

The two bulls were so securely attached to each other it was almost certain they would die even without our help. If they were lucky, some other predator would have taken them down; however, if not, it would have been a very unpleasant lingering death from starvation. Bull mammoths do not eat during the summer rut; therefore, by the end of the season, they are already compromised by several moons of fasting and the rigors of mating with cow mammoths, compounded by strenuous battles with other bulls.

"Pitiful, perhaps, but not unimpressive," Puh said. "Ria, this is a good place for you and the boys to stay. This is far enough away to keep out of the fray, but close enough for you all to see what is happening."

"Yes," Ria agreed, putting an arm around Mror and drawing him to her.

"We stay as well?" Swift River asked, meaning himself and his brother Hawk.

"Yes, both of you," Black Wolf said.

This had already been discussed, but I suppose Black Wolf's sons hoped there might be a change of plan that would allow them to come. However, leaving them with Ria and the younger boys not only kept them away from potentially being injured an angry bull mammoths, but would allow them to help protect their little group while the adult men pursued the two mammoths. Black Wolf's sons might be too young to tackle a pair of mammoths, but they should be able to discourage most other creatures that might threaten Ria and the boys, or be interested in raiding our supplies, which would also be left on the knoll. Those of us taking part in the attack quickly divested ourselves of our packs and any extraneous gear. We carried only our spears.

As Puh and Black Wolf took leave of their families, I also wished to speak with Fox.

"Keep an eye out for predators, and keep your spear handy," I told him. "With luck, the river will prevent the mammoths from going too far to avoid us. Hopefully, we will be back soon."

"I still do not see any movement from them," Swift River said, staring toward the now discernible shaggy hulks.

"It is probable they are resting," Puh told him. "No doubt they have spent the past three or more days pushing each other around. Their thirst must have driven them to the river; even in their current predicament, they must drink or they will perish."

Before setting out once again, I put an arm around Fox's shoulder and gave him a brief squeeze before I walked away with the others.

"Have a care, Puh-Puh," Fox called after me.

"I will," I assured him.

Fox's companions called out similar sentiments and received similar replies, but then their voices faded as we closed the distance between the knoll and the mammoths.

As we neared, I could see the mammoth's eyes following our movements. Their sides still rose and fell with each breath. The bulls seemed resigned to a fate of perpetual entanglement, but when we were about ten steps away, the beasts suddenly stood and regained their feet.

They stood face to face; their tusks clasping each animal to the other. Now that they were standing upright, they were imposingly tall. Even from where we had halted I could smell their musky, earthy odor.

Here, out in the open, there was no feature in the landscape we could use to aid us; there was just the slim hope that the river was too deep for them to cross on foot. All that was in our favor was that the mammoths were hampered by their weakened state, and the fact that they were physically attached to each other.

"Let us go behind the one on the right," Black Wolf said, edging toward the rear of that mammoth.

"Half of us might go behind him and the other half head toward the one on the left," Puh suggested. "If they do not know which way to move to meet us, it will cause them to work against each other."

"Good plan," Karno said with a nod. "*Woofmen* go this way, you go other way."

The rest of us nodded as well, and we parted our group to set about opposite ends of the bulls. As Puh had predicted, the mammoths did not know which way to turn. A mammoth's instinct is not to flee, but to turn to face any threats, counting on its immense size and strength for protection. However, since they were locked together, neither could successfully turn to face us. They rumbled and grumbled with frustration and fright, but they were at a loss as to how to fend off these annoying humans.

I was beginning to think this might be easy. Then, just as we lunged forward with our spears, the mammoths unexpectedly moved away in unison. They sidestepped our assault and now stood in the river. Again, we attempted to reach their backsides, but once more, the bulls moved away.

A bull mammoth has long legs, and one of its steps was probably equivalent to at least two of ours. A few steps put them out of reach of our spear thrusts. I realized this was not going to be a leisurely stroll up to a pair of disabled creatures that could be done in with a number of quick stabs.

For a moment, we stared in disbelief and dismay. The mammoths stared back as they awaited our next move. The canny beasts had tapped into some innate skill; that, coupled with a strong sense of self-preservation, had allowed them to coordinate their movements.

"They have figured out that we are coming at them from the riverside," Puh told us. "We must move in different directions, and then turn and come at them from all sides."

"Good plan," Karno said again.

We splashed through the cold waters of the river and came at the mammoths from all angles, plunging our spears into their tough hides as often as possible. We had only one spear each, so the weapon must be tugged free after each strike. Sometimes the spearhead was well lodged and it took a few tries to retrieve the spear, especially after the shaft became slippery with blood.

This at last seemed to fluster the mammoths. They bellowed with rage, and their breaths came in great gasps and snorts. We came at them again and again, panting for breath as well. It was hard work to continuously force our way through knee- or even waist-deep water. My feet and legs were chilled, and my muscles burned with effort.

The river bottom was littered with stones and gravel, which rolled underfoot and made it difficult to stay upright. The bulls had no such problem, their wide feet easily steadying their stance. Each time they attempted to evade our attack their movements sent up large splashing waves that thoroughly drenched us. They were deceptively fast, and they soon learned to move in an unpredictable manner as well, taking advantage of the unwary to knock them over with a furry shoulder or hip, or a swing of the trunk.

I was gratified when one of the bulls finally sank to his belly. He was still alive, but his life was quickly ebbing away. Miraculously, none of us had been crushed under one of the mammoth's ponderous feet. The water swirling around our legs was now stained red with the mammoths' blood. It would not be long before the second mammoth also dropped.

"Let us leave the river," Puh said as he started to walk away.

The rest of us waded to the bank, as well. We were wet and tired, and breathing as heavily as our prey.

"They are all but dead," Puh said. "We can catch our breath and wait for it to be over."

Karno was grinning.

"This good!" He said. "This prove we are strong! We are brave! When we go to People Gathering, they be happy to see us. They tell us we good hunter."

A flash of insight told me that this was why Karno had been eager to make an impressive kill. Not because of his love of daring feats and – possibly best of all – having something to brag about, but to demonstrate the Wolfmen's worth to those who might otherwise be reluctant to accept them at The People from the East's Gathering. The rest of our party was silent as they too presumably absorbed this thought.

The second mammoth then went down with a splash. I turned to see ripples of water chase one another to the shoreline. The first bull was now motionless. The second groaned loudly, and struggled to rise to his feet, despite the awkwardness of still being fixed to the mammoth that was already down.

"I will go to the knoll to let Ria and the boys know what has happened," Puh announced.

"I will go with you," I said.

 **Chapter Seven** 

We set up camp on the riverbank. It would take days to process all the meat and harvest various additional materials from the mammoths, but the warm daytime temperatures meant we must work as quickly as possible. There was so much to be taken off the animals it was unlikely we would be able to remove of all of it before it started to spoil; nevertheless, the remains would feed countless creatures. Ultimately, nothing would go to waste.

We worked night and day, keeping an eye out for creatures that might hope to steal our kills. It was inevitable that they would come. The breeze carried the news of our good fortune to all who tarried downwind. They had only to follow their noses to find a bustling butchering site, complete with smoking racks, a fire pit, and lean-tos.

Other than driftwood scavenged at the riverside, the closest wood was at the large tree that Fox and Mror had climbed. We were able to collect some deadwood from under the tree, but it was not enough to maintain a fire. The Wolfmen left us to travel farther afield to seek more wood — at least enough to preserve the meat so it would still be edible by the time it could be consumed.

It was an extremely laborious process. And when we had processed as much as we could before the carcasses spoiled, the meat would then be transported to our respective homes. Even if everyone carried as much as they could physically manage, there was no way we could bring away more than a small fraction of the mammoths' resources.

One the second day of butchering, I knew we would not have much more time before the meat still on the carcasses would go bad. Puh and I were standing by a smoking rack, on which we had just placed strips of mammoth flesh. We were thoroughly begrimed with blood and other bits of mammoth gore, and we reeked of smoke and sweat intermingled with strong elements of slightly rancid bull mammoths. It was then when I had an epiphany.

"Puh," I began. "Do you know how a leaf floats on the water?"

Puh looked up at me, his face betraying surprise at the seeming randomness of the topic.

"Yes, I do," he answered.

"When I was a boy, sometimes I would set leaves on the water and add an acorn or two and watch them float down the stream. Sometimes I would load them up with several acorns to see how many they could carry before they sank or dropped their load."

"What makes you think of that?" Black Wolf inquired.

Black Wolf had come to join us, bringing with him an armload of meat. Like the rest of us, he looked weary and he was covered with filth. We had been working almost nonstop since the mammoths were killed.

"I was thinking," I said, rubbing an itch on my nose with my forearm, my hands being too slimy for such a task. "It occurred to me we sometimes use animal skins to make water bags, so why not use the mammoth skin to build a big leaf? We could then load it up with all the things we have taken from the bulls and use the leaf to float everything up the river, rather than pack it out on our backs. The river will not take us all the way home, but it will take us quite a way and it may make the journey easier."

Black Wolf and Puh exchanged glances.

"*Build a big leaf?*" Black Wolf repeated. "Tris, do these thoughts include ideas on how to actually construct a big leaf?"

"Yes, actually – well, a little bit of an idea, anyway," I admitted. "What if we used the mammoth skins, even in their raw condition, and stretched them over their ribs. The mammoth fat on the skin will make a waterproof leaf, and the bones will keep it in shape. If it floats and we load it up with meat, fat, sinews, and all, and attach a rope to it, we could walk along the riverbank and tow the big leaf toward home."

Puh and Black Wolf again traded glances.

"I suppose it is possible," Puh said. "But the structure, even empty, would be extremely heavy. What if it will not float?"

"Perhaps it will not work," I conceded, shrugging. "It was just a thought."

Black Wolf peered over our campsite, to view to river beyond, seeming to ponder the notion.

"We would have to pull against the current," he mused. "But then, there are many of us to pull. It might be less onerous than lugging all this home on our backs or dragging it on travois sleds, which we would have to make from the only spare wood available here, our smoking and lean-to frames. Plus, we could still use the hides and the ribs after the leaf is disassembled. Let us give it a try."

Black Wolf, Puh, and I walked to the river and stared at the sad remains of the two bulls. The mammoths had been stripped of their most prized bits; we had already eaten the hearts and the tongues, and some of the flesh, but we had also smoked most of the best cuts of meat, sliced off great slabs of fat, and harvested some of the longest tendons. The hides had been rolled up and left on the river bank. We had not planned to bring them home; they were too heavy to carry the distance. Now, however, they might provide the means to bring our load closer to its final destination.

Flies buzzed around the scene. Crows and ravens needed to be waved off every so often, but other scavengers seemed content to wait until we departed before encroaching. Still other animals were keener to bully their way in, but so far, none successfully. Earlier that morning we had had to put up a strong, united front to ward off a large bear. The bear approached, sniffing the air and occasionally standing on his hind legs to get a better view. He was a large beast, but he seemed unsure of pitting himself against a gathering of armed humans. A group of us came to stand between him and our bounty, spears in hand. He must have decided it was not worth the risk, and he left us to seek his fortune elsewhere.

"How much more will we smoke?" Bror asked upon joining us.

"Not much, if any," Puh answered. "I do not know that we will be able to transport any more than we already have cured or still have curing on the racks. But Tris has an idea about floating everything home, if we can stretch the mammoth hides over a frame of rib bones and make the thing float on top of the water."

"Do you mean make it float like a raft of deadwood floating downriver, and pile all our meat in it?" Bror asked. "And assuming this river eventually winds its way to our compound?"

"Exactly," Black Wolf replied. "This last batch of meat will be smoked by nightfall. Let us start building the raft, as you say, and see if it will float."

"We must stay here until the last of the meat is smoked, anyway, so we may as well give it a try," Bror concurred.

When the others agreed that we had taken all we could reasonably expect to use from the now very odiferous mammoths, we took turns walking upstream in small groups and bathing in the clean water. We would find ourselves dirtied again before it was time to depart, but it felt good to scrub away the layer of crud that had accumulated on our bodies.

The copious amount of fresh meat meant we were still eating heartily off the fallen beasts. Now that we were relatively clean, we ate once more and talked about our plan to make our way home. Karno was intrigued at the idea of making a raft.

"It like mammoth swim upside down in river!" Karno said, gleeful at the thought. "We make hollow mammoth float and ride him home!"

"I was thinking we would pull it up the river with ropes," Black Wolf explained to Karno. "The raft will be full of meat and such. I do not think there will be room for people in it."

"Plus, it would be a revolting vehicle in which to ride," Ria pointed out. "A smelly mammoth hide, several days after it was removed from the carcass, filled with slabs of fat, piles of tendons, and sacks and sacks of smoked meat. *Pew!*"

"I would not mind to ride in it!" Fox volunteered. "I think it would be fun to be out on the river like a goose or a duck!"

"Will we make two rafts, one from each hide?" Bewok asked. "And will we have enough rope to tie the rib frames together and attach the hides to the frames?"

"We make one first," Karno said decisively. "If enough rope, we make two."

This seemed a good idea. Some of the ribs had already been removed from the carcasses. Bits of flesh still clung to them, but they had dried in the sun, so at least they were not slippery to handle. It was fairly simple to stand them up in place and tie the ribs into the correct shape, albeit upside down. The raft would have to be righted when it was completed. The hides were another matter. It was difficult to get a good grip on them. The hides were quite weighty and still coated with a layer of fat, which made them difficult to grip. The task was easiest when we grabbed the long fur at the edges. It took almost all of us to drape one of the hides over the frame. Then the excess skins were cut away, lightening the raft considerably. Using our knives, we cut holes where the hides would be attached to the upper part of the raft, and lashed them as securely as we could, considering we could not be generous with our limited supply of rope.

Finally, the raft was flipped over. It rocked back and forth as it settled into its upright position. It was a clumsy-looking thing, resembling an enormous turtle on its back. And we still did not know if it would float.

"Shall we try it in the water?" I asked.

"We may as well find out if our work will be fruitful," Bewok responded.

The raft was too heavy to carry – not because we could not tote its weight, but because the stress of its own unsupported weight might break it apart. We carefully rocked it in one direction, then the other, until the raft was at the river's edge. The trail left behind on the muddy riverbank looked as though a massive centipede had made a mad dash for the water.

We soon found it was not enough to get it off the riverbank; we had to coax it farther, to where the water was deep enough that it would float. And float it did.

The raft settled into the water, with half its depth submerged, and the other half bobbing above the water's surface. In fact, it appeared to be extremely buoyant — but also rather unstable. A single man grasping one side and pulling down easily tipped the raft to an alarming extent. The raft would need to be loaded with care so that the weight was evenly distributed. I hoped it would then be less tippy.

"Now we just need to keep it from floating away," Black Wolf observed, holding onto one of the sides.

Puh was already approaching with a length of rope, which he passed to Black Wolf.

"Here you are," Puh said. "See if this will help."

Black Wolf looked at the rope blankly.

"What am I to do with it?" he asked.

"Tie it to the raft," Puh instructed. "Then, I suppose you might try tying the other end of the rope to one of the mammoth's tusks."

Without a word, Black Wolf waded over to the mammoth carcasses, which remained where they had fallen, in several feet of water, and tied the rope to one of the curved tusks that poked out of the river.

"It moves in the breeze! It wants to float away!" Black Wolf lamented. "I hope the rope will hold it."

"I hope so too," Bewok said. "I would not like to chase the object of all our hard work downstream until it fetched up on something."

The raft strained at the rope, but it did not break away.

Since the first raft appeared to be a success, we began work on the second one. This meant removing a few more ribs from the bulls – a less-than-pleasant job, considering that the animals had been dead for nearly two days, but there was no getting around it. We then repeated the process, and by nightfall we had a second raft tied to the same tusk as the first.

By then we had been working almost without stop since the beasts had been killed. We were exhausted beyond measure. The last of the meat had been smoked and the rafts had continued to float, so now we had only to load the rafts and start the journey homeward. We decided to get a night's sleep, even though that meant having to take turns keeping watch to hold predators and scavengers at bay, and then prepare to leave in the morning.

The night was rather restless. The slowly rotting mammoth hulks were sending out pungent waves of scent that broadcast the news of a potential feast to any creature that might be in the vicinity. This brought visits from the curious and the hungry; some were easily discouraged. Others, like the number of lions that emerged from the darkness during the depths of the night, were more determined. I was sound asleep, Fox lying beside me, when I was awakened by shouts, quickly followed by a loud roar. I had been sleeping so heavily that at first I was not sure if I had dreamed it, but as more roars rang in my ears, I knew this was real.

"Puh-Puh!" Fox cried out, "There are lions! They are so loud!"

"Get on my back," I instructed Fox.

"But my spear . . ." Fox protested.

"Just get up on my back!" I insisted. I did not add that I feared it would be more probable that he would accidentally poke me with his spear rather than strike one of the lions.

With my help, Fox quickly clambered up on my back. Lions are most apt to try to drag away the smallest and most vulnerable members of a group. I hoped they would be less eager to attack Fox if he was riding on my back or shoulders. Mror was mounted on Puh's back, as well. Each of us carried our spears, poised for action. We shouted at the lions and waved our arms. Our fire was little more than embers and a few burning sticks at this point. The firewood was almost gone. We could only count on our weapons and our physical presence to ward them off.

The lions feigned a few charges, but we met each one with a line of sharp spearheads. Ria armed her bow, and although it was not powerful enough to kill a lion, it could launch its little spears into a tender spot and sufficiently annoy the beast to cause acute dismay. Ria shot some of her arrows into the lions, and at last they left us alone.

A glow at the eastern horizon told us that dawn would not be long in coming. We decided there was no point in trying to go back to sleep, so we broke our fast and readied to begin loading the rafts. We hoped to tie the rafts together so they could be pulled through the water as one. By the time the sun peeked over the horizon, the loading process had started. Passing the harvests from our hunt along from one person to another, we managed to get everything on the rafts in short order.

I was pleased to see that the rafts were working out so well. I was rather amazed that my idea about the floating leaves might actually lead to something as remarkable as this. Granted, the rafts were ugly and a bit ungainly – not to mention constantly shrouded in a cloud of flies because of their eye-wateringly foul smell. But if they allowed us to bring home such a load without needing to carry it the whole distance, it would be a tremendous boon. Who knew if we would ever need to try this trick again, but it was good to know that it did work. It was a shame we had never tried this with the seal hides that were harvested at the coast. They were much smaller, of course, but they also had a hefty layer of fat and, being lighter and less hairy, would be easier to fashion into a raft.

I pushed the thought from my mind. I doubted I would ever see the ocean again. It was too far away from our new compound, and we were fortunate to have plenty of resources nearby, thus negating our obligation to make an annual hike to the coast. Plus, it was time to leave and I needed to devote my thoughts and energies into moving forward with our travel plans.

Puh, Bror, and I took hold of the rope at the front of the lead raft and began to pull. The rafts did not move. An inspection brought to light that the loaded rafts were sitting on the river bottom, as comfortably seated as a frog in a puddle. We pushed them into deeper water and once again pulled the lead rope. Almost immediately, the rafts struck a shallow spot, and stuck fast. This time, the rope parted. Luckily, our companions who trailed behind us plunged into the river and held on to the rafts, lest the current work them loose and cause them to float away.

"What happen?" Karno asked. "Raft float good, then stuck."

Puh pushed at the rafts until they were in water deep enough to make them float once again, while I quickly mended the rope.

"We will need to tie another rope, so that its breaking point is doubled," Puh said. "And I think we will need to find a way to keep the rafts from becoming affixed on the shallows."

"Some of us can walk alongside the rafts and help to guide them," Bewok suggested.

"That would make sense," Black Wolf agreed.

We recommenced our slog through the river, dragging and pushing our ungainly rafts as we went. I had been proud of my idea to construct these rafts, but I had to admit that this was not a fast way to bring goods from one place to another. We could not walk quickly, for we needed to fight the water's natural resistance as we trudged along. And the river's current pushed against the rafts as well.

Despite our being a noisy procession, we still managed to surprise a bear that was dozing on a grassy bank. The bear lifted his head as we came into view, and seeing what must have been a startling sight, he sprang to his feet. He paused only a moment, snapping his jaws at us, before bounding off to seek a more restful place to resume his nap.

Around midday we changed places. Puh, Bror, and I relinquished the rope to Black Wolf at the lead, followed by Fish Hawk and Swift River. The pushers were also relieved and replaced by fresh hands. I was grateful to once again tread on dry land, even if we were being swarmed by insects and frequently had to navigate around brush, rocks, and tall reeds.

In fact, sometimes we lost sight of the rafts as we were forced to go around riverside obstacles. While we were skirting an area thick with bulrushes, we suddenly heard a chorus of honks and then a series of shouts, just as the rafts and their handlers once again came into view.

The cacophony continued as we charged to the scene. Our friends had halted in place, apparently finding their way blocked. Flashes of brilliant white exploded amongst the bulrushes, and loud flapping filled the air as though someone were energetically shaking out a fair-sized hide. Other creatures had apparently taken note of the disruption, too. Nearby, crows cawed raucously and several ducks quacked with alarm as they launched themselves into the air from their formerly placid paddle downriver.

We soon found ourselves opposite our traveling companions, looking across a large swan's nest, just in time to see one of the swans lunge toward Black Wolf, its wings flailing mightily, and causing Black Wolf to tumble backwards into the river.

There were two indignant parents and four scarcely less aggrieved but almost full-grown cygnets. Upon perceiving our presence they swiveled their heads from atop their long necks to spy the new intruders. The swans hissed at us, displaying their rough pink tongues, and set up honking once more. They then turned their malicious scrutiny back toward Black Wolf, who had taken advantage of the swans' momentary inattention and regained his feet. He was looking decidedly wet and unhappy.

"I do not know who was more taken aback, us or them," Black Wolf said when he noticed that we had rejoined the procession. "They are most aggressive," he went on. "I think I would rather meet another bear than these creatures."

"We will distract them while you pass by," Puh offered. Then he added to me and Bror, "Let us engage them, invite them to come at us." Turning briefly to Ria, the boys, and all those still coming along, he said, "See if you can go behind us, and continue to follow the raft. We will catch up in a few moments."

I could appreciate Black Wolf's sentiments, but I could also appreciate that these fowl were simply protecting their family and their nest. I would do no less if my loved ones were under threat. I did not want to hurt them; I just wanted them to let us pass unharmed. Out of the corner of my eyes I could see the rest of our group making their way past Puh, Bror, and me. At least they would be able to rejoin the others unscathed.

We poked our spears toward the swans and called to them, hoping to incite their wrath. They responded with enthusiasm, thrashing the air with their great wings, honking and hissing, and generally making us feel unwanted. We waited until the others had safely escaped and then backed away from the irate fowl, leaving them to preen their ruffled feathers back into place.

When we caught up with our friends and the rafts, they had paused to allow us to regain the procession. Black Wolf was still showing signs of his impromptu dunk in the river. He presented a forlorn sight indeed. He dripped as he stood on the riverbank, and his many stiff braids were now somewhat less orderly than usual, leaving some sticking out straight and others appearing as the bent legs of a deceased insect.

"Are you injured?" Puh asked Black Wolf, with concern.

Black Wolf shook his head.

"No," he answered. "Except for my dignity. My father had always told me to beware of swans. He said one of his uncles was attacked by a swan that hit him so hard with its wings that it broke his arm. The arm swelled to grotesque proportions and took on vile colors before he died from his injury. This story has left me with a great respect for swans. So when they came at me I stepped back and tripped over a rock and fell backward in the water. I feel silly to have been caught unawares and to have panicked like that, but I was glad you came along when you did so you could keep their attention while we got away."

"*Gah.* Dumb birds," Karno said with disgust.

"Dumb they may be," Black Wolf retorted, "but I did not see you leap forward to meet them."

Karno shrugged.

"Karno say birds dumb, not Karno dumb," Karno said – then he grinned at his own jest.

Black Wolf muttered something inaudible and looked at Karno darkly. It seemed the day's events had strained his sense of humor. I then noted something that would help to cheer him.

"Look! Swallows!" I said, pointing overhead.

The birds flew in graceful arcs, chasing the many biting flies that had been plaguing us for days. But it was their musical cries that caught my attention. I hoped they had hearty appetites and that we would now find some relief from the flies' vicious nibbling.

"Perhaps we are nearing the forest," Puh said. "The swallows need to nest up off the ground, so their homes must be within an easy flight's distance from here."

"Yes, these flat grasslands offer little shelter for them," Ria agreed. "Once we can see trees, we will know that we are nearing the edge of the grasslands and we are almost at the end of our journey."

Black Wolf seemed pleased at the thought. We all smiled as well. We were suffering from lack of sleep, continuous toil, and exposure to sun and insects, and we were all quite ready to end this excursion.

The multitudinous swallows must have been voracious, because the number of insects now diminished considerably. As the sun set, however, mosquitoes replaced the flies. The swallows continued their feeding until darkness overtook the day, but then the bats came out to take their place. They were not as numerous as the birds, but I was grateful for any kind of reprieve from the mosquitoes' stings.

We made a camp at a bend in the river, using driftwood scavenged from the river's shore to build a fire. We had actually collected quite a bit, throwing the wood into the rafts as we went, so there was plenty to keep a fire going all night long. I was glad for this, as we would have to once again take turns standing watch all night. A good fire would not only warm us throughout the cool night but help us see any marauding creatures that might want to attack us or steal a meal from the rafts.

As usual, Puh, Bror, and I took the first watch. Smoke from the fire helped to discourage the mosquitoes that had escaped the bats' notice. We were serenaded by crickets, while late fireflies flitted around the edge of our camp. If I had not been so exhausted, it might have been a pleasant evening.

"Do you think we will reach home tomorrow?" I asked Puh.

"Probably," Puh replied. "If not tomorrow, early the next day. I do not think we are far away. It is just that the river does not flow in a straight line, so we cannot take the most direct path home."

"I am beginning to wonder if the rafts were really a good idea," I said. "I had not thought it would be this hard to bring them upriver."

"There was no easy way to transport so much meat," Puh responded. "If we had packed it out on our backs, we would not have been able to carry nearly as much and we would be even more tired than we are already."

"I was not overly optimistic we would even find the mammoths," Bror chimed in. "I agree with Tor. It was not going to be an effortless task, no matter what method we used. Besides, I was impressed, Tris. The rafts may look and smell hideous, but thus far they have proved to be watertight."

* * *

When morning came we found we were packing up to resume our trip just in time to avoid an impending visit by a couple of bears. They appeared to be eagerly swimming across the river to investigate this mobile feast. Bears are not lightly built or sleek like many aquatic animals, but they are in fact quite good swimmers. The bears paddled determinedly in our direction, compelling us to hasten our efforts to leave the area. Fortunately, we were gone before they landed on the shore where we had camped.

We soon left the grasslands behind and reached the edge of the forest. The river shallowed here, making it tricky to keep the rafts afloat. Sometimes it took all of us to maneuver them through narrow channels, between rocks, and up a few small rapids. At last we came to a point where we could proceed no farther without going too far out of our way. We chose to unload the rafts and divvy up the goods among our packs. And now that we had access to plenty of wood, we constructed several travois sleds.

We arrived at the compound well before sunset. I was glad to be home. Jura and little Mino had stayed at my home with Morning Star and our girls while Fox and I were absent. It appeared Jura and Morning Star were now good friends, and little Mino was enjoying the company of our girls, who were pleased to have a visitor with whom to play.

I was relieved to step out of the sled harness that Puh, Bror, and I had been pulling and greet my family and friends. The others in our group were similarly divesting themselves of their burdens and enjoying a heartfelt welcome. We had brought home an immense amount of stores and had returned safely. We were bidden to sit and rest, and we happily complied.

It was only when Morning Star gently awakened me that I realized I had fallen asleep. I had slept so soundly that I did not know Fox had curled up against me and fallen asleep as well.

"Tris," Morning Star said, putting a hand on my arm, "the evening meal is almost ready. Rouse Fox, too, so you both can clean yourselves before we eat. You both must be so hungry."

"Many thanks, Morning Star," I told her, smiling at the irony of her last remark. While it was true I was almost always hungry, we had gorged ourselves on copious amounts of mammoth meat ever since we had butchered the beasts. We had actually eaten extremely well for the past few days. I then touched Fox's shoulder and said, "Fox, it is time to wash up. Our evening sup is almost ready."

Fox stretched a bit, letting out a little groan.

"I am so tired," Fox mumbled. "Must I wash?"

"Yes, you must. After you eat a bit, you can go to bed then if you would like," I said to him. "You do not need to stay up if you do not want to."

Nevertheless, Fox managed to rally after a bit of food and drink. He eagerly listened to the telling of our journey, at times exchanging glances with me as if to acknowledge our camaraderie in this adventure. It was good to know our sleds had been unloaded during our prolonged naps and all we had to do was sit and enjoy the meal and the company of our loved ones.

After the sup, the Wolfmen regaled us with some of their music. They had not played for us in some time, but our success warranted celebratory songs. They gathered up an assortment of rocks and heavy sticks and beat out a rhythm as they chanted in their native tongue. We did not understand the words, but as always, it was so agreeable to hear.

Morning Star and our daughters sat with Fox and me during the evening, but when our youngest daughter Lily had drifted off to sleep, Morning Star whispered to me that it was time to put the children to bed.

We wished the assembly a pleasant evening and took of leave of the company.

"What about Jura and Mino?" I asked Morning Star after we had arrived at our home and settled our children in their beds.

"Jura said she would stay with Karno in his lean-to after his return," Morning Star informed me, rubbing a salve into my bug-bitten, sun-scorched skin. "She is a nice woman. And Mino is a sweet boy, just like his father was."

"You liked having her stay?" I asked.

"Yes," Morning Star answered. "She was very quiet at first; I suppose she has not met many from The People from the East's tribe, never mind lived in their homes. But I think she was comforted by the fact that my mate is a fellow Old One, and she soon got over her shyness. Besides, little Mino was so full of fun and he so happy while he was playing with our girls. Jura was delighted Mino was having such a good time."

"I am glad," I said to Morning Star, pulling her close to me. I nuzzled her hair, taking in the scent only she bore. It may have been a blend of a thousand aromas, but it had always intoxicated me. "I have missed you." I added.

"I have missed you as well," Morning Star said, reaching up to embrace me and then kissing me on the lips.

"Come to bed, then," I whispered in her ear.

Chapter Eight

Howling wind whips snow through the air. Icy blasts sting our eyes, and every step requires great effort as we trudge across the frozen landscape. Suddenly, a small group of people comes into view.

I had not had that Dream in many moons, and yet now it had reappeared. Who were those people? And why were we out in such harrowing conditions? I tried to purge the Dream from my mind. It was useless to concern myself with such thoughts; our current weather was still relatively mild, and winter would not be upon us for some time.

Karno and his companions stayed with us for several days after our return from the hunt, resting before embarking on their homeward journey. It was a happy time for all of us, celebrating our success by stuffing ourselves with food and evenings spent listening to the Wolfmen's music. Now that we were home again, we felt pleased to know that the tremendous bounty we had brought back to the compound would take much of the pressure off us to bring in additional meat before the end of the fall rutting season.

I thought the autumn reindeer migration might be ignored completely this year, except that we needed their hides. Reindeer bore fur that made wonderfully warm coats, leggings, mittens, and boot liners. Deer skins, on the other hand, were covered with stiff hairs that tended to shed, thus requiring us to scrape the hides clean before curing them for future use; it was fine for day-to-day wear, but real cold-weather garb required a good thick layer of fur. Nevertheless, these hunts were still several moons away. I could put aside those concerns, at least for a while.

* * *

One afternoon Puh, Bewok, and I were hafting new spearheads onto wooden shafts, working in companionable silence as we dipped the base of the knapped spearheads in melted glue and then seated them in the spear shaft sockets. Next, we tightly wrapped wet sinew fibers over the joint where the stone head attached to the shaft. When the sinews were dry, we would slather a layer of hot glue over it and then smooth it over, taking care not to burn our fingers on the hot glue.

"Tor," Bewok said to Puh, breaking the silence. "I would like to speak with you about Twie. She is not spoken for?"

"No," Puh answered. "She is of age, of course, but she is not spoken for. I have been awaiting a request either from either her or a suitor."

Bewok hesitated a moment before going on.

"If you give your permission, and if she will have me, I would like to be her suitor," Bewok told Puh.

Puh smiled at this.

"You are a fine man and you have been a good friend to our family," Puh said. "I would be pleased if you were joined with Twie. I wish you luck when you approach her. She is wise and gentle-hearted; I believe she will give you the consideration you deserve."

I did not feel it was my place to say anything, but I hoped Puh was right.

"I am ten winters older than Twie," Bewok said regretfully. "She may wish to be paired with a man closer to her own age."

"There is only one sure way to know," Puh replied.

"Yes, that is true," Bewok conceded. "I will ask her now."

"Good luck, Bewok," I said to him.

Bewok finished smoothing hot glue over a hafting and then abruptly rose to his feet. He hurriedly gathered his spears, some of them only half-finished.

"Perhaps leave the spears elsewhere before you ask her," Puh suggested, still smiling.

Bewok distractedly looked at the spears and then laughed.

"Yes," he chuckled, "I do not want Twie to feel she must accept under duress."

At that, Bewok left us.

"I am glad he has finally asked for Twie," Puh said. "I have been expecting this for some time. He would be a good match for her."

"I think so, as well," I agreed. "I am a bit surprised neither of Black Wolf's sons has shown an interest in her, or she them, but she would be better off with Bewok. Swift River and Hawk are well on their way to becoming men, but they are still very young, in spite of their ages. Twie would have a mature man with Bewok, one who is able to provide for a family."

"That is my thought, too," Puh said.

A little while later, Twie came to Puh and me.

"Puh," Twie said softly. "Bewok has asked for me?"

"Yes, my pretty one," Puh answered.

"I have told him I would accept him," Twie announced. "I have known Bewok since I was a girl, and I hoped he would one day ask you for me. We would like to be paired soon. He wanted to come with me to talk to you about it, but I told him I wished to speak with you first. What do you think, Puh?"

Puh looked at Twie as she stood before us. She was tall and graceful, like her mother, with the same dark red hair. She did not have Muh's exceptional beauty, but she did have a pretty face and a kind demeanor. It occurred to me that Puh was right: Twie was indeed wise. More than that, she was sensible; people can be wise but not necessarily sensible. Many of her contemporaries might still be a bit silly and flighty, but even as she hovered at the precipice of becoming forever joined with a man she had long wished for, Twie appeared calm and self-assured. Perhaps she had inherited those traits from Puh.

"I think you and Bewok should make the decision about when you will be paired," Puh responded. "You are an intelligent young woman, and I trust you and Bewok to make the plans that will be best for you both." Puh embraced Twie. "I am so very proud of you and so very happy for you, as well. You will be a wonderful mate and a good mother to your children."

Twie beamed at Puh's words.

"Many thanks, Puh," she said. "I will tell Bewok and we will settle on a day to be paired."

* * *

Twie and Bewok's pairing was to happen soon, indeed. They chose to be joined the next day, while Karno and the other Wolfmen were still with us. We quickly pulled together everything needed to put on a feast, even if the menu heavily favored smoked mammoth meat. Twie had no special gown, so she wore her best summer garment and decorated her hair with flowers, wearing garlands of flowers around her neck, wrists, and ankles.

I did not know The People of the Wolves' pairing rites; however, Bewok seemed content to do whatever was required of him. According to our traditions, the parents are present to formally give the couple to each other, but since Bewok's parents were not here and only Puh was still alive of our parents, it was just Puh, Twie and Bewok at the center of the assembly.

"Bewok, son of Wudther, I give you my daughter Twie," Puh began. "May she bring you much happiness

151

and many children, and may this pairing bring you both many years of love and well-being." Puh then placed Twie's hands in Bewok's, symbolically giving her to him.

"Thank you, Tor," Bewok replied. "I accept her with all my heart."

Bewok then leaned awkwardly toward Twie, who appeared equally unsure about what was going to transpire. But when Bewok's lips reached hers, she smiled and returned his kiss.

"*Gah!*" Karno uttered in disgust.

Karno may have been the only one in attendance who was taken aback by Bewok's kiss, but it was hard to say, since the other Wolfmen did not comment. I was happy for Twie. I admired Bewok for being willing to depart from their long-held cultural norm to please his new mate. And Twie gave every evidence of being extremely pleased with him.

"*Gah!*" Karno said again. "Bewok no longer *Woofman*. Bewok grow hair long. Bewok smoosh faces. Next Bewok scrape off tattoos!"

"I think you have little fear of that," Black Wolf told him.

Karno grumbled under his breath in response, but he soon forgot his disapproval as the pairing feast commenced. He sat by the newly joined couple, with Jura at his side. It seemed to me that he sometimes looked at her thoughtfully. Did he wonder if she wished to be kissed as well? They were not outwardly affectionate, but I was heartened to see he was unfailingly kind to both Jura and little Mino.

"I am so happy for Twie," Morning Star remarked to me. "I do not believe she could have made a better match."

"I think you are right," I concurred. "Puh is quite pleased, too. He still has two more daughters to be paired, but they have some years before they will be old enough."

Morning Star smiled at this.

"Yes, they are still playing with dolls," she said with a laugh. "But now that Saree is the oldest daughter at home, she may find she has more responsibilities. And Mi, as well. Twie was a hard worker, and someone will have to take up her chores."

"They will learn," I assured Morning Star. "For now, though, they are certainly enjoying themselves. Summer is in full bloom, there is plenty of food, and everyone is in good spirits."

It was true that the children and the dogs were joyously capering with one another, the dogs barking and the children shrieking with pleasure as they chased one another across the compound. Even little Mino joined in the fun, despite having only recently learned to run.

I then observed Bewok place an object in Twie's hand. She held it before her to admire the item. It seemed to be a necklace, with a circular ivory pendent suspended from a cord. Twie smiled brightly and slipped it around her neck. I was sure she was thrilled to receive the gift, but I was eager to examine it so as to look at Bewok's handiwork. He was a skilled craftsman, and in particular very skilled at carving.

From my seat, the pendant seemed very simple in design, but it appeared to be completely smooth. It would take many days to create such a fine piece, but then, that was the point of a pairing gift: to demonstrate the depth of your devotion to your new mate.

My pairing gift to Morning Star had been a necklace made up of hundreds of tiny shells, all laboriously drilled and strung on a fine cord. The cord had broken and been reknotted many times now, and many of the shells had been lost. I had offered to replace the necklace with something better, but Morning Star demurred, saying she wanted to keep the one she had. I was almost embarrassed that she still wore the pitiful-looking thing, but it was gratifying, at least to some extent, that she still valued the present. I mused that one benefit of becoming paired with a somewhat older man is that you are likely to receive a better pairing gift, unlike the now-shoddy necklace I had given my mate on our pairing day.

The festivities continued as day turned into evening. The Wolfmen sang songs, and when everyone had settled around the fire, Bror told a story about a maiden who came down from the stars. When the moon rose high in the sky, the new couple wished everyone a pleasant evening and retired to Bewok's home, which would now be Twie's home, as well.

We were all full of food and good spirit, surrounded by our families and friends. Morning Star was still at my side, with our sleeping tot, Lily, on her lap, and our next-youngest, Raven, on mine, thumb in her mouth and a tad droopy, but still awake for the moment.   As Bror launched into another story, Fox and Pony listened, spellbound.

When the tale was over, Karno shifted in his seat, and I thought perhaps he might want to lead another song, but instead, he turned to Black Wolf.

"We speak of Gathering now," Karno said.

"What about it?" Black Wolf asked.   He looked rather tired, but he smiled indulgently.

"Karno speak Willow about Gathering," Karno told him.

"And what did she say?" Black Wolf questioned.

"Willow tell Karno all people come," Karno said. "Karno want go, too. Willow say much care needed to bring in new people. What *Back Woof* say?"

Black Wolf pondered this.

"It is not up to me to say anything," he admitted. "I suspect many will not be happy about including those outside our tribe, but that is up to Willow."

"But now *Back Woof* can tell them about mammoth hunt," Karno said with great enthusiasm, his arms mimicking the motions of stabbing with a spear. "*Back Woof* speak about *Woofmen* have strong arm. *Woofmen* brave. *Woofmen* work good. And now, *Woofmen* paired with Old Ones" – he vaguely waved a hand in Jura's direction to indicate his pairing with her, in addition to today's pairing of Bewok with Twie.

"All true," Black Wolf agreed. "I will speak for you, but be patient."

"What mean?" Karno asked.

"I mean that it may take several – many, perhaps – Gatherings for the issue to be resolved," Black Wolf said. "But never fear, I will speak for you at each Gathering until it is."

I had a sense that Black Wolf dreaded the prospect, but I knew Willow Woman was determined to have her way.

"Do they not like Wolfmen at the Gatherings, Grandpa?" Fox asked Black Wolf.

Black Wolf seemed to think on this before answering.

"They do not know Wolfmen, just as they do not know many Old Ones, either," Black Wolf explained. "Some are suspicious of those they do not know. Like when a stranger enters the compound and the dogs bark at them. But once the dogs realize that the newcomers are friendly, they settle down. I hope for the same at the Gathering."

Fox nodded that he understood.

"Puh-Puh, will we go, too?" Fox inquired.

"I must go, but whether or not the whole family goes is up to your mother," I replied. "It is a long journey to reach the Gathering Hall, and it will be cold by the time it takes place, and even colder yet by the time it is over."

"I think we will go," Morning Star stated firmly.

I should not have been surprised by her response after knowing her for all these years; except for Willow Woman, she was the most strong-willed and resolute woman I had ever known. All the same, it would be a daunting journey.

"Are you sure?" I asked.

"Yes," Morning Star said. "I know it will be a long, hard trip, but I want to go places and see things while I am still young enough to make the journeys."

"I see," I then added. "I suppose it would be good experience for the children, too."

"I also think of my mother," Morning Star whispered, so her mother, Little Fawn, would not overhear. "My mother is lame now. She cannot travel. The time may come when I cannot leave the compound, either because I have too many children to care for or I am too old. And I have never been to a Gathering. I know it is just for men, but even if the children and I have to stay in our rooms, I still want all of us to go."

"Then you all shall go," I promised.

* * *

The following days gradually returned us to our usual routines, but once we caught up on our neglected chores, Puh, Black Wolf, and I ventured back to where we had abandoned the rafts to see if anything was salvageable. The mammoth hides and ribs might have many uses, and we also hoped to reclaim the rope we had utilized to create the rafts and tow them upriver. We had recently endured several days of torrential rains, so we hoped the rafts had not been washed into the river and subsequently swept away.

We could hear the river before we saw it. What had been a reasonably tranquil body of water was now swollen by the copious rainfall. The riverbanks were under water and the rushing current bore an assortment of tree branches and other debris downstream. I worried that this was a bad sign for our rafts, but I was thankful that we had not had to cope with these conditions while we were towing them.

What we found was a scene of total destruction. The rafts had not been carried away on the river, but they were completely torn apart. A number of crows feasting on the scant remains took to the air as we approached. The culprits that had dismantled the rafts were identified by the numerous bear tracks in the muddy, well-trampled ground. They also had left a fair bit of excrement; they must have been in the area for some time.

"Bears!" Black Wolf exclaimed. "They have destroyed our rafts!"

"I see that," Puh said. "Watch your step," he cautioned Black Wolf.

Black Wolf looked about him.

"I will," Black Wolf assured Puh. "It seems there were quite a few of the beasts. They must have come in to eat the flesh that was left on the mammoth hides."

The sad remains of our hard work lay strewn about the site. It looked as though the rafts had been tipped over, rolled around until they collapsed, and finally tugged apart.

"They must have been big bears," I observed.

The bears' huge paw prints stood out plainly amongst the many smaller ones made by other animals that had come to scavenge what little was left behind.

"We can still bring back sections of rope," Puh said. "And perhaps some pieces of the hides are still good enough to clean and cure."

We did not stay long. Not only were we concerned about the bears revisiting the scene of their misdeeds, we also had to worry about time. We had embarked at sunrise and hiked swiftly to this location, and it was now midday. We hoped to make it home before nightfall, so we quickly collected all the bits of rope that were still worth saving and hacked free a few sections of mammoth hide that had not been too badly damaged; these were rolled up and then bound securely to an improvised travois sled to make their transport home easier. This was probably the best we could hope for, anyway, since a full mammoth hide is not only huge, but extremely heavy. We could not have hoped to bring even a single intact hide home between the three of us, anyway.

* * *

Summer ran its course and the autumn days sped by, bringing fiery colors to the landscape and several moons of frenetic rutting and hunting activity. The annual fall Gathering of The People from the East would start at the first full moon following the rutting season, so after the new moon began to wax once again, we began to make our final plans for the trip.

We could not all go, since some of us had to stay behind to keep up with maintaining the compound and defend it against any potential threats — even if those threats were just the rodents that were always intent on stealing our stores.

It had been decided some time ago that this would be Black Wolf and Little Fawn's sons' first Gathering. They were old enough that they should be introduced to the ways of their tribe. Little Fawn, ever the protective mother, disliked the fact that Swift River and Hawk would soon become men. It was not so much that they would become involved in the tribe's operations, but that they also would be expected to take part in the more dangerous aspects of life. They had accompanied us on many of our hunts, but except for the most mundane expeditions, they were simply observers, or helpers after the animals had been dispatched. Every child was different and assumed responsibilities at different ages, but most sons had already made kills on their own by the time they had reached the ages of these boys. However, as determined as Little Fawn was to keep her sons safe and prolong their childhoods as long as possible, those days were nearly at an end.

Since this Gathering was to be a societal debut for some of the attendees, it was therefore an especially auspicious occasion. Each family was going to send at least one representative. Representing the Old Ones in our clan would be Puh, Ria, and Mror, my family and me, and my Uncle Inlee. Black Wolf and his sons, and Fish Hawk, who was the mate of Black Wolf's daughter Petal, would also attend. We were to go to the Fen of Falls, Willow Woman's summer lodge, to meet up with Willow Woman's entourage, as well as Karno, along with some of his Wolfmen. From there we would commence the last leg of our journey to the Gathering Hall.

We set out on a cool, clear morning, dragging travois sleds so we could carry all the impedimenta required by a family on the trail. Puh and I also brought our dogs, Auchs and Raena. A frost blanketed the landscape, and a slight breeze rattled the branches of the trees. I wondered if the snow was in the offing. We had seen a few flakes now and then, but they had not yet amounted to much.

Cries from a migrating flock of geese drew my gaze skyward as Puh and I dragged our sled over the pathway. The huge flocks, so vast that they darkened the skies, had already winged their way south. These were the stragglers that hoped to make it to their destinations before winter set in.

This trip would be slower than our usual trek to the Fen of Falls. We hoped to hunt, if the opportunity presented itself, so our families would not be restricted to the dried stores we most often consumed when we were on the trail. We also would travel for shorter periods of time, not only because the sun set earlier, but so we could make a comfortable camp while we still had light rather than throwing up a quick lean-to just as darkness overtook us.

Black Wolf was in high spirits, as he always was when we were on our way to see Willow Woman. He led our processions through a forest bedecked in late-autumn hues and sang at the top of his lungs as we trekked along.

The Mighty Hunter has a heart strong and true

No matter what happens, he knows just what to do
The Mighty Hunter dreams of small pleasures and big deer
Of hot sunny days and streams that run clear
If the Mighty Hunter is lucky he may do as he please
If he is unlucky, he may come down with fleas . . .

"We will *only* be dreaming of deer if he keeps this up," Fish Hawk said, bringing up the rear, just behind Puh and me.

"We make so much noise, what with all the talking and the sound of dragging sleds, Black Wolf's singing may not matter," Puh speculated.

"I suppose that is true," Fish Hawk replied. "I guess I cannot blame him for being inspired to sing. He has been waiting a long time to see Willow and Oak, and now he will have more than a moon to be with them."

"And we get to visit with Oak, too," Fox piped up cheerfully as he and Mror strode along together in the procession. "That makes me happy, but I cannot say that I want to sing."

"I am glad we will see Oak, too," Mror agreed. Then Mror turned to look at Puh and me, as we steadily dragged the sled down the path. "Puh-Puh," Mror said to Puh. "Do you never sing while we are on the trail?"

"Not often," Puh replied.

"You do not like to sing?" Mror persisted.

"It is not so much that I do not like to sing," Puh began, "but that I prefer to listen. If I sing I cannot hear other sounds as well. Sometimes it is important to be able to hear if an animal is following you, if birds suddenly cry out in alarm, or if a prey animal approaches. Besides, I do not have a voice for song like Black Wolf."

Morning Star chuckled at this.

"I do not suppose there is another person who can achieve Da's volume," Morning Star said with a wry grin. "Except, possibly, Willow Woman. Dear though she is, I have never yet heard another with a voice like hers."

"It is the only way she can be heard at the Gathering; she must project her voice over the rabble," Fish Hawk stated. "It must be a requirement of every Head Elder. I have great respect for Willow Woman. It is not a position I would want. Little Oak has quite a future to look forward to if one day he becomes Head Elder."

"He will not be so little by then," Morning Star pointed out. "If Oak grows up to be like his parents, he will be a formidable man."

This was true. Black Wolf was the tallest man any of us had ever seen, and Willow Woman was one of the largest women, being both impressively robust and statuesque.

"Muh-Muh, will I be formidable, too?" Fox asked his mother.

"No doubt, you will," Morning Star answered.

This seemed to please him. I was not sure he knew exactly what *formidable* meant, but he seemed happy at the thought, nonetheless.

* * *

We arrived at the Fen of Falls after five days of hiking. The next morning, Karno arrived with Jura, little Mino, and a few followers. We would rest at Willow Woman's lodge for several days before starting out for the Gathering Hall.

We helped Willow Woman's staff to load their sleds for the trip and close up the lodge for the season. We planned for at least five more days on the trail. As before, we would be traveling relatively slowly. What with heavy sleds and small children in our company, we would have to proceed at the pace of the slowest among us.

On the second afternoon we flushed a sleeping boar out of his nest and managed to bring down the animal. We set up camp early and had fresh meat for our evening sup. It was a pleasant time, despite the cold, windy weather. The boar's flesh sustained our travels until we reached the valley that was home to the Gatherings.

When we came to the top of the hill overlookng the Gathering Hall, we were stunned at the sight. A collective gasp escaped our lips. The new Hall sprawled across the landscape, but in the background where the old Hall had been located, stood a partial skeleton of wooden frames. Once a magnificent structure, now it was just a few strips of wood poking up haphazardly from the ground. Even the old hearths had been removed; the only evidence of their onetime existence was the evenly spaced blackened pits amongst the weeds. We had not known that the old Hall had been taken apart since our last visit to this place. Many small homes had been erected nearby; so it would seem the old Hall had been sacrificed for its materials.

Willow Woman seemed frozen in place. Tears ran down her cheeks.

"This is a terrible sight," I said quietly. "I am sorry the old Hall has been destroyed."

Willow Woman finally spoke.

"I thought I could stand anything," she said, her voice choked with grief. "My father presided over that Hall, and his father before him."

Black Wolf put an arm around her.

"I am sorry, too, dear Willow," he said comfortingly. "I know this must be a shock. It is a shock to all of us. But it is cold. Let us go down to the new Hall and start a fire or two to warm up some of the rooms."

We somberly walked down the hill to the new Hall, passing through a field of tree stumps where trees had been hewn to build the grand new structure.

Willow Woman walked straight back to her rooms at the far end of the building, accompanied by Black Wolf. The rest of us loitered in the enormous main chamber, where the Gathering was to be held, to give Willow Woman privacy while she grieved the loss of the revered former Hall.

It was a relief to get out of the wind, but the only light was that which came down through the chimney holes in the roof. The room had two hearths, but Puh walked to the large hearth at the center of the Hall and, removing his iron pyrite and flint from his pack, began to strike the two stones together over a few well-crumpled shreds of birch bark. When sparks ignited the tinder, he watched the smoke curl up from the bark, occasionally encouraging the ember with a gentle breath. At last the birch bark seemed to be burning steadily, so Puh set it amongst dried grasses and larger pieces of kindling. As the fire increased in strength, Puh added more wood until a healthy blaze had been created.

In the meantime, we had dragged our sleds into the storage wing off the center of the Hall. This segment of the structure consisted of a juncture where short wings jutted out off the main building. It appeared that one wing was used for general storage, the other for food storage. At the one and only Gathering I had attended, I had observed that most of the Gathering attendees had brought food and other supplies, at least enough for themselves, but the more generous brought extra to feed their less fortunate fellows. It seemed to fill them with great pride to be able to provide for others or to gift their excess to their Head Elder's household. Others hoped to trade for goods from some of the many vendors who set up lean-tos where they could display their various wares, which might consist of foods, tools, articles of clothing, or trinkets.

The doors to both storage wings were wide open, and I noted that the food chamber had little in it. Willow Woman's sleds were loaded with many foodstuffs, so that chamber would soon be at least partially stocked. The opposite chamber, where our sleds now resided, also had little in them except our vehicles.

The lone window in each of these chambers had been left cracked open, presumably to allow for ventilation, but now I thought it a good idea to close those windows to prevent animals from gaining access to our food. I walked to the window and raised my hand to push the panel closed, but something just outside the window caught my eye. Instead of closing the panel I opened it wider. I had expected to see the collection of new homes in the distance, but not this.

"Puh, you might want to take a look," I said, calling Puh to me.

Puh obligingly approached and looked out the opening. His eyebrows promptly rose.

"A Challenge Circle," Puh said. "I did not realize they had made one here. It appears much has gone on we did not know about."

Fish Hawk and Uncle Inlee had come to peer out the window, too.

"The village where I was raised had a Challenge Circle . . . as you well know, Tris," Fish Hawk said. "But I have never known there to be one at the Gathering Hall. I guess it would be another way to settle disputes amongst the disgruntled."

"The ground within the Challenge Circle is still rough," Uncle Inlee pointed out. "And it is dotted with stumps. I would not care to tussle with anyone in there."

"Nor would I," I agreed.

* * *

By the time we had lighted torches and settled ourselves in spare rooms, evening was upon us. The vast Hall seemed much friendlier now that it was inhabited and warm. The children played, dogs snoozed near the hearth, and the aromas of cooking food filled the air.

"White Cloud will not let me help him," Morning Star announced to me, seeming a bit put out that she was not allowed to participate in producing our meal.

"He is making a meal without much time to prepare it," I said, hoping to soothe her. "This will probably be something simple he had planned to put together quickly. Perhaps he does not need any help."

Morning Star shrugged.

"I will help clean up after the nightly sup," she said. She then grinned. "I will not give him the option to say no."

"I would think you might like a break from cooking," Ria said to Morning Star.

"I do like a break," Morning Star acknowledged. "But I cannot find a way to get a break from my guilt at having someone else do my work for me."

"Enjoy it while you can," Willow Woman said, she and Black Wolf having rejoined us at that very moment. "You work hard every day; you deserve to rest. I have instructed White Cloud not to let you, Ria, or Jura assist him in anyway."

I was pleased to see that Willow Woman appeared to have regained her good humor.

"What about me?" I asked. In the past I had sometimes given White Cloud a hand.

"I gave White Cloud no instructions regarding help from anyone else, so you are free to do as you please," Willow Woman responded, smiling. "White Cloud is unlikely to reject your offer of help."

"Then I shall," I said, leaving them to go to White Cloud's side.

"Puh-Puh, I will go, too," Pony said, accompanying me to the hearth.

White Cloud was delighted to have a few extra sets of hands to bring off this meal, even if one of those sets belonged to a small child. Pony had often assisted her mother, and she was an eager and able helper.

After the food was consumed and the children put to bed, we adults sat around the fire.

"I did not see much activity around the homes that have been built down by the old Hall," Uncle Inlee noted.

"Many of the residents will be getting in some late rutting-season hunting before the Gathering starts," Black Wolf informed him. "But they will return before the moon is full."

"The vendors will start to arrive in a few days," Willow Woman added. "Those who come here first have the best chances to set up in the most opportune spots. They seek to position themselves in the places where people must pass by to reach the Hall's entrance. Soon after, the earliest attendees will start to arrive. It will not be long before our peace and quiet is gone."

Again, I recalled the Gathering from many years ago. It had been in the old Hall, and I had found it to be almost unbelievably crowded, stiflingly hot, and the air filled with many loud voices. I hoped the additional space in the new, bigger Hall would lessen the claustrophobic effect.

"What is vendor?" Karno inquired, looking perplexed.

"They are men who bring things they wish to trade for other things," Fish Hawk explained. "You might trade a knife for a parcel of dried meats, a pile of cured hides for a coat."

"Ah, Karno see now." Karno nodded that he understood, but then seemed to have another thought. "Sometimes trade meat for mate?"

We sat in silence for a moment; I, for one, was not sure I had actually heard Karno correctly. Willow Woman cleared her throat before speaking.

"If anyone has made such trades, it would not come as a complete surprise," Willow Woman admitted. "But I do not have knowledge that would allow me to vouch one way or the other."

"Just so long as they do not trade their mate for some meat," Fish Hawk said jovially.

"No, not do that," Karno agreed, laughing at the idea, and looking over at Jura fondly.

"When the Gathering begins, what do you want the Wolfmen and Old Ones to do?" Uncle Inlee asked Willow Woman. "Are we to stay in the Head Elder's wing where our rooms are located until we are called to join in?"

"To start, I believe that would be best," Willow Woman replied. "My hope is to take care of the attendees' most pressing concerns first. They will want to air their complaints and seek my decisions on these matters. It may take a number of days to get through them. But after that, I wish to present the case for allowing other peoples to be part of the Gathering, and do it in a way that will not cause an all-out brawl."

"How will you do that?" Uncle Inlee questioned.

"I will talk about the hard times many have recently endured," Willow Woman answered. "I will speak on the benefits we might see from cooperating with one another. If nothing else, I will speak on my belief that our survival may well depend on our ability to work together."

"I believe that is so, as well," Black Wolf concurred. "There is also the fact that we must concern ourselves with future generations. Think on all the children of mixed tribes, like my daughter Morning Star's children with Tris. One of the reasons I am determined to see this through is so that they will live in a society that welcomes all peoples."

"What part will be our part in the meeting?" Puh asked.

"Your presence as rational, competent human beings should help our cause," Willow Woman replied. "You may be called upon to answer questions. You may have questions, yourselves. It might be helpful to listen to the proceedings through the wall so you can get a feel for how things are going."

"If it does not put you to sleep to do so," Black Wolf quipped. "After the tenth man gripes about his neighbor impinging on his hunting grounds, it all starts to sound the same."

"Or who will win whose daughter," Fish Hawk said, suddenly solemn.

Fish Hawk was a friend and, by his union with Black Wolf's second-eldest daughter, Petal, he was also extended family. Many years ago, I had been challenged to battle his brother Snow Leopard for Morning Star. Most pairings did not include a challenge in order to win one's mate, but matters that could not be otherwise settled sometimes found resolution in the Challenge Circle. There, men fought until one capitulated or was killed.

His brother had surrendered rather than be killed, but Snow Leopard had continued to pursue Morning Star and had stolen her from our pairing ceremony. Puh, Black Wolf, and I had then been forced to track Snow Leopard and his band to retrieve my new mate, finally killing Snow Leopard in the fracas.

Fish Hawk graciously overlooked this and, in fact, had later sought me out to apologize for his brother's behavior. After all, Morning Star had been promised to me, and Snow Leopard had issued a challenge and lost, and then abducted a newly paired woman. I had not wished to fight Snow Leopard or to kill him, but I had no choice, unless it was to lose my one love from boyhood. Fish Hawk knew all this, and I had never once doubted his friendship, but that did not stop him from being sad over what had transpired.

 **Chapter Nine** 

The coming days consisted of readying the Hall for the event. The huge building showed signs of casual animal and human inhabitation, and needed – at the very least – a cursory cleaning. Our sleds were unloaded and foods were stashed in the food storage chamber, while our personal possessions, such as bedding and spare clothing, were brought to our rooms. We adults were often preoccupied with these tasks, leaving the children free to play in the great room where the Gathering would eventually assemble. For now it was mostly empty, and it gave them a huge area in which to run after one another in breathless abandon. Since most of our dwellings were cramped and crowded, to play indoors in this way was a novelty, and they gave every appearance of enjoying it immensely.

The Hall was laid out thus: the huge first chamber hosted the Gathering's assemblage, while the second half of the Hall was at Willow Woman's disposal, accommodating her household, plus any guests she might be entertaining. The area at the center of the Hall that separated the public main room from Willow Woman's private rooms housed a large hearth, and it was from there that the two shorter storage wings branched off. Willow Woman's lodgings consisted of many rooms, but the only one who had a room to himself was Willow Woman's healer, Gray Owl. The rest of us shared rooms: Morning Star and I shared our chamber with our children and our dog; Uncle Inlee, Puh and his family and dog were in another room; Willow Woman, Black Wolf, and Oak in another; and the Wolfmen in yet another. Fish Hawk and Black Wolf's sons Swift River and Hawk even shared a room with some of Willow Woman's staff. It was a bit crowded, but no one seemed to mind.

Much firewood had to be brought in; it was a priority to make sure we had enough fuel to see us through the Gathering. Soon, stacks of wood were piled along many of the walls. The sight made me think back to the Gathering I had witnessed so long ago. No wonder the old Hall had seemed so packed-full, what with all the supplies it held. Wood had been heaped everywhere, and bags and baskets collected in a mound at the far end of the main room. Everything had been in such disarray back then that I had not at first noticed Willow Woman as she lounged on a pile of sacks.

In addition to firewood, we would also need a lot of water. Many trips were made to and from the nearest stream to fill numerous water bags. We wanted to bring in as much water as possible before the onslaught of attendees potentially fouled the closest water sources. This was a chilly chore. Nighttime temperatures dipped below freezing, so the creeks and ponds were skimmed with ice by morning. Even though the ice thawed as the day warmed, our fingers still ached with cold as we filled each bag.

The vendors started to arrive a few days before the night of the full moon, which would signal the beginning of the Gathering. Those of us who did not belong to The People from the East's tribes had been careful to hide our presence, only coming and going from entryways that were out of sight from the newly sprung village on the far side of the Hall. But now that the vendors had set up right outside the Hall's entrance, we were more or less trapped indoors, unless we wanted to stir up gossip about our occupancy and potential intrusion on The People's annual Gathering.

I became bored. We were often confined indoors for long periods of time over the winter, but at home I always had projects to work on. The other seasons kept us busy harvesting foods and hides and collecting materials we would need to make tools, clothing, and household items. The only good part about being shut in the Hall was that I was able to enjoy the company of my friends, and most especially, my mate. Our children were often occupied in playing with Oak and Mror and were carefully supervised by several of the adults. Morning Star and I would take advantage of these times to slip away to our room, where we could simply enjoy being together. The life of a hunter requires much time away from his mate; this provided the first opportunities in a very long time that we could while away an afternoon in each other's arms. I had hoped that Morning Star might conceive another child soon to ease her mind about the loss of our little Wren. And ease my mind, as well.

We knew when the early attendees began to arrive, because they let themselves into the Hall and loudly announced their presence. If they had brought supplies to contribute to the Gathering, they deposited these items into one of the storerooms. As time went on, it became more apparent why the new Hall had been built. Willow Woman may have been dismayed at the demise of the old Hall, but the new Hall had many advantages. It was big enough to accommodate many more people, the firewood and food could be stashed in areas other than the main chamber.

Whereas the old Hall was too small to house the attendees, the new one had enough space for all to settle in for the duration of the Gathering, just so long as they did not mind living cheek by jowl. As the moon waxed fatter, the sounds of many voices drifted through the walls to reach our ears. The noise carried on late into the night as men who had not seen one another since the previous year caught up on all that had transpired in the intervening time. By the day of the full moon, the level of sound emanating from the Hall's main chamber was incredible as the men shouted their conversations to be heard over the din.

Most of those who were not participating in the Gathering sat in the room that abutted the central hearth, listening to the goings-on through the wall. I was amazed to hear silence descend upon the room as soon as Willow Woman, Black Wolf, and Oak entered the Gathering's main chamber. She owned a voice that carried a great distance, and now she addressed the assembly in a tone that brooked no nonsense.

As Black Wolf had predicted, the initial proceedings mostly consisted of Willow Woman listening to complaints. There were the usual sorts of grievances regarding someone's repeated attempts to take game or harvest foodstuff from lands not his own. I was amused to hear one man take exception to a neighbor's daughter who teased his son. He wanted Willow Woman to instruct the man to tell his daughter to mind her manners. Willow Woman did not speak for a moment, but I could imagine the dour look on her face. Regardless of clan, I knew of no people who did not cherish their children. Children were our most important clan members, as they were the future of our people. That being said, they were not generally coddled, either, and I knew Willow Woman to be a strict but affectionate parent.

"We do love our children, do we not?" Willow Woman responded at last. "And we want to protect them. But it is also our duty to teach them how to function in a challenging world. Sometimes you will catch the bear; sometimes the bear will catch you. And sometimes, you will find that the person who is teasing you only wishes to know you better. Perhaps your son needs to get to the root of the cause and work it out with the girl. Without any adult interference, that is, beyond encouraging him to face his tormentor in a dignified and civilized manner."

No one spoke for several moments.

"That is wise, Willow Woman," the man concurred. "Thank you. I will do as you say."

The low murmur of voices seemed to indicate general approval, as it did after each time Willow Woman rendered a decision or offered advice. I was encouraged that the meeting was going so well. So far, there had been none of the discord or brawls for which the Gatherings were so well known.

When no one else came forward with a complaint, Willow Woman began to speak again.

"Now that our early business has been taken care of, I want to bring up a subject that has troubled us at many of our past Gatherings: the problem of dwindling resources. The wildfire that killed much of the plant and animal life has only exacerbated an already perilous situation. Additionally, several unusually harsh winters have compounded these difficulties. Not only have we lost some villages because the residents have died off or moved away, but some of the Old Ones' settlements recently lost many of their inhabitants, as well. It was fortunate for them that Karno, leader of The People of the Wolves, has stepped in to help one clan. These problems belong to all of us."

The undercurrent of muted discussions became louder now, but Willow Woman raised her powerful voice to speak over them.

"We all live on these same lands," she went on. "And I think it is only prudent to work together for survival."

"What are you suggesting?" someone asked. "Do we not work together now?"

"Not as much as we could," Willow Woman replied. "However, I am not suggesting that anyone be forced to do anything. What I want to see is a spirit of cooperation among all peoples and clans, and to do this, there must be exchanges of ideas, pulling together in large hunting parties to bring down more game, and trading foodstuffs and supplies. It would be helpful if each clan, including those of the Old Ones and the Wolfmen were represented at the Gatherings."

Now the crowd began to shout. Black Wolf and Oak shared the platform with Willow Woman at head of the assembly, and I wondered if poor Oak was frightened at the hostile reaction. Then I remembered Oak had sat through every Gathering since his birth, and he might have been thinking it was about time someone began to holler. Nevertheless, since this was Swift River's and Hawk's first Gathering I speculated that they might not share Oak's serene frame of mind. Since they were on the other side of the wall with the rest of the attendees, I could not see their reactions to the current rancor, but I was sure they found it an unusual, if somewhat disconcerting experience.

Morning Star was at my side as we listened, holding my hand. Her grip tightened, and I glanced over at her. This was her first Gathering, as well.

"Do not worry," I whispered to her. "I have been expecting this."

"I do not like it," Morning Star told me. "I am glad the children are in the far-back rooms with White Cloud and Gray Owl — dear men that they are, to be willing to entertain a passel of little ones! But I think they would be afraid at all the shouting. It is fortunate Jura decided to keep herself and Mino in the far-back rooms, too. She would be terrified to hear all the commotion. Poor Oak; he is out there in the thick of it!"

"I am sure Oak is taking it in stride," Puh said to Morning Star. "He is a most remarkable child. Like his mother, he is incredibly self-possessed."

"And unlike his Da!" Morning Star added with a little giggle. Black Wolf had a famously volatile temperament.

"Did you hear?" Karno interrupted. "She talk of Karno! She say Karno leader!"

Willow Woman had resumed her speech.

"We cannot deny that we would benefit from interacting with one another at the Gatherings. Let us invite all our neighbors to participate."

"Yes!" someone called out. It sounded much like Fish Hawk.

"No! No!" someone else cried out vehemently in response.

"You already let the Old Ones speak at one Gathering many years ago," another said. "What did that do for us? They only wanted our help; they did not contribute anything to the common good of our peoples."

The rest of the shouts were unintelligible, being lost in the sea of voices – until Black Wolf's deep bass penetrated the uproar.

"*Silence!*" Black Wolf ordered.

Quiet descended upon the Hall.

"What ails you all? Why must every Gathering devolve into an utter brouhaha?" Black Wolf demanded. "I agree with Willow. We have everything to lose if we do not include our neighbors at these meetings. If the Old Ones asked for help, it was only because some of our people had been ransacking their undefended homes. What would you have done, if you never knew what you would come home to after each hunt? The Old Ones and the Wolfmen have often come to our aid. They have repaid us many times over for the favor of speaking at a Gathering."

"You only say that because you associate with these other clans," someone spoke up.

"Yes, and I know them to be fine people," Black Wolf answered. I thought it good of him not to mention the men of the Old Ones who had once aspired to eat us, or the one who had clobbered him on the head with a club. Black Wolf went on, "They are honorable, smart, strong, and brave. And who of us has not envied the Old Ones their extraordinary insight that allows them to find game when no one else can? And we of The People have much to offer them as well. We would be fools not to ask them to join us here."

"I have invited some of them to come here," Willow Woman stated.

This brought about another round of emotionally charged and highly vociferous replies, some positive, some most definitely quite negative. The door panel leading to the room where we stood listening to the exchange suddenly moved, opening the doorway, causing all of us to jump. We had been so intent on following the exchanges that we taken by surprise. It was Oak.

"Mother asks that you men join us now," Oak said with a smile. Just as Puh had said, Oak was completely unperturbed.

I bent down to give Morning Star a quick parting kiss.

"I am afraid," she stated. I could feel her tembling.

"Everything will be fine," I said as calmly as I could, but I too was trepidatious.

Uncle Inlee walked out first, tall and proud, his white hair marking him to be a man with much knowledge and experience. He was followed by Karno and his fellow Wolfmen, then Puh and me. My senses were immediately assaulted by the thick air. It was not just from the smoke that curled up from the torches and fireplaces, but also from the aroma of cured hides, sweat, and the combined breath of the several hundred people who had occupied this chamber since the start of the Gathering. Because of the crowded and hot conditions, the attendees were in varying states of undress. My gaze was also drawn toward the cluttered walls of the room and upward to the vaulted ceiling, all of which had been utilized to hang or store the belongings people had brought with them for the duration of the event.

Conversation hushed upon our emergence from the back room, but only temporarily.

"Snow Leopard's killer!" a man called out.

I had already felt conspicuous, thanks to my fiery red hair and freckled skin, weathered to a deep pink, but now I cringed inwardly. It seemed I would never be free from that fateful series of meetings with Snow Leopard. I scanned the sea of hairy faces. Some were friendly, others guarded, still others appearing outright hostile. Fish Hawk pushed his way through the crowd to stand by me.

"Who said that?" Fish Hawk shouted back angrily. "I am Snow Leopard's brother. I loved my brother, but he was wrong to steal a woman he had rightfully lost in the Challenge Circle. Tris did what he had to do to get his mate back. Snow Leopard would still be alive if he had left well enough alone."

"Many thanks, Fish Hawk, for coming to my defense," I said to him, but I was not sure he could hear me over the commotion.

Fish Hawk glared fiercely into the crowd. I was both honored and humbled by his response. I had ever known Fish Hawk to be an extremely amiable, good-humored man, and the dramatic change that had overcome him shocked me.

This seemed to mollify at least some of the attendees, who now looked to one another unsurely.

"Snow Leopard committed numerous offenses when he stole my daughter from her pairing celebration," Black Wolf roared, apparently not content to give up on the subject yet. "His actions did not do credit to our People!"

"That is just it," a man near the front of the assemblage said. "There are many Old Ones whose actions do not do them credit, either. And what do we know of the Wolfmen?"

Karno stepped forward to speak, no doubt wanting to tell about our most recent mammoth hunt, but Black Wolf held up a hand to stop him. Some instinct halted Karno from following through with his impulse. Karno put aside his usually brazen behavior and simply nodded to Black Wolf, stepping back to resume his former place.

"We cannot waste time airing grievances for offenses dating back to when we first began to occupy these lands," Willow Woman spoke up. "Neither The People nor the Old Ones are entirely blameless for the current mistrust and resentment some harbor. And about the Wolfmen, they have only been here a short time and thus far they have been good friends and have shown they are skilled hunters and also an industrious people."

"And we have music," Karno blurted out. I was quite surprised he said not a word about the mammoths we had brought down. I would have thought it would be foremost in his mind.

"Hashing over old grievances may be a waste of time, but nevertheless, the old hatreds will not just evaporate like a puddle after the rain," another man said.

"Why not?" Willow asked. "Those who carry hate hurt only themselves. Are we to tear at our skin and wail and pull out our hair over past wrongs? Are we to hold an entire people culpable for misdeeds done by a few of their race, misdeeds that in some cases were done long ago? He did this, he did that? Are any of them still alive? We must make sure the old hatreds die out with us, with our generation."

"We will burn this Hall before we let others into our Gathering!" a voice from the back of the chamber yelled, and others joined in, chanting *burn, burn, burn*!

Terrible images of Willow Woman's burning summer lodge sprang to mind. The awful event and the bloodshed during the subsequent attack were forever seared into my memory. I squelched a feeling of rising panic and forced myself to remain calm. I hoped that Morning Star and the others listening from the back room were not becoming too alarmed.

"We will fight them until we are all that is left alive on these lands," another voice rang out.

"Stop! That is enough!" Willow Woman bellowed. I saw that she was shaking with rage. Sweat beaded on her brow, and she seemed to be struggling to maintain her composure. I edged toward her to touch her hand comfortingly. She smiled at me only slightly, and then continued. "Those of you who think you should burn this Hall, what will that accomplish, except to waste the years of work that went into building this magnificent structure and all the materials that went into making it? Who would you hurt except your neighbors who congregate here every fall? And regarding battling the Old Ones and the Wolfmen until they are all gone, what makes you so sure you will be the victor? The last men who tried did not succeed. They had been exiled as Outsiders. When they did not abide by the terms of their exile, and attacked, they met their deaths, killed by the cooperative efforts of a group of Old Ones, Wolfmen, and men of The People. I will also add that when Oak and I were under threat, a woman of the Old Ones stood before us with her bow and arrows and fended off our attackers. Do you not see what we can achieve if we work together? To attempt to resolve the issue by fighting would just bring about a colossal waste of life. Right now, our aim should be to diligently preserve life – which is already under constant threat by the forces of nature – not to rashly extinguish it."

The room had fallen silent at Willow Woman's words. Now, some of the men discoursed with those around them to discuss her remarks.

"Perhaps there is a simple solution to this," one man said. "What if a man of The People and a man, either of the Old Ones or the Wolfman, were to meet in the Challenge Circle?"

"Yes!" another agreed. "If everyone is willing to abide by the result of the bout, then there would be no need to battle it out with one another."

"We would be honor bound to accept the result," yet another quickly added.

Willow Woman and Black Wolf traded glances, seemingly surprised at this suggestion. I wondered if Willow Woman had simply expected to just deem it so as Head Elder, and she had supposed any disgruntled attendees would to allow her to have her way. I also wondered who would be selected to meet in the Challenge Circle. As someone who had already endured the experience, I could empathize with those chosen. This was hand-to-hand combat, and Old Ones did not fight like The People. The People fought with fists, while Old Ones used their whole bodies – almost like two bears wrestling, except Old Ones also used their heads, elbows, knees, and feet to achieve a victory. I still had a scar on my forehead from where Snow Leopard had split open my brow.

"What say you, Willow Woman?" questioned someone from the midst of the crowd.

"If we win, they will respect the decision," Black Wolf said to Willow Woman in a low voice. "It may end the quarreling for good."

Willow Woman appeared to be deep in thought.

"*For good?*" She said at last. "I do not know if it will ever be ended for good. But if it gives us even a temporary period of peaceful coexistence during which most of The People will learn the real qualities of their neighbors, it will be a good start toward moving forward." Willow Woman then locked eyes with me, "Tris, you must do this for me."

"Do what . . . ?" I asked, peering into her sweaty face.

"Do you mean the Challenge?" Puh asked anxiously.

"Yes," Willow Woman replied. "I can think of no one else who would be most likely to settle this matter in our favor."

"When would this take place?" Uncle Inlee asked. "Would we have time to prepare?"

Willow Woman still held my gaze.

"Tris, will you do it?" she asked again. "If so, I will tell them we will go to the Challenge Circle. If not, we will have to think of something else."

"I will do it," I told her.

Not that I actually wanted to do it or was sure I could win. After all, I had no idea who I would be up against. But I agreed simply because Willow Woman requested it of me. She had been my friend for many years now, and friends come to the aid of one another. That was an unspoken rule of the land.

"We will go to the Challenge Circle," Willow Woman announced to the assembly. "Choose your champion. We have ours." Willow Woman indicated me.

"Will it be now?" Puh inquired.

"Shortly," Black Wolf answered grimly. "As soon as they have chosen someone to meet Tris in the Challenge Circle."

"Tris, do you remember how they fight?" Uncle Inlee asked me, clearly not pleased with this turn of events.

"Yes," I replied. I remembered only too well.

"Do you know how to hit with your fists?" Uncle Inlee persisted.

"Well, I have given out two punches," I admitted.

"*Two?*" Uncle Inlee said incredulously. "You won the previous bout against Snow Leopard with two punches?"

"Only one," Black Wolf said with a chuckle. "He mostly battered Snow Leopard into submission. The second punch was when Tris thumped his cousin for disparaging Morning Star."

That one punch to Snow Leopard had not won the bout; I was only seventeen winters old at that time, and I was well pummeled before the whole thing was over. I had only managed to succeed by being stronger and heavier, and by my sheer determination to win.

It took a little time and a lot of arguing before the other contestant was selected. Like Snow Leopard, he appeared little taller than I, but he was broader through the body than Snow Leopard had been. Black Wolf stared at the man in dismay.

"Who is that?" I asked Black Wolf.

"He is called Little Weasel," Black Wolf answered.

Black Wolf's reply momentarily flummoxed me. Some of The People's names could be unusual and less than flattering to the owner, but if I had heard him correctly, this was possibly the most unlikely moniker of all time ever gifted to a recipient.

"Are you joking?" Uncle Inlee said, his tone betraying his disbelief.

"No," Black Wolf responded. "I guess if a giantess like my mate Little Fawn can have a similarly incongruous name, then so can he."

"I would not like to speculate on how appropriate his name might be," Puh said dryly. Then he asked Black Wolf, "Do you know him?"

"I do not know him except by reputation," Black Wolf informed us. "He and his clan are from our southern border. They seldom come to the Gatherings because it is such a long hike to get here. I have not heard that he is a bad sort, but he is known to be exceptionally tough. And perhaps wily, too, although he does not appear to be terribly smart. All the same, I would have a care, Tris."

We were each given a brief amount of time with which to prepare ourselves. No weapons would be allowed, and each of us would be required to strip to the waist so that no knives might be concealed within our long-sleeved tunics.

Those of us who had stood with the Head Elder now retreated to the back room, where our families and friends awaited us. Morning Star's face was strained with anxiety as she came forward to meet me.

"We heard everything," she said, tears starting to run down her cheeks.

"I am sorry; it must have been upsetting to listen to," I responded, wrapping my arms around her and kissing her forehead.

"I still have nightmares after your bout with Snow Leopard," Morning Star told me. "It was the most awful thing I have ever seen. I want to ask *why you*? Why should you be the one to go to the Challenge Circle? But I know the answer. Who else would be a better choice? Da has always said it was a good thing you owned a placid nature, because if you ever decided to get really angry, you would be like a bear on a rampage."

I smiled at this.

"If only I had a bear's teeth and claws," I mused aloud, trying to lighten the mood.

I pulled my tunic over my head and slipped my knife from its sheath at my belt.

"Keep the children indoors," I instructed Morning Star, assuming she would stay in the Hall as well.

Puh seemed almost as distressed as Morning Star, but he just stayed at my side, taking possession of my tunic and knife as I removed them.

"I will hold onto these until after the bout," Puh said quietly. "You will want your tunic as soon as it is over. It is cold out there."

I nodded to him.

"Many thanks, Puh," I answered.

"Tris, remember to keep your hands up," Black Wolf said while motioning how to position my hands before me. "If you strike with your fist, keep your thumb on the outside of the fist; else you might break it. Do your best to avoid his blows."

"You may be sure I will do my best," I promised.

"You are too calm," Willow Woman said to me with concern.

"I am not sure anyone can be too calm," I replied. "This has all happened so quickly that I have not had time to become unnerved. Let us get this done so we can put it behind us."

I embraced Morning Star once again and gave her a long kiss.

"I will be back soon," I said to her. "Try not to worry."

"I cannot promise not to worry," Morning Star responded, wiping more tears from her eyes. "I feel sick about this."

"I am sorry," I said, kissing her one more time before hastily breaking away.

I left the room without looking back. I could not bear to see her distress. The sight of Morning Star's tears tore at my heart. My companions accompanied me as we pushed our way through the mob of men. I was somewhat encouraged to see that I was taller than many of them; perhaps Little Weasel would not be so big, after all.

The throng followed us outside as we made our way to the Challenge Circle. This one was unlike the Challenge Circle in the Village, where the ring had been constructed from mammoth tusks. This one consisted of crudely hewn timbers, and it was a circle in name only, because it was in no way round. It was approximately nine or ten paces across, and it was dotted with tree stumps and clumps of weeds. A few men who had come out before us were swiftly cutting a few small bushes to ground level and taking the bits of brush away, thoughtfully providing a few last-moment improvements. They seemed very proud to contribute their efforts toward perfecting the grounds within the Challenge Circle, even if the jagged stumps still stood out as glaring obstacles.

I stepped over the Challenge Circle's wooden boundary and studied the area in which I would be fighting. Once the bout began, I would have little time or attention to spare for my surroundings. I took special care to take note of where each stump was located. The stumps were about knee-high, and their tops came to splintered points; I would not care to fall on any of them. The stubby remnants of the newly chopped bushes and the withered grasses crunched under my boots. As the cold began to seep into my skin, I wondered when my opponent would present himself.

I did not have long to wait. Just as a light snow began to filter down from a gray sky, I saw Little Weasel approach. I studied him, trying to get a feel for how he moved and what manner of man he might be. The first thing I noticed was that he had a shambling walk, head down and arms swinging. His black hair was cropped unevenly at about shoulder length, and his long beard was unruly. I mused that he was about as unlike a man as Snow Leopard as any two men could be. Snow Leopard had been lithe, but powerfully built, almost elegant in his appearance. He had been handsome and fastidious in the care of his person and clothing. Little Weasel's face and chest bore the scars most hunters wore, and he was covered with copious body hair. Despite being generally unkempt, he seemed vigorous and healthy.

Little Weasel raised his head only after he had stepped into the Challenge Circle and stood opposite me. His nose was somewhat flattened and bent to one side of his face. He gave me a disarming grin, exposing a huge gap in his smile. All of his front teeth, both top and bottom, were missing.

"You are Tris?" Little Weasel said to me, still grinning pleasantly. He had a deep, raspy voice and enunciated his words oddly; *you are Tris?* came out sounding like *you ah Twish?* I supposed it was his lack of front teeth that caused this unusual phenomenon.

"I am" – I hesitated a moment – "and you are . . . um . . . Little Weasel?"

"*Ha,*" he waved my words aside, "most people just call me Weasel. I was named for my revered grandfather, Big Weasel, so I was called Little Weasel to distinguish me from him. But I have grown since then. Call me Weasel."

Weasel then peered at me more closely.

"I have never been this close to an Old One before," he admitted. "I have never seen hair like yours before . . . and green eyes! And you have speckles all over your skin!"

"I do look a little different," I agreed. "But I think underneath we are all the same."

Weasel looked me up and down. I suppose he wanted to assess his opponent as well.

"You must be quite strong. You have lots of scars," Weasel stated. "I am the best fighter among The People. Are you the best fighter amongst the Old Ones?"

I was surprised by Weasel's unhurried and amiable chatter. I was actually starting to regret that I would have to try to hurt this congenial man.

"I do not know," I answered, but I stopped myself adding that we Old Ones did not do this kind of fighting. There was no use telling him what he would soon find out for himself.

"Well, before we start, I want to let you know that I am not fighting because I dislike you or your people.

Or the Wolfmen," Weasel said, continuing to grin engagingly. "I volunteered because I have always been curious how I would fare in a fight against a man of the Old Ones."

Weasel then paused to cast a glance around the Circle with all its impediments and idiosyncrasies.

At that juncture, shouts from outside the Circle diverted my attention while Weasel continued to inspect the grounds.

"*You cannot enter!*" an indignant man bellowed.

I turned to see Morning Star and Ria trying to join the crowd around the Circle.

"Get out of my way!" Morning Star replied, brushing past him.

How well I knew that tone. My beloved mate might be only half my weight, but when I heard that timbre in her voice, I knew better than to argue. The man looked around helplessly, as though hoping someone might come to his rescue and make Morning Star obey. Apparently that tone was well known to everyone else as well, since no one came to his assistance. Morning Star took advantage of his momentary inattention and quickly melted into the mob. Weasel had missed this, but he happened to look up when Ria tried to brush past, too. The man stopped her as well, and he tried a more tactful approach.

"I am sorry, Grandmother, but women are not allowed," the man said.

Ria glowered at him.

"I will go where I please," she told him.

"But Grandmother, no weapons are allowed," the man tried again, pointing to Ria's bow and quiver of arrows.

"I will leave them in the Hall. But then I will return," she said firmly. "And I am not a grandmother!"

Weasel laughed aloud at this exchange.

"You tell him, Grandmother!" Weasel called out cheerfully. "Um, *not a grandmother!*"

I then saw that Morning Star had reappeared to stand next to her father and Willow Woman, who were accompanied by Puh, Uncle Inlee, and the Wolfmen. Ria soon joined them. I felt relieved: Morning Star and Ria would be safe there.

By now, many in the crowd were becoming impatient, and they were yelling to us to commence the Challenge.

"Well, I guess we should start," Weasel said, still smiling.

Each snowflake that landed on my skin seemed to impart a little sting of chill to my body. The longer I stood still, the colder I felt, so for this reason, and the desire to get it over with, I too was eager to begin.

"I guess we should," I concurred.

Little Weasel stepped back.

"I was told not to let you get your hands on me," he said. "How about you?"

"I was told to stay out of the way of your fists," I replied.

Little Weasel chuckled at this.

"Good advice," he said.

We began to slowly circle one another, carefully avoiding the stumps. I waited for Weasel to come at me, watching him closely to see if he leaned one direction or the other so I could turn to meet him. However, Weasel did not seem to employ any particular strategy. He suddenly darted forward, his right fist lashing out.

I had to admit, he was quick for a big man, but I ducked his fist and stepped toward him, just as he once again danced backward. This brought me up close to him, and I locked my arms around his torso, simultaneously wrapping my right leg around his and jerking it back, so that Weasel's leg was pulled out from under him, enabling me to throw him to the ground. Weasel went down heavily. A roar went up from the crowd – some were pleased, some obviously displeased.

"*Ooph!*" Weasel said as he landed. "*Ouch!*"

I was amazed to see he was still smiling.

"That was a good move!" Weasel marveled as he regained his feet. "You must teach me how to do that."

But then Weasel resumed his fighting stance, and he came at me once more, this time attempting to land a few quick jabs. The first hit me in the chest, and the others I blocked with my forearm and swatted away. I knew I was supposed to hit him too, but my inexperience, coupled with my reluctance to do him an injury held me back. Nonetheless, Weasel's flurries of blows continued to rain on me and soon ate away at my hesitance. When the old scar on my brow opened-up again, I finally found my resolve to fight back, and without a second thought I slammed Weasel on the side of his head.

Weasel staggered for a moment, and although his grin had faded, it soon returned as he shook off the effects of the impact.

"So you do have a punch," Weasel said as calmly as if he had simply observed that I had two eyes and a nose.

I could think of no reply, so I just nodded. Blood ran down the side of my nose from my forehead and probably oozed from other sites, as well. Weasel was also bleeding from his left ear. I hazarded a glance around us to see where the nearest stumps were lest I find myself dropping onto one of them, either by accident or design. The snow was starting to collect on the ground, making the footing a bit slippery. I could see red splashes of our blood dotting the otherwise pristine white covering.

Weasel rushed at me anew, and this time we traded punches, Weasel getting in two hits to each one of mine. He hit hard. His knuckles were now split open and bleeding freely. I was frustrated at my lack of proficiency, so I reverted to the tactics I had learned as a boy. I ignored Weasel's blows and grappled him by the torso to pin his arms by his sides. I just wanted to stop him for a few moments so I could gather my wits enough to formulate some kind of a plan.

Weasel struggled against my hold, but he could not break free. He writhed violently in my grasp, so I butted my head against his and I was gratified to see his eyes roll back. I dropped him on the ground, probably more gently than most would expect, and then stepped back, wiping away the blood from my face. While I tried to think, I bent to grab a bit of snow, and rubbed it onto my hands to clean off the blood.

The mob of spectators were on their feet, shouting at us, but I could not tell what most of them were saying. Then I came to realize that some were calling out, "Finish him! Finish him!"

Finish him? After being knocked around, in my semi-addled state I could not fathom what they meant. Then it occurred to me that they wanted me to kill him. The idea was repellent to me, but the Challenge would have to be resolved one way or the other. Either death or capitulation.

Weasel slowly roused himself. He seemed surprised to see me nearby, just watching him as the voices continued to shout at us from outside the Circle. Weasel gave me a sheepish grin and he rubbed his head.

"My head aches," Weasel said to me, without a trace of malice. "It was good of you to let me recover for a bit."

Then Weasel stood and again raised his fists in a defensive pose.

"You are not a fighter, are you?" Weasel went on.

"Not in the way you know it," I answered. "Not with my fists."

Weasel began to circle me. He was slightly crouched, and he seemed wary of what I might do next. All at once, he stopped in place and let his hands fall to his sides. Weasel's mouth dropped open and he gasped, once again exposing the conspicuous absence of his front teeth.

"Look! Over there!" Weasel said to me, motioning toward Willow Woman.

At first I wondered if this were some type of ruse to make me look and then take me unawares, but then he added, "Look at that pretty little thing . . . so dainty!" Weasel gushed. It took a moment for me to realize to whom he was referring; it was not Willow Woman he meant, but Morning Star, my own mate! Weasel, as if in a trance, went on dreamily, "She looks like a juicy tidbit! I wonder if I might take her out to the bushes and introduce her to my hairless weasel!"

In my still somewhat muddled state, my brain strove to work out what he was saying, and I pondered what parts of this hirsute individual might not have a thick covering of hair, when his meaning suddenly dawned on me. My hand seemed to fly of its own volition. My fist connected with Weasel's head once more, and he collapsed like a grouse struck with a stone. As I trembled with fury, guilt began to overtake me. I supposed his reaction to a woman like Morning Star, even if many men would have chosen to keep their thoughts to themselves, was natural. As my sense of ire eased, Weasel began to groan and he moved his head slightly from side to side.

Some of those outside the Circle, including Puh, Ria, and Morning Star, stepped over the border and looked down on Weasel, staring at him wide-eyed. Puh handed my tunic to me so I could don it against the cold. Puh studied my well-battered physique without comment, but he patted my shoulder. I thought he seemed relieved to find me all right, even if I was a little worse for the wear. Morning Star also looked up at me searchingly, as though trying to ascertain my condition. She touched my face tenderly.

"Are you badly hurt?" She asked. "Your poor face! You are bleeding."

"I do not think I am badly hurt," I answered.

"Is he alive?" Morning Star inquired, indicating Weasel.

"Yes," I answered, "he has made a little noise."

Weasel moaned more loudly this time and tried to raise himself on one elbow.

"I am done; I am done," Weasel said hoarsely. Then he saw Morning Star standing at my side. "Who is this lovely, lovely . . . um . . . vision of beauty?"

Morning Star exchanged glances with me.

"How hard did you hit him?" she asked incredulously.

"Why do you say that?" I asked. "That is what I ask myself every day."

Morning Star looked at me skeptically.

"No mother of four young children often feels worthy of such high praise," Morning Star said flatly. "But I do appreciate the sentiment."

"Who are you?" Weasel persisted, this time speaking directly to Morning Star.

"I am Morning Star," she introduced herself. "I am Tris's mate."

Weasel was momentarily struck mute, and then he started to laugh. He flopped back onto the cold, snowy ground and continued to laugh heartily.

Morning Star seemed both confused and a bit miffed.

"Why is that funny?" she asked.

By now, Willow Woman, Black Wolf, and many of the others had come into the Circle as word was passed around that Weasel had declined to go on further.

"It is not really funny," I told her. "It was just that he had made a remark – admiring you from afar, so to speak – just before I hit him that last time. Perhaps he has only now realized that it was not a prudent thing to say in my hearing."

"No, it was not," Weasel agreed. "Oh, my head, my head!" he held up a hand to me, "Help me up!"

I turned to raise Weasel to his feet.

"Thank you," Weasel said to me while brushing himself off, "and I apologize for what I said. I had not heard that Old Ones took mates who were from The People's tribes. I would never have guessed that she might be your mate."

"Come and meet the rest of my family," I said with a smile.

Chapter Ten

As we walked through the mob, I noted a wide variety of expressions on the visages we passed by. Some seemed amused, others confused. Some appeared to be quite unhappy. Weasel talked all the while. Whatever his injuries, his vocal capacities were entirely unaffected.

"You know, Tris, the good thing about having no front teeth is that the inside of my lips do not get cut during a fight," Weasel told me. "If the snow starts to collect on the ground, you might hold some of it to you face. It will dull the pain and take down the swelling."

Willow Woman, Black Wolf, and Oak had taken their places at the head of the congregation. Willow Woman waved to those of us who were her household guests.

"Tris, Tor . . . all of you, come up here," she said, bidding us to join her.

I turned to take my leave of Weasel; he touched my arm.

"I will meet your family later," he said to me.

I nodded and smiled to him.

"Yes, later," I agreed.

We rejoined Willow Woman but made a point to stand well to the side, wanting to be close enough to make a show of support, but not so close as to appear to be unduly influential.

"Well," said Willow Woman. "The Challenge is over. Little Weasel has conceded."

"I have conceded the Challenge," Weasel called from his place in the crowd. I could no longer see him, but his voice and unique style of pronunciation were unmistakable.

"You put up a good fight," Willow Woman assured Weasel. "I have seen what Tris can do, and I believe you are lucky he is a kind and merciful man."

"Yes, I am fortunate in that," Weasel agreed humbly. "He could have killed me several times over; I do not believe I could have done more than wound him."

I was not so sure that Weasel was incapable of doing more than injuring me. He was a formidable opponent. It had to be acknowledged that when it came to fist fighting, he was far superior to me. I guessed that it was my unusual way of countering his maneuvers that won the bout — that and his eccentricities: his humble good nature and his weakness for attractive women.

"You could have used those stumps to your advantage!" a man said angrily to Weasel.

"That would not have been fair," Weasel replied simply.

By now, I could tell where Weasel was standing. He had a group of men around him trying to tend his wounds while he still attempted to take part in the meeting.

Willow Woman's healer, Gray Owl, was sent for, and he soon entered the main chamber. He came up behind me and gave me a gentle nudge to alert me to his presence.

"Let me look at you, Tris," Gray Owl said quietly. "But you will have to sit down. You are too tall for me to treat you, otherwise."

I followed Gray Owl to a place near the edge of the platform, with Morning Star trailing along behind us. I sat down, as instructed.

"Many thanks, Gray Owl," I said. "I do not think anything is too amiss."

"I have asked White Cloud to bring in some snow," Gray Owl told me. "I will just clean you up and assess your injuries to make sure nothing is broken. What is it that hurts?"

"My brow, my eye, my cheek, and my nose," I said. I then put a hand on my chest. "Some places on my chest are sore."

Puh, Ria, Uncle Inlee, and Morning Star stood by. Gray Owl looked up at them from where he hovered by my side.

"Would you bring a torch or two?" he requested of the group.

"I will," Uncle Inlee volunteered. "There should be a few extras in the back rooms that I can borrow." And he left us.

"Would you look at Weasel as well?" I asked Gray Owl.

"What weasel?" Gray Owl responded absently, pushing back my hair to examine my forehead. "I do not usually treat animals, especially ones that are apt to bite me."

"The man who fought me," I clarified. "His name is Weasel."

"It is?" Gray Owl seemed surprised. "How extraordinary. Yes, I will look at him, if you like. Oh, here is the snow I requested. Thank you, White Cloud. Tilt your head that way," he motioned to my right, "and I will make a cold compress you can hold to your face while I see to the rest of you. Um, you will need to remove your tunic again."

I slipped the tunic over my head once more. I then gratefully accepted the snow-filled cold compress, nodding my thanks to White Cloud. I pressed it first to my left eye, hoping to keep it from swelling shut. As the snow inside the compress melted, water dripped down my wrist and then ran down my arm, but I did not mind. It helped to dull the pain. When that spot began to ache with cold, I moved it to my nose, then my brow, and thus moved the compress around to whichever part of my body hurt the most.

Uncle Inlee soon returned with two torches. He was accompanied by my children, along with Mror. Puh and Uncle Inlee each held a torch near Gray Owl and me while the others looked on solemnly. I was glad Gray Owl had wiped off all the blood from my face and body before the children came out, but all the same, they looked at me in horror.

Lily climbed into my lap and put her arms around my neck, while Pony and Raven clamored about me, each weeping and trying to put their arms around me too. Gray Owl patiently worked around them as best he could. Fox and Mror stared at me as though I were something grotesque. I regretted they had to see me like this, with my face bruised and cut. However, I supposed even if they did not see me now, they would see me soon enough, and the bruises would just become more swollen and colorful as time went by.

"Do not be too upset," I said to console them, "I am not hurt too badly." I smiled at them. "See? I am fine."

"Puh-Puh has ouch," Lily said, beginning to sniffle as tears formed in her eyes.

"Puh-Puh, what happened to you?" Fox asked.

"You have heard of The People's Challenge Circle?" I replied. "Well, it was requested that I take part in a Challenge."

"But why, Puh-Puh? Why?" Pony said, wiping her eyes and renewing her grip on me.

"Because there was a question about all of us being able to attend The People's Gathering. If I won, we all can attend." I answered.

"And you won?" Fox pressed me.

"I did," I told him. "Now all of us can come."

"Just let me put some salve on your Puh-Puh and he will be all right," Gray Owl said kindly to the children.

The children reluctantly moved out of the way so Gray Owl could finish his work.

"Muh-Muh, did you see the fight?" Fox wanted to know. "We heard a lot of noise outside. We wondered what it was all about, but we were not allowed to look out there."

"I did," Morning Star grimly replied. "And I sincerely hope that is the last time your Puh-Puh has to go to the Challenge Circle."

"Is the other man . . . dead?" Mror asked. Apparently he knew the rules of the Challenge.

"No, he is in the room. You will get to meet him soon," I said to Mror.

"Is he a bad man?" Raven asked fearfully, as though he might be scary to behold.

"No," I said, shaking my head and moving the cold compress to my cheek. "He does not seem to be a bad man. I wish I could have met him under pleasanter circumstances."

While this conversation occupied my thoughts, my attention to the ongoing meeting had lapsed. But I then heard Gray Owl speak to Willow Woman, requesting that Weasel be asked to join us so he could treat his wounds. Willow Woman called for Weasel to come forth. There was a stir as the crowd made a path to allow him to walk the length of the chamber.

After a few moments Weasel presented himself before us, still grinning even though one side of his head was now distended and starting to turn a troubling shade of purple. He had a wisent hide cloak over his shoulders, which made him appear broader than ever. He held his cloak around him by grasping the edges with his hands, thus prominently displaying his bloodied knuckles. The children gaped at him in astonishment. When Weasel gave them a wide smile, they seemed even more taken aback. Fox found the courage to speak.

"I have lost many teeth over the past few years," he said to Weasel. "But they grew back. Will your teeth grow back?"

"Me, too!" Pony chimed in. She made a grimacing smile to show Weasel her teeth. "See? One is still missing!"

Weasel laughed merrily at this.

"When I was child, I lost and grew teeth too," he told them. "But these lost teeth are gone for good. When you are a grown-up and you lose teeth, that is the way of it."

The children relaxed as they chatted with Weasel. Just as I had, they seemed to like him instantly. In fact, it was a bit disconcerting how quickly they forgot me. The children eagerly gathered around him while he talked and made them giggle.

Now poor Gray Owl had to once again try to work around a number of small beings. He asked Weasel to doff his cloak. Weasel obliged, baring his hairy, blood-splattered chest as he dropped the garment. He submitted to Gray Owl's ministrations with unflappable good humor.

"You will have to keep a cold compress on the side of your head off and on for the rest of the day, and even into the night if you feel it will help," Gray Owl instructed Weasel. "And take this." Gray Owl gave him a small satchel. "Take a large pinch between your fingers and put it your mouth. Chew on it for as long as you can stand it and then spit it out. It will help relieve the swelling and pain. I will forewarn you; it tastes terrible."

Weasel shrugged.

"Taste makes no difference. I thank you for tending to me," Weasel said. Then he turned me. "So, Tris, which of these little ones are yours? The big red-haired boy looks like you."

"Yes, that is Fox. He is my eldest," I said to Weasel. "The taller black-haired girl is my daughter Pony, the smaller one, my daughter Raven, and then the littlest girl with the red-brown hair is my Lily."

"You have a nice family," Weasel stated. His gaze wandered over to Morning Star. "And there will be more to come, I am sure. I have two children, myself. Two boys. My mate passed a long time ago, shortly after our youngest son was born. They live with my brother's family now so they will have a mother to care for them. I see them when I can."

For the first time since I had met him, Weasel appeared downcast.

"You must miss them," Morning Star said sympathetically.

"I do, indeed," Weasel admitted. Then his smile returned. "But I do enjoy seeing other people's little ones when I can. They remind me of what I have to look forward to when I go home. Come to me, my little flower!" When he said *little flower* it sounded like *widda fow-wah*. Weasel pulled Lily onto his lap to give her a cuddle, and she laughed with delight. "How I miss hearing that soft sound, the sound of children's laughter."

I suddenly noticed that all conversation within the Hall had stopped except for the words spoken by those around me. I glanced up to see that every eye was upon us, and people were gazing at us, looking as though they had come to a realization. It must have seemed incredible to view two men who had been pounding each other just a short while ago, now sitting together completely amicably, surrounded by smiling and laughing children. It occurred to me that this might do more to aid Willow Woman's cause than anything else we could have contrived.

Uncle Inlee left us to speak with Willow Woman and Black Wolf. They seemed to come to some agreement, and then Uncle Inlee began to address the assembly.

"I am Inlee," he started. "I have asked Willow Woman if I may speak to you. I wanted to tell you I understand why many have reservations about including others at your Gathering. When you are used to your own people and strangers are suddenly thrust amongst you, who does not wonder at the newcomers? Just as when you find a fruit you have not seen before, you may wonder if it is safe to eat or if it will harm you. My hope is, now that The People from the East have been on this territory for several generations, that you will come to know that most Old Ones have no idea of harming you. That not only are we able to contribute toward working together, but also, perhaps most importantly, that you will accept our friendship. I believe it is this bond that will be the most likely to help us endure hard times. I know I would not be standing before you now if not for the help I had received from my fellow Old Ones, and also from our Wolfmen friends, and from The People." Uncle Inlee then motioned toward Weasel and me. "I think the Challenge has been settled in the best way possible. The outcome has proved that Willow Woman is right to want us to work in cooperation with one another."

Uncle Inlee then looked to Willow Woman, who smiled and nodded approvingly.

"We will see what happens," a voice said skeptically.

"What Inlee say, Karno agree," Karno added. "*Woofmen* good friend. Good hunter. We make good music."

"Can we hear the Wolfmen's music?" someone asked.

"Yes! Please play your music!" Fox called out.

The other children quickly chimed in, pleading for the Wolfmen to play.

"I think we should quit for the day and, if the Wolfmen are willing to play, to listen to their songs," Willow Woman said, clearly pleased to find a convenient way to end the proceedings.

Karno spoke with his comrades, and they momentarily disappeared to collect an assortment of rocks borrowed from the edges of the hearths and chunks of wood taken from the stockpile of firewood. They soon began to strike a cadence on the wood and stones and chanted in strong voices. The Hall, so crowded and fuggy with smoke from the torches, now seemed like a magical place, as the chamber filled with the Wolfmen's songs.

We all listened enraptured, taking in the Wolfmen's rhythmic sounds and their amazingly well-harmonized voices. It was even more inspiring when a larger group of the Wolfmen was present, but nevertheless, it had had a wonderfully happy effect on all in attendance. After a few tunes, Weasel turned to me.

"Karno talks funny, but I do like his music," Weasel said without a trace of irony. He then noted that Mror was sitting in Ria's lap. "You said you are not a grandmother," he said to Ria. "The boy is your son?"

"This is Mror. Yes, he is my son," Ria said, still seeming rather displeased at being taken for a grandmother earlier. "I suppose it was an honest mistake; I was old when I became a mother. I did not think I would ever have children, so I am very grateful to have Mror."

All at once I remembered that I had promised to introduce Weasel to my family. I quickly presented him to all those he had not yet met. Weasel seemed impressed.

"Your mate is Black Wolf's daughter?" Weasel asked me. "That is a powerful alliance. But never mind, I am glad to meet your family,"

"I hope you will introduce me to your family as well, before the Gathering breaks up," I responded.

"I made the trip with one of my brothers and two cousins," Weasel said. "I will have them join us."

Lily had fallen asleep in his lap, but Weasel stood up gingerly so as not to wake Lily, and he carried her on his furry shoulder to where his relatives were standing. A moment later he returned, with his family coming up behind him. Lily was still sound asleep, looking delicate and pale in the powerful arms of this large, dark, hairy man.

We rose to our feet to meet these people, who, like Weasel, seemed to be quite genial. His brother and cousins were nowhere near his size, but they shared his rather disheveled look. We did not want to talk through the music and thus spoil the effect, so we did not converse much, but we did enjoy a pleasant evening together. Morning Star managed to coax Jura and her son Mino to come into the Hall's main room, too. Jura was still very shy of strangers, but now that things were much more tranquil – though it may have been only a temporary illusion of tranquility – it was a good time to encourage her to take part in the Gathering.

The threat to burn down the Hall niggled at the back of my mind. I suspected we would discuss it once we retired to Willow Woman's private rooms. We would need to be vigilant. When the Wolfmen stopped their music to partake in the evening sup, Willow Woman waved me to her. Morning Star had risen to collect a tray of food to feed all of us, just as she did every day when we were at home, so I spoke to the children first.

"I am going to speak with Willow Woman," I said. "I will be back in a moment. Do not wander away."

"We will watch them," Ria said hastily, knowing that Willow Woman was waiting for me. "Go ahead and talk with Willow."

Willow Woman sat with Black Wolf and Oak, just a short distance away. The many loud conversations in the Hall made it difficult to hear, so I sat close to her and leaned in to listen to her words.

"Tris, I am amazed by you, and I am truly grateful to you for going into the Challenge Circle," Willow Woman said, her hand on my arm. "Not only did you win, but you showed that there does not have to be animosity between our peoples."

"Weasel deserves half the credit," I admitted.

"Well, by losing, he certainly does," Willow Woman said with a laugh.

"I did not mean that he deserves credit because he lost," I began. "I meant that he proved we do not have to hate. I do not think he knows the meaning of the word. He must be one of the most good-natured men I have ever met."

"That amazes me as well," Willow Woman said. "His family has had very hard times. He knows only too well how many clans are on the edge of survival. There has been talk of their moving north."

"As did we," I pointed out, since my family had relocated to Uncle Inlee's lands in the North Country.

"Probably not as far north as you are," Willow Woman speculated. "You are almost at our northern border. But maybe closer to here. I would welcome them; they are good people." Willow Woman paused for an instant. "But that is not why I wanted to talk to you. As I watched the Challenge I was reminded of many things. Of how much I have come to rely on you and your family; how much I care for you. And it makes me so ashamed of how I treated you when we first met."

I took Willow Woman's hand and gave it an affectionate squeeze.

"We have spoken of this before," I said gently. "You have nothing to feel bad about." In truth, I did not feel that she had been ill-mannered – although I might have said she was perhaps a tad forward. Admittedly, at the time I had been taken aback, but I was not offended.

"I was so rude to you," Willow Woman told me, with tears glinting at the corners of her eyes. "I had never known any Old Ones before. I thought of your people as just curiosities who looked and spoke differently from us. I did not give you credit for being fellow creatures who had intelligence and feelings. You have been so kind in spite of all that, but I hope you can accept my apologies and that you know in what high regard I hold you. Especially now that I look into your poor face. Does it hurt very much?"

"I am fine," I said. "And there is no need to feel sorry. Not then, not now. We all can be forgiven if our first impressions turn out to be incorrect. At least, I hope so, because I have been guilty of harboring at least a few wrong impressions." Today's meeting with Weasel sprang to mind. If I had stuck with my initial hunch about Weasel's character from when I first laid eyes on him, I would have done him a real injustice.

Willow Woman surrendered a small smile.

"There are no words that can adequately express how much you mean to me," she said. "I can only hope that somehow you know, even without them."

"I feel the same," I told Willow Woman earnestly. "I am very glad I know you."

Slow Bear then approached me with a fresh compress filled with snow.

"Gray Owl asked me to give this to you," Slow Bear said. "I think the snow has stopped falling, but the wind has picked up. It will be a cold night. We will need to be diligent about feeding the fires."

"Many thanks, Slow Bear," I said to him. "It may be a good idea to keep watch on more than just the hearths."

Slow Bear nodded.

"I agree," he said, looking first to me, and then at Willow Woman. "I would not want the fires to get out of hand."

Willow Woman seemed to ponder this.

"Yes, I have thought on that, as well," she said. "I fear the threat of burning down the Hall may come to more than just a threat." She sighed. "The People have been very tolerant of me as their Head Elder, but I believe they would prefer Black Wolf to me. They respect him and they have become used to his sharing the platform with me. When Oak's turn comes, I am confident they will welcome him; he is the best of both of us." Willow Woman sighed again. Her eyes scanned the huge chamber. "Nothing lasts," she said. "This new Hall is nice, but I still miss the old one. I cannot understand how they could destroy the old Hall for its materials. I loved that place . . . for its memories and because it was where I met my dear Black Wolf. However, although it has taken me a long time, I have come to realize that not all people think the same way I do, and we do not always share the same values."

I did not know what to say, so I simply nodded.

"Willow Woman, do you want me to set up watches to keep an eye on things during the night until the Gathering closes at the end of the moon?" Slow Bear inquired.

"Yes, thank you, Slow Bear," Willow Woman responded, roused from her musing. "That would be wise."

* * *

The days of the Gathering passed without any further problems, possibly because of the vigilance of those who kept watch. Once the main business of the Gathering had been settled, it turned into a social event. Pairings and barters were arranged. Vendors did a good trade, but they soon left, as the worsening weather inspired them to pack up and return to their homes. Karno and his companions took their leave not long afterward. I worried about the weather, too. After all, we would be traveling with our families. It was difficult enough for grown men to slog through harsh conditions, never mind for our women and children. But we had agreed to wait until the end of the Gathering so that Black Wolf would be able to make the journey with us. We hoped to have a sufficient period of good weather when the time to travel came about. Else-wise, we would have to await fair skies.

In the meantime, Gray Owl continued to look after Weasel and me. I still had a headache, but I was healing well. Weasel's head remained alarmingly swollen and bruised. He did not complain; nevertheless, I felt concern for him. Even after the Gathering crowd started to thin out as more and more attendees took their leave, Weasel and his brother and cousins remained encamped in a corner of the main chamber. Gray Owl did not want Weasel to begin their long homeward trek until his condition had substantially improved.

When the end of the Gathering was drawing near, everyone had left except for Weasel and his relatives, and those of us who were still Willow Woman's guests. The main chamber was now dark and empty without the horde of people occupying it, and the stacks of firewood had diminished to one modest pile at the end of the room. The fires and torches in the chamber were no longer kept lighted, so the once-lively space became cold and dark.

Weasel and his kin then settled themselves around the large central hearth, awaiting Gray Owl's decision on when it would be advisable for Weasel to travel. I asked Gray Owl why it was taking so long for Weasel to recover.

"Do you remember when Black Wolf was clubbed on the head?" Gray Owl responded.

I thought back for a moment and recalled Black Wolf's long recovery.

"Yes," I answered.

"Well, this is similar," Gray Owl replied. "A little too similar, in fact. I am going to speak with Willow about taking Weasel with us to her winter lodgings. It is only a day's trek from here, which would tax Weasel, but it would not be as bad as attempting to walk all the way down to our southern border. That would take them at least half a moon, probably longer, given the weather we have been experiencing."

I was astounded at this news. Weasel was a large, very strong man; how had he been laid low by only a few strikes to his head? After all, Weasel had struck me in the head any number of times.

"Will he eventually be all right?" I asked.

"Yes," Gray Owl said. "I believe so, anyway. It will just take time. The swelling and the nausea have begun to recede, but when pressed, he still tells me that his head aches, his eyes hurt, and his left ear hurts, too. And he does not appear to be able to hear out of that ear."

"Will his hearing return?" I asked anxiously. To lose hearing, even in one ear, was a devastating loss for a hunter.

"No, I do not believe so," Gray Owl said, shaking his head. Then he looked up at me and held my gaze for a moment. "Do not feel bad, Tris. Remember, you took part in the Challenge only because Willow Woman requested it of you. Weasel volunteered. He knew the terms, and he was lucky to escape with his life. I did not witness the bout, but I was informed that you had several opportunities to kill him, if you had chosen. You spared him and he survived with a protracted severe headache and deafness in one ear. He was lucky. I, for one, would not get into a Challenge Circle with you, no matter what the impetus."

"How long will Weasel have to stay at the winter lodge?" I asked, thinking that his clan would not be able to exist for long without the support of so many of their hunters.

"He should be much improved in a few moons, but it is likely he will have to stay with us until the end of winter," Gray Owl explained. "His family can go home from the winter lodge without him and then return to collect him in the spring."

"That would make the most sense," I agreed. "I hope it will not be too hard on them to lose him for the season. With luck, he will be back to full health in time for the spring hunts."

"Yes, with luck," Gray Owl said with a smile. "It is fortunate that luck seems to favor him."

Chapter Eleven

The cold and snow are a heavy presence on the landscape. The winter's day is bright and sunny, but then a black spirit begins to overtake the sun. Darkness sets in.

I awoke from another night of restless sleep. A peek out the hide-covered doorway showed that the sun was just beginning to creep up to the horizon, staining the otherwise dark sky a pale pink. I had almost forgotten about the Dream of the sun's apparent demise. The spectacle of seeing the sun being blotted out filled me with dread. What would happen if the world were plunged into unending blackness? Would we then have to live by the light of the moon and the stars? I fervently hoped that this Dream was some vision from the Ancient Memories that my great-grandmother had told me about, and not something we would actually experience.

The journey home was long and arduous. The snow was not yet very deep, but the ground was frozen hard as rock. The air was so frigid that Black Wolf was not inclined to sing, as he often did when we were traveling from one place to another. I suspected that even though the cold prevented Black Wolf from singing, he was privately delighted to have an excuse to don his winter kit, which consisted of a hooded coat, mittens, and leggings, all of which were constructed of hyena pelts. The deep orange with black dots made for a distinctive outfit, and he was very proud of these articles. Black Wolf did not seem to mind the quizzical glances he sometimes received, nor the fact that the suit of clothing often caused dogs to stiffen with fear at the sight of him, barking and growling to voice their disapproval.

We had to allot extra time for setting up camp in the evening, to ensure that the trailside huts we erected would provide us with adequate shelter to ward off the freezing temperatures. Simple shelters such as those we had slept in on our way to the Gathering would not do in these conditions. We built our huts in areas that had enough saplings to bend into frames for our little enclosures, which we then covered with layers of pine boughs, and also used the pine boughs to carpet the floor, thus keeping us up off the cold ground. The children were especially glad to have Raena to snuggle with at night, as she provided extra body heat.

Our trip was somewhat shortened by the fact that we did not have to stop at the Fen of Falls, as we had on the way to the Gathering, so we used a trail that gave us a more direct route home. We did choose, however, to make a slight detour to spend one night at our former compound. We had not visited there since relocating to the North Country several years earlier, and we did not know what we would find.

I was excited to once again see the place where I was born and had spent most of my life. We had barricaded the doorways to our homes to prevent animals from taking up residence in them, just in case we were one day forced to return. We cleared the doorway from only one of the dwellings, Puh and Ria's old home, which was one of the few places where there was sufficient space for all of us to pass the night.

I looked around me while we worked to remove the branches and rocks that blocked the entryway, and I was saddened to see the neglected and desolate look of the compound. This place that once bustled with life was now littered with deadwood, and small naked bushes and clumps of winter-wizened weeds sprouted up in odd places. I was very curious to see how the home I had shared with Morning Star and the children had fared, but there was no time to take a look. As it was, we had much work to do before we settled in for the evening. After we unblocked the entryway, the chimney would need to be cleared. Puh had left a large stone over the opening and brush had to be cut back, too, before we could start a fire within the fireplace.

As we labored, I suddenly heard a familiar sound: the caws of a crow.

"*Kaw!*" Fox cried out happily.

I was not sure I could distinguish her call from that of any other crow, but Fox certainly knew his old friend. She flew to his shoulder, greeting Fox warmly. Fox seemed overwhelmed with emotion at the sight of

Kaw. When he took her off his shoulder so he could wrap his arms around her, she calmly let Fox handle her. After a moment, Kaw began to nudge at the edge of Fox's coat, and it became apparent that she was trying to find her way inside it.

"Kaw, I no longer have the sling in which you used to ride," Fox told her. "But you can go in my coat. It is warm in there. You must be cold."

Fox held open his coat just enough for Kaw to wriggle inside.

"Close up your coat, Fox," Morning Star admonished him. "You will get a chill."

"But Muh-Muh, I want to look at her," Fox protested. "I cannot believe she is here. Kaw must have heard our voices and came down to say hello. Perhaps she returns now and then to see if we have come back."

When we were able to enter the house, Fox brought Kaw in, too. It was dark inside, except for the light that came in through the doorway. Puh and Ria had left a few lamps behind, but we discovered that mice had eaten the fat within them, so the lamps were now useless. A fire at the hearth soon lent both warmth and brightness to the main chamber. Ria lighted a few curling pieces of birch bark and placed them in the bowl of a lamp and carried it around the home to determine its habitability. There were signs of mice, but no indication of larger creatures. The air within the house was musty, but at least there were no dead beasts or large droppings with which to contend.

I was struck by the thought that this place, once so well known to me, no longer felt like home. Generations of my clan had lived and died here, but it was strange to me now. Except for the things we had brought with us, all the items and furnishings that normally outfitted the dwelling were gone. Our voices echoed off the walls, adding to the general feeling of barrenness. I could only imagine how it was for Puh, whose history here was longer than mine.

The next morning, we closed the entryway and chimney opening once again, and Fox regretfully let Kaw go. She followed us to the nearby field where our deceased kin had been interred: my Muh, four of my siblings, Great Gran, and so many others. Kaw perched on Fox's shoulder while we paused to remember our loved ones. I was grieved when it was time to leave. Who knew when we might next come to this revered place; it almost felt as though I were losing them once more.

When we recommenced our journey, Kaw trailed us along the path for quite some distance, but eventually she turned back. Tears welled up in Fox's eyes as he watched her fly away.

"Farewell, Kaw," he said. "I will come back. Someday I will live at our old home again."

* * *

When the familiar sights of the river leading to the North Country came into view, we were buoyed to know our excursion would soon be at an end. I was thankful the snow had not yet fallen in any amount. There was just enough to cover the ground, but not enough to make it tedious to walk through, nor require snowshoes.

On the last full day of our trek we were intent on covering as much distance as possible before the sun began to set. The sun was about halfway through its decline when the dogs began to utter soft woofs of alarm. As usual, Puh and I were dragging our sled, which on this trip had runners attached to the underside to make it easier to pull over the snow. The dogs had run up ahead of our group; I could see them sniffing the ground on both sides of the trail, hackles up and ears facing forward. Black Wolf, Swift River, and Hawk were at the front of the procession, following by Morning Star, Ria, and the children, while Fish Hawk and Uncle Inlee brought up the rear behind Puh and me. Black Wolf signaled that we should stop for a moment.

"What is it?" Fish Hawk called to Black Wolf.

"Fresh tracks in the snow," Black Wolf answered. "Looks like a she-bear and a couple of cubs have passed by here recently."

We often saw animal tracks on the trail, but we usually liked to avoid a bear with cubs. I hoped the dogs and the noise created by our procession had motivated the bears to move off as soon as they heard our approach. We set out once again, keeping a sharp eye out for any signs of an irate mother bear. Her tracks had been well trampled by our feet by the time I saw them, but it did not look as though she was a large bear. Nevertheless, even a modest-sized sow can put up a surprisingly fierce defense of her offspring. If we had not been accompanied by our families I would not have been concerned, but I was always wary of potential threats when they were with us on the trail.

Morning Star turned to look at me, seemingly to gauge the level of danger by my facial expression. I smiled at her encouragingly. She gave me a wan smile in return and called Lily to her. Lily obediently went to her mother, who promptly picked her up and carried her as we walked.

We had not gone far when the dogs began to give out small woofs once more. This time they had halted at the base of a tree and were looking up into its branches. Black Wolf once again signaled for everyone to stop in place.

Perched up in the tree were a couple of very plump cubs, their eyes wild with terror, crying out pitifully as they peered down at the clearly vexed dogs.

"Tris, we must call the dogs off them," Puh said to me.

I nodded in agreement; the mother bear would surely be nearby. The dogs reluctantly responded to our orders to leave the cubs alone. We had just started to move forward again when the sow came bounding out of the forest. She froze in her tracks as soon as she saw us, vocalizing her displeasure, stamping a forepaw, and snapping her jaws.

"Her ears!" I said to Puh. One of her ears was missing, and the only evidence of her other ear were a few lumps of flesh and scant tufts of fur. Her head and upper body were deeply scarred. This must be the mother bear we had met in the spring, when she and her cubs were attacked in their den by the big boar bear. The sow had taken quite a beating before the whole thing was over, but it was good to see she had survived, even though she obviously was not pleased to see us again.

"Yes," Puh began, "I recognize her. She has only two cubs now. Let us back up a little and see if she will take her cubs away from here so we can continue on."

"Good idea," Uncle Inlee agreed.

We all slowly moved back, allowing the mother and her youngsters to leave the area without feeling we were encroaching on their space. We waited some while after the bears had disappeared from sight before we resumed our hike.

"Have good winter's sleep, little mother and cubs," Puh said as we passed the place where they had vanished into the woodlands, "and better luck with this year's den."

* * *

Our arrival at the compound was heralded by Black Wolf's dogs, which had remained behind with the rest of Black Wolf's family. Snow was falling once again, but our families and friends greeted us joyfully, embracing us as best they could amongst the excited dogs, which vied with the humans to give us the most enthusiastic welcome. Little Fawn seemed overcome with both relief and happiness at the return of her absent children, even if Hawk and Swift River were well on their way to being men and Morning Star was an adult with a family of her own. Little Fawn also had warm words for me and the children.

We had been away for only the better part of two moons, but I was saddened to see the change in Little Fawn. She looked haggard and thin, and her back more bent than ever. Little Fawn had once been a very tall, robust woman, but toil and strife seemed to have aged her beyond her years. Great Gran had once told me that Little Fawn brought about much of her own troubles, but still, I felt for her. She had been my mother's closest friend and someone I had known since my birth.

"Mama, you look tired. Did you not eat and sleep while we were away?" Morning Star asked her mother. "I would have hoped you might rest a bit without Da and the boys to keep you busy."

Little Fawn smiled at this.

"It is true your father and brothers make a lot of work for me," Little Fawn admitted. "Your sister Petal did much to help me with my chores and with caring for your younger sisters, but I worried the entire time you were gone. I did not sleep much, but I will sleep very well tonight, I think."

Swift River and Hawk approached their mother and embraced her, causing her face to light up with pleasure.

"My young men are home!" Little Fawn said happily. "How did you like your first Gathering? Did anything especially interesting happen?"

"Nothing much," Hawk said briefly, "It was crowded and hot."

"And noisy," Swift River added.

"But what happened during the Gathering?" Little Fawn persisted.

The boys exchanged glances and shrugged.

"Um . . . nothing," Swift River said, breaking away from his mother to go indoors. Like most of us, I expected he was eager to remove his pack and a few layers of heavy clothing, and finally get off his feet for a while.

"*Nothing?*" Little Fawn echoed as she watched them walk away, apparently surprised and disappointed that they did not come home with a lot of stories with which to regale her. "Tris, what happened to your brow?" Little Fawn suddenly asked me.

My face had almost completely healed by now. Gray Owl assured me I had only a few shadows of bruises, but the cut to my eyebrow was still evident. I did not want Little Fawn to be upset, so I hesitated as I cast about for a way to explain without raising her concern.

"I will tell you about it later, Mama," Morning Star promised, saving me from replying.

"You and Tris must bring the children over for the evening sup," Little Fawn said as we, too, left her to go to our own home.

Our dwelling had been unoccupied all this time, and it would have become very cold in our absence. While Morning Star took our children to rekindle the fire and light a few lamps within our abode, Puh and I maneuvered the sled to a place near our homes. The sled had been mercifully lighter during the trip home, since much of what it carried was food stores and warm clothing. The food stores had been almost completely consumed by now, and we had donned most of the extra clothing to keep us warm during the trek. Puh and I unpacked the sled, helped by all those who came to retrieve their belongings from the load.

As it happened, Little Fawn invited everyone on the compound to have their evening sup at the house she shared with Black Wolf and their four youngest children. It was a bit of a squeeze, but their home was the largest of any of the structures in our compound, so if we were to eat an indoor meal as a group, they were the ones most likely to host it. I worried that Little Fawn had taken on too much, but many hands contributed to lighten the workload. It was a jolly evening, with many stories and much laughter shared.

I have sometimes heard people say they *took a nap.* I thought this a novel expression, because it always seemed that *naps took me.* More often than not, if I slept during the day it was because I had nodded off, usually just before or just after a meal. Morning Star sometimes teased me about it, and the children looked upon this habit as an oddity to be casually shrugged off. In truth, it was not so much that I simply liked to sleep – after all, my sleep was often plagued with terrible Dreams – but apparently when my body craved it, it simply gave in to the urge if I sat still for too long. This night was one of those occasions. I was dozing soundly when Morning Star woke me to say it was time to go home.

I rubbed my eyes and rose to my feet.

"I am sorry to fall asleep during your supper," I said to Little Fawn in apology.

Little Fawn smiled and hugged me.

"Do not worry," she said. "This time you were not the only one. At least you did not snore like Black Wolf."

"I was just resting my eyes," Black Wolf retorted sourly.

"It has been a very long excursion, we all have good reason to be tired," Puh stated.

"And we still have much work to do to prepare for winter," my brother Ty said.

Ty had been one of few adult men left at home to do the heavy chores while we were away. He must have been glad for our return – not only to know we had survived the trek, but to know that he, Bewok, Bror, and Uncle Trae would now have assistance. The many tree trunks and branches, laboriously dragged to the compound, testified to their industriousness while we had been at the Gathering. The nine households on the compound would use a lot of firewood over the coming season, making the business of procuring wood a constant occupation.

By the time we were settled in our own dwelling for the evening, the fire had taken the chill off the air, and lamplight made it feel cozy once again. The children were wiped down and tugged out of their clothing before being sent to bed. It was not long before they were sound asleep. Raena, too, was snoozing in her favorite spot near the entryway. It was good to be home.

During the coming days we worked to set up winter windbreaks outside our doorways to help keep the warmth in and the cold out of our abodes. Although we had built windbreaks outside our old homes as well, this area was more open to the breeze than our former woodland dwellings, making the breaks even more of a necessity.

Our old homes had been dug out of a hillside, whereas these were only partially earth-bermed, so they tended to be draftier. During construction we did our best to seal any leaks with a combination of sticks, grass, and a muddy mixture of soil, pulverized grass, and water. Adding desiccated herbivore droppings helped to make the mud stickier, but we did not always have ready access to sufficient amounts to make it a regular addition.

We had no sooner finished with this seasonal chore when we were treated to a stretch of bright, sunny weather. The wind abated, making the days feel relatively balmy. On the second day of the fine weather, some of us decided to go hunting.

Puh, Black Wolf, Bewok, and I met shortly after sunrise. Our footsteps scrunched over a snow-covered landscape. We talked quietly to formulate a plan, our words coming out accompanied by foggy clouds. We would skirt the forest by the lake, and set up waiting by the game trails, hoping to intercept whatever animals might come to drink. The animal tracks showed us that a few deer and elk were moving through the area; we had plenty of smoked and dried mammoth meat, but fresh meat would be most welcome.

We located a spot where we could conceal ourselves on either side of the trail, Puh and I on one side, and Black Wolf and Bewok on the other. We were upwind, so we hoped our stillness would hide our presence from any potential game. We waited, motionless.

As the morning wore on, small woodland creatures that might normally take pains to avoid us began to forget our presence. Birds sang and flitted around us. Squirrels took advantage of the glorious weather to collect nesting materials and foodstuffs against the long freezing days that were not too far off. They capered around our feet, completely ignoring us. I listened carefully for the footsteps or the snapping of twigs that might signify the approach of a prey animal. But I heard only the sounds of my own breath, the gentle breeze in the branches of the trees, and the rustling of the few frosty leaves still clinging to the brush. Sometimes my ears caught the sounds of a squirrel's claws as it scrambled up and down a tree trunk, or the fluttering wings of a bird as it alighted on a limb nearby.

Without moving my head, my eyes occasionally wandered up toward the sky. Watching the changing position of the sun was the easiest way to judge the passing of time. The rising sun was behind us, but when it reached its apex, I would know midday had arrived.

Scarcely a cloud dotted the vast blue firmament overhead. Oddly, the day seemed to be slowly darkening. I could not yet see the sun, since it was still behind me; perhaps a cloud had arrived to temporarily filter out the brilliant sunlight. The shadows became deeper and deeper. It must be quite a large cloud to cause this darkness to set in. I was eager to turn and look, but it was paramount that we remain absolutely motionless while we waited.

Finally, I could not resist the urge to chance a quick look at the sun. I was stunned to see the horrible phantom orb of my Dreams starting to overtake it.

Puh noted with some alarm that I had momentarily turned around.

"Do not look behind you," he whispered to me.

I was mystified at this, but I nodded faintly in response. I sensed slight movement across the trail, where Black Wolf and Bewok must have also noticed the change.

"Do not look behind us," Puh said to them, speaking just loud enough to be heard.

"What are we not looking at?" Black Wolf replied, not bothering to lower his voice.

I heard them push through the brush and they soon joined us, carefully facing the same direction we were. All the while it was growing darker and darker.

"Puh, I have had Dreams about the sun going dark," I said to him. "What is happening to the sun?"

"Do not look at it," Puh instructed us. "I believe this is something that Gran once told me about. She said sudden darkness during the day meant that something very important was going to happen. When the sun hides, it is a sign for us to prepare."

"What sort of something? And why should we not look at it?" I questioned.

"Gran said that if you look, the view will take away your sight." Puh's words seemed illogical, but he spoke so very seriously I did not doubt him. "I saw you take a brief glance; are your eyes hurting you? As to what this might portend, I have no notion."

"The glare did burn for a moment," I answered, "and I saw a strange image of the sun in my view, even after I had turned away. It was as though the image had been burned into my sight. But it has faded away now."

"That is good," Puh responded.

"If we cannot look, how do we know what is happening?" Bewok inquired.

It was now almost as dark as night. The singing birds had gone silent. Stars began to materialize in the sky. I wondered if the sun had been completely consumed, but I dared not hazard another glance.

"We might walk to the lake and try to look at the reflection of the sky," Black Wolf suggested. "Would that be dangerous?"

"Clever idea, Black Wolf," Bewok said with a smile.

Bewok seemed intrigued by the phenomenon; he was clearly eager to take a peek.

"I would not want to risk losing my sight, not for even a glimpse," Puh answered.

"Should we return home?" I asked, worried that our families would be upset by the sun's ominous disappearance.

"We may as well," Puh replied. "I do not know how long this darkness will last. It will soon grow cold, and the animals will bed down as though it is night."

Thus, we turned for home, carefully shielding our eyes from the spectacle overhead. We had not walked far when it seemed the deep shadows that had overtaken the land were now receding. The stars blinked out, one by one, and birds began to sing once more. I was immensely relieved to see the earth come to life and the day begin anew.

"I believe the sun is now returning. The forest seems brighter, already," Black Wolf stated. Then he asked, "Do you still want to go home?"

"Yes," Puh said. "It did not last long, but I hope no one stopped to stare at the sun. I will be worried until we check on our families."

Just a few moments later, the sun shone as brilliantly as before. It was as though nothing had ever happened. We did not have far to travel, and we returned to find life going on at the compound much as usual. Uncle Inlee met us as we returned.

"You are back early. I assume you must have seen the darkness, too?" Uncle Inlee asked.

"Yes, we saw the sky turn to night," Black Wolf replied. "We became worried and broke off the hunt to come back and make sure everyone was all right."

"My parents had told us never to look at the sun when the sky grew very dark during the day," Uncle Inlee said. "So when I saw the darkness suddenly begin to creep across the landscape, I told everyone not to look. Some of them may have glanced for an instant, but no more. I must admit, I too wanted to look, but my parents said to look was to lose your eyesight."

"Tor said it portends an important event," Black Wolf said to Uncle Inlee. "Did your parents say that as well? Did they say what kind of event?"

Uncle Inlee appeared thoughtful.

"I do not recall that they specified," he finally answered. "I can only hope it means something very good will happen."

"That would be pleasant, indeed," Bewok agreed.

I was now slightly annoyed with myself that I had wasted so much time and worry over the frightening Dream. The terrifying prospect of losing the sun forever had ended up being a considerably less worrisome reality; merely relatively short period of darkness. Of course, had Puh not been there to warn us not to look, that might have indeed brought about tragic results. I was thankful Puh and Uncle Inlee had previous knowledge about these episodes of black suns, and that they were there to advise us to avoid looking at them.

By now, others began to join us, all eager for information about the unusual incident.

"Have you seen this before, Inlee?" Bewok inquired.

Uncle Inlee shook his head.

"I have seen the moon change shape during the night," Uncle Inlee replied. "It was never blotted out, but it did seem to wax and wane within the span of a few moments. But this is the first time I have seen this happen to the sun. Then again, it is a far different thing to stare at the moon. It does not make your eyes ache, which the sun certainly does. However, I believe my parents may have seen it. Or if not them, someone they knew had. Maybe even their parents. Perhaps Bror can make a story of this so it will go into the Old Ones' repertoire of tales."

Bror, my sister Ru's mate, was a Keeper of Stories, a role he had inherited from his father. Most of the stories were generations old, but Bror sometimes created new tales when inspiration struck. Bror had just come to join us.

"You want me to make a story about the sun faltering?" Bror said, having overheard this last bit of conversation. "That would make a good yarn. I will think on that."

Bror was accompanied by Fish Hawk and Uncle Trae. All three carried axes and were covered with splinters of wood and scales of bark. Now that the crisis had passed and the rest of the day was before us, I was reminded that I must find something to occupy myself.

"If we are not going to hunt today, I may as well help you with the firewood," I volunteered, turning to walk away, so as to retrieve axes from home. Puh began to walk with me.

"I will, too," Puh added. "We can try again tomorrow to bring in fresh meat."

"Puh," I said, "I am glad you and Uncle Inlee knew to alert us to the dangers of looking at the darkening sun. I had Dreamt of this, but my Dreams brought no foresight regarding the danger of viewing the sun, only the feeling of worry over what it might mean for us to live in a constant state of nighttime."

Puh shrugged.

"It is part of life to learn," Puh said. "I am still learning, too."

"I hope that is true for me, as well," I responded. "I also aspire to attain your level of restraint. You are always outwardly calm, even when I know you are not. You scarcely batted an eyelash when the deep shadows overtook us. No one would have guessed at your concern, had you not spoken of it."

Puh smiled at this.

"It is good to have command of your emotions," Puh said. "That does not mean that you are never to show your feelings, but that you can exercise control over them. It is important to show love, warmth, and joy when the situation warrants it. But it is also important to restrain your emotions when appropriate. Sometimes the trick is not to suppress or express your feelings, but to know what action is required for each situation. Thus far, you have behaved in a manner that makes me very proud of you. To be calm always is not possible, and sometimes a little temper has its uses: would you have been inspired to wallop Weasel as you did had you remained completely unperturbed at his . . . um . . . colorful remark?"

Chapter Twelve

The stinging snow pelts my skin as we hike. It catches in my eyelashes, causing me to wipe my eyes to clear them every now and then. I hear a sound and look behind me, but all I see is a trail of blood.

A moon had passed since the sun did its trick. I was pleased that no one lost their sight, but I still awaited the arrival of whatever momentous happening it might portend. Like Bewok, I was hopeful we could look forward to discovering that it might be something wonderful. Bewok himself certainly had good news for us: he and Twie were expecting their first child. While this was very fine, it did not seem to be the kind of event that would cause the sun to disappear behind a shadow, a shadow so large that it also darkened the earth below.

We were now entering the depths of winter. This was the season of spending most of our days confined to our dwellings. The penetrating cold probed our homes for any tiny inlet that might allow some of its frigid temperatures to sneak in, and raging winds shook the trees and piled up snow in deep drifts.

When the weather abated sufficiently for us to work outdoors, we drew water from the stream, first cracking the ice with our axes so we could access the running liquid underneath.   After we cleared away excess snow from our chimney outlets and pathways, processing firewood was another never-ending chore. After many days of being inside a dark and cramped structure, it was pleasant to spend time outdoors, even if the cold air made it almost painful to breathe.

Fortunately, we had so much mammoth meat to consume that we hunted only when the best conditions were present. We were therefore dismayed when Puh, Bewok, Bror, and I were on a hunt and the snow began to fall fast and thick.

We had managed to ambush a roebuck, and, after being struck by our spears, he had run into the dense brush as he tried to escape. We were obliged to follow his trail and finally found the collapsed animal where he had perished in a thicket. We gutted the deer and tied its hoofed feet to a branch, carrying it suspended between us. Using our spears as walking sticks to steady us and leaning into the wind, we trekked homeward.   The wind increased in force until it whipped the snowflakes into our faces, causing us to blink against the onslaught.

"I am regretting not bringing my snowshoes," Bror said as we laboriously made our way through yet another snowdrift.

"We will regain the path before long," Puh said. "It is not yet midday; we should be home well before sunset."

"If the snow were not so light and fluffy, I would suggest making a sled to carry this deer," Bewok started, "but it is difficult enough to drag ourselves through these drifts, never mind a deer's body, too."

Just as Puh had said, we soon found the trail once again. Our tracks, laid not long ago, were almost obliterated by the fresh snowfall. However, we were able to make better progress now that we did not have to fight our way through a tangle of undergrowth.

We had gone some distance when we heard a deep voice call out *"Halloo! Halloo!"*

The four of us stopped in our tracks and exchanged glances.

"That voice sounds familiar," Puh said.

"Yes, it does," I agreed. "It is not quite deep enough to be Black Wolf's . . ."

"Halloo! Halloo!" reached our ears again.

We stared into the wind-driven snow, squinting our eyes and blinking frequently.

"Who would be out here in this weather?" Bror asked. "We are a long way from anywhere, except our own compound."

"I guess the only way to know is to let him catch up with us," Puh responded. "Let us set the deer down while we wait."

Puh then let out a long, loud whistle to let the caller know we had heard him.

"*Halloo!*" then it occurred to me why the voice sounded so familiar. The husky shout sounded like *haw-woo*, rather than the usual *halloo*.

"That sounds like Weasel," I said, astonished that he should be so far from Willow Woman's winter lodge and so very far from his home. "I wonder what would bring him all the way out here."

"*Who?*" Bror asked.

"He must have recovered from his injuries," Puh mused. "He cannot have traveled all that distance alone. He must have some of Willow's people with him."

A moment later, a small band of humans came into view. At first, they appeared to be only shadows amid the falling snow, but then I was able to distinguish their forms as they fought to make headway in the storm. It was not until they were nearly upon us that I realized they were three men and one child, or possibly a small woman. Their faces were hidden behind frosted beards and icy mustaches, except for the smaller person, who was almost entirely enveloped in furs and clothing, so that only the eyes were exposed to the elements.

"I am so glad we found you," said a voice belonging to Slow Bear, Willow Woman's head of household and foremost advisor after Black Wolf. "We had been traveling for several days when the weather suddenly turned foul."

"I am glad you found us as well," Puh said. "What has happened to bring you here?"

The men seemed hesitant to speak. It was the child who replied.

"Mother has died," Oak told us. "Slow Bear, Gray Owl, and Weasel are bringing me to Father."

Tears formed in the corner of Oak's eyes, but he hastily wiped them away. It would not do to weep in these temperatures; tears would soon freeze on one's face.

We gasped at this news. I felt as though the air had been stolen from my lungs. I was speechless. I had last spoken with Willow Woman only a few moons ago; how was it possible she could have passed? We stood huddled together in the cold and swirling snow, trying our best to maintain our composure.

My mind reeled. It could not be. It just could not be.

"We must not cry," Weasel said in his peculiar bass. *We mus nah cwy.* But he was absolutely right. Then Weasel went on, "When we came upon your tracks and saw the fresh trail of blood, we knew you must be close by. So I began to shout, hoping you would hear us and guide us to your encampment."

"Of course we will," I said, finally finding the presence of mind to respond. Then I realized that Weasel did not know Bror and Bewok. "Weasel, this is Bror, mate to my sister Ru, and Bewok, mate to my sister Twie."

Bror gaped at Weasel.

"Now I recall where I heard that name," Bror said to me. "This is the man you met in the Challenge Circle."

"*Bah*, do not remind me!" Weasel said, wearing a small grin. "The next time I want to be thrown around and have my hearing knocked out of one ear, I will tackle a woolly rhinoceros."

"Let us recommence our trek," Puh suggested.

Now that we had been standing still for a little while, my feet were beginning to feel cold. Those of us carrying the deer hefted him up once again and we began to walk, doing our best to stay on the trail in the blinding blizzard. I speculated it was a good thing they had found us. As the snow obscured more of the landscape, it was becoming increasingly difficult to stay on the path. When Oak began to founder, Weasel picked him up.

"I will carry you, little man," Weasel said to Oak. "You just hang on."

The sun was well into its decline when we reached the compound.

"Bror, Bewok, will you hang up the deer while Tris and I take our visitors to Black Wolf's home?" Puh requested.

"Yes, Tor," Bror answered. "We will take care of the buck."

"Many thanks," I said to Bror and Bewok.

"Yes, many thanks," Puh added. Then he turned to the exhausted group that had followed us home. "Come this way."

"Thank you, Tor," Slow Bear responded.

We waded through the snow across the compound to Black Wolf and Little Fawn's abode. Puh whistled once again to announce our presence, and then we ducked into the weather break outside their entryway, and finally, through the thick hide curtains that covered the door to their home.

Black Wolf was sitting by the hearth, apparently resealing the seams of his boots with birch tar. He rose to his feet with a smile as soon as he saw Puh and I enter, but his expression quickly changed to one of apprehension as he realized that we were accompanied by Slow Bear, then Gray Owl, and finally Oak and Weasel. Black Wolf rushed to Oak's side.

"What has happened?" he asked as he knelt by Oak, brushing the snow from him and starting to help him out of his many layers of clothing.

"Father, I am so glad to see you," Oak said, flinging his arms around his father's neck and holding onto him tightly.

Black Wolf returned his embrace.

"I am so glad to see you, as well. So very glad, in fact." Black Wolf continued to hug Oak, who now openly wept.

"What is it?" Black Wolf questioned, becoming alarmed. He looked up at the rest of his guests. "Something has happened?"

By now, all the members of Black Wolf's household had gathered around us. Hawk and Swift River seemed unsure of how to greet the new arrivals, especially their half-brother Oak, while Little Fawn and her two young daughters, Sky and Dewdrop, looked on in bewilderment.

The men who had brought Oak to his father seemed reluctant to be the ones to deliver the awful news to Black Wolf. I did not feel it was my place to relay the message, either. No one spoke for a moment. Black Wolf seemed frozen in place. Puh then appeared to draw on some inner strength and then he took a few steps to close the distance between them. He put a hand on Black Wolf's shoulder.

"My old friend," Puh said sadly. "We come with the most terrible tidings. I am deeply sorry to tell you the beloved Head Elder has passed."

Black Wolf's eyes went wide and his mouth dropped open. Then he suddenly let out an anguished wail, the like of which I had never heard from man nor beast. Black Wolf cradled Oak and wailed again. It was a heart rending and yet frighteningly inhuman sound. No such noise could ever be issued from even the fiercest animal's throat. Black Wolf rocked Oak in his arms while both sobbed inconsolably.

My eyes ventured to scan the startled faces around me. Both little girls began to weep as well and immediately went to their mother for comfort. The boys appeared shocked to see their father, a huge and powerful man, so wracked with grief. I myself was beset by my own feelings of desperate sadness at the loss of my friend.

Little Fawn seemed to slowly grasp the significance of Puh's revelation, and the identity of the child in Black Wolf's arms. My esteem for her increased substantially as she appeared to gather herself up and approached Slow Bear, Weasel, and Gray Owl.

"Slow Bear, is it not?" she said, giving him a slight smile. "If you do not remember, I am Little Fawn. You and your friends must be so cold and hungry. Please set your packs and outer clothing here, then you may sit by the fire and I will get you food and drink."

They nodded to her with words of quiet thanks and began to shed their now-dripping clothes and packs. She then bent to pick up Oak's things from where they had been deposited on the reed mat floor covering and hung them up near the fire where they might dry. Pausing briefly to soothe her daughters, she issued quick orders to her boys to collect a number of food items from their storage area for her while she began to fill gourd cups with water. The first cup she offered to Oak.

"Have some water," Little Fawn gently said to Oak.

Oak stopped crying and, still sniffling, looked up at Little Fawn. She must have appeared so different from his mother. Willow Woman had been tall and quite stout, but despite her bent back, Little Fawn was even taller, and she was comparatively slim. Willow Woman's face had been full and most often quite merry, whereas Little Fawn had a very long, lined, drawn face that did not often smile. But now she smiled kindly at Oak.

"Thank you," Oak said, taking the proffered cup from her hand. Oak took a long drink.

"You will soon have something to eat, as well," Little Fawn told him.

"You are Little Fawn?" Oak guessed. "Mother told me about you. She said if I was ever to meet you, I must be very nice to you and respect you as a great lady."

"Yes, I am Little Fawn," Little Fawn said, seeming genuinely touched by his speech. She then left us, disappearing into the storage room from which her sons now emerged, toting a basket of tubers and slices of smoked meats. When Little Fawn reappeared, her eyes seemed damp as well. I could only imagine the conflicted feelings she now must harbor. She had eventually learned about Black Wolf's involvement with Willow Woman, but this was the first time she had been forced to confront the relationship, or at least the child that had resulted from the relationship.

Black Wolf seemed to struggle to master his emotions.

"How did it happen?" he asked, his voice breaking with grief.

"Our revered Head Elder passed in her sleep," Gray Owl replied, his own voice strained. "She did not suffer."

Black Wolf appeared somewhat relieved at the news Willow Woman had not been ill or met with an injury. He was silent a moment.

"I am grateful to you all for bringing Oak to me, and carrying this weighty news to me as well," Black Wolf said quietly. "I realize that some you have known Will . . . the Head Elder for most, if not all, of your lives and that she meant a great deal to you, too."

Slow Bear and Gray Owl thanked Black Wolf, but Weasel then spoke up.

"I did not really know Willow until recently," Weasel began, "but she was a very kind woman and she insisted I stay in her household until either spring arrived or I was healed. If not for her and her healer, Gray Owl, I do not know if I would still be alive."

Weasel pointedly looked at Gray Owl and nodded to him, as though to offer a nod of thanks.

"We are all indebted to her in some way," Puh stated.

"She was a great Elder," I added, feeling a tear run down my cheek. "And a great friend to all of us."

"Was she . . . interred?" Black Wolf inquired.

"She was," Slow Bear answered. "Much wood was needed to melt the frozen ground. We dismantled part of the winter lodge and began to dig where the room had been, since the top layer of soil was not frozen there. We burned all day and all night to melt enough of the permafrost to create the proper-sized grave. The rest of the staff is still there, erecting a suitable cairn to mark her place. The stones are all frozen to the ground, so we have taken apart the fireplace and hearth from the dismantled section of the lodge with which to build the cairn. The lodge is now only half its former size; I hope you are not upset at how we handled the situation."

"No," Black Wolf replied, shaking his head. "As I said, I am grateful to you. I hope you will stay with us for at least a while. You may have my room for as long as you would like."

* * *

Thus, Slow Bear, Gray Owl, and Weasel stopped over at the home of Black Wolf and Little Fawn; there, they decided to remain at least until winter had abated. It was a deeply sorrowful time. I could scarcely believe that Willow Woman was really gone from our lives.

One morning I met Black Wolf at the wood cache, where we both sought to collect an armload of firewood. The sight of the orange-and-black fur coming through the trees always gave me a start at first, but I was relieved to see it was only Black Wolf in his hyena-fur winter coat.

"Pleasant day to you, Black Wolf," I greeted him. "I have already picked up some wood from this pile . . . the logs are less frozen to one another over here."

"Pleasant day, Tris," Black Wolf returned. "Thank you. I will pick from there."

Black Wolf still looked perpetually aggrieved, but he had progressed from appearing to be in the throes of desolation to a resigned mournfulness.

"How are your guests settling in?" I asked. "My children are certainly pleased to have Oak living nearby. Fox, most especially."

"The men seem to be content to stay with us, and I am glad for it," Black Wolf told me. "I owe them much for bringing Oak to me. I hope they will remain here to be with Oak, as they once stayed with Willow. I suspect they will."

"I think so, too," I said. "It would be pleasant if Weasel could stay on, too. Although I suppose he will want to return to his family when the weather allows such a long journey."

"Weasel has not spoken of leaving us, yet, but I know he has two sons. I am all too aware how hard it is to be parted from those you love," Black Wolf said, kicking at some of the logs with the heel of his booted foot to loosen them from where they were still frozen to their neighbors. "I still have to remind myself that Willow is really gone. Over the years I was always waiting to be with her. But I knew it was just a matter of time and crossing the distance to see her. It is hard to believe that she is not simply at one of her lodges and that one day we will be together. But then, it is true that she is indeed at some distant place – a far distant place – where one day I will make the journey to be with her once again."

"That is a comforting thought," I agreed.

"In the meantime," Black Wolf started, "I am amazed not to have received one look of reproach, not one ill word, from Little Fawn. Initially, I was too absorbed in my own despair to think of her reaction to all this, but I have to give her credit for her generous behavior, to both me and Oak. Fortunately, Oak is an extremely amiable child, and he has managed to charm not only Little Fawn, but also our little girls, who are delighted to have a new playmate. I do not believe they yet understand that he is their half-brother. However, since Oak calls me *Father*, I think they will soon come to the conclusion by themselves."

"I believe you are right," I concurred.

Crunching footsteps in the snow made us turn our heads to see who was approaching.

"Hallo, pleasant day to you both," Uncle Inlee greeted us.

"Hallo," Black Wolf responded. "You have come for wood, too? Tris and I have been picking from here. Try this wood."

"Pleasant day, Uncle Inlee," I said to him. "How is Aunt Soosha today?"

Soosha was Uncle Inlee's mate, and I had frequently seen her bustling around the compound over the past few days. She, like Uncle Inlee, was about fifty winters old, and I thought she was being rather active considering her age and the inhospitable season.

"She is well, Tris; many thanks for asking," Uncle Inlee answered. "I believe she hopes to have everyone over for an evening sup, perhaps today or tomorrow. She has been gathering, borrowing, and trading all sorts of foodstuffs."

"She has?" Black Wolf said. "Is this about having a ceremony for Oak and Willow?"

"Yes. Plus, I think she just misses having our evening meals together, as we do when the weather is mild," Uncle Inlee said with a shrug. "We have not had our evening sup together many moons since. Also, I hear Bror has a new story for us. It should be an auspicious evening."

Black Wolf brightened at this.

"That sounds like an important evening, indeed," he said. "Please let us know if we can contribute anything to the meal. I will prepare Oak for the event."

"Good," Uncle Inlee said with a grin, "I will let you know if we need anything, but I believe Soosha has already gone to Little Fawn to raid your storage room several times."

We soon broke up our impromptu meeting, but later that afternoon I learned that we would be taking our evening sup at Uncle Inlee and Aunt Soosha's home that night. Morning Star claimed she had already informed me that we were to dine at Uncle Inlee's, but it must have slipped my mind. Also, it was possible she had told me while my thoughts were engaged elsewhere. It happened sometimes.

"Mama is helping Soosha with the food," Morning Star explained as she picked up the children's toys that lay about the floor of our home. Fox, Pony, and Raven had gone to play with Oak at Black Wolf and Little Fawn's home. Now we were left with Lily, who had just been put down for a nap. "I think Mama is excited that we will all be getting together. Mama seems happier lately."

"Little Fawn always did like to prepare food," I said. "Some of my earliest memories are of times spent eating with your family. Your mother is an exceptional cook." Morning Star gave me a look. I hastily added, "As are you."

Morning Star grinned at this.

"You flatter me," she responded with a laugh. "I know I am not as skilled as my mother as a cook or a homemaker. But she did try to teach me; I am sure she was frequently dismayed that as a child I would rather run around outdoors than tend to my chores at home."

"You do an admirable job taking care of me and the children, and our home," I said, kissing her cheek.

"Mama mentioned something about having a ceremony for Oak and Willow Woman," Morning Star resumed our prior topic.

"Yes, your father said something about it earlier today while we were speaking with Uncle Inlee," I said. "Is this about Oak becoming Head Elder, now that Willow Woman has passed?"

"I think so," Morning Star said. "Women are not included in these things, so I can only guess. But seeing as Oak is only a boy, I believe Da will be the one to actually take on the tasks — at least until Oak becomes a man. Mama is very proud of Da's new role." Morning Star then glanced at the children's sleeping alcove to make sure Lily was not still awake and listening. Lily was only very young, but she was at an age leaving her capable of echoing words and phrases she had overheard, sometimes much to our regret. "I also believe Mama is secretly relieved that she no longer has competition — that is, competition for Da's affection."

I was surprised at this. Black Wolf and Little Fawn had not truly lived as mates for many years, not since even before Black Wolf first met Willow Woman.

"Does your mother wish to . . . um . . . rekindle her relationship with your father?" I asked, skeptical that there was any hope of this ever coming to pass.

Morning Star shrugged.

"I do not know," she replied. "Of course, I do want Mama and Da to be happy, and I would be so pleased if they could come to terms, but they are so different. I am not sure it is possible. That being said, they are older now. Perhaps they both will have mellowed enough to find at least a sort of contentedness together."

"I would like that for them as well," I agreed.

When the time came to cross the compound to go to Uncle Inlee and Aunt Soosha's, Morning Star informed me that we would be toting our water bag, a basket containing our collection of gourd cups and several birch bark platters, and another basket full of roast tubers and onions. I carried the water bag and two baskets, and we stopped to collect our older children on our way to the home of our aunt and uncle. The basket of steaming tubers and onions threw off a tantalizing aroma that followed in my footsteps.

"Oh, Puh-Puh, that smells so good!" Pony called from where she walked behind me.

"I am so hungry," Fox joined in. "I will eat lots and lots! I will eat even more than Oak!"

Oak had a hearty appetite, but I was fairly certain Fox ate more than Oak did on a regular basis. I could not chide Fox for his appetite – after all, throughout my lifetime I have sometimes been noted for the amount of food I can devour. I had to admit that when it came to food and making love to my mate, my appetite was almost unlimited. Nonetheless, even I was occasionally startled at the quantity and frequency of Fox's consumption.

"It is not a competition," Morning Star said to Fox. "Just eat until you are full."

"Hungry, Muh-Muh," Lily spoke as she waded through the snow. "Have sup?"

"Of course we are going to have sup, you silly," Raven said, giggling at Lily. "Why else would we take our cups and platters with us?"

We had reached the weather break outside Aunt Soosha and Uncle Inlee's by now. It was a bit tricky to carry my load through the narrow, low-ceiled entryway, but Fox helped by holding the hide curtains aside to make my passage easier.

The stifling warmth of the room and the wonderful smells of cooking foods greeted us upon our arrival. Most of our neighbors were already here, so the space was rather crowded. Chatter filled the room, lending a very pleasant air to the assembly, but I felt myself beginning to sweat under all my winter clothing and I soon became eager to remove at least one layer of clothes. I could see where many of the attendees had already stripped off some of theirs, so I put down my burdens and added my winter coat and long-sleeved tunic to the heap. Morning Star, too, shed her coat and helped the children out of theirs.

Morning Star turned to look at me, and she blinked with surprise.

"You have removed your tunic," she said.

"It is hot in here," I stated. "If I get cold I can put it back on, but I can see that almost every other man has also removed his, so I cannot be the only one who feels the heat."

Morning Star simply shook her head.

"It is warm in here, but I would not say it is hot," she said. "You men are so used to being in the cold that you cannot take the warmth of being indoors."

This was true. We had discovered early on in our relationship that she very often tended to be cold while I tended to be hot. Even so, I knew Willow Woman frequently had complained of feeling too warm, and she very seldom spent much time outdoors, so these differences did not seem to apply to all men and women uniformly.

Aunt Soosha hurried over to welcome us. She was a congenial, energetic person whose industriousness never failed to impress me, even at her advanced age. She relieved me of the basket of tubers and onions and bade us make ourselves comfortable, wherever we could find space.

"Let us sit over there," Morning Star said, pointing to a wall where her father was already ensconced with Oak on his lap. My Puh, Ria, and Mror sat on one side of him, while Slow Bear and Gray Owl sat on the other. I nodded and followed her through the throng of people, wishing our friends and family *pleasant evening* as we passed by.

As soon as we sat down, Oak hopped off Black Wolf's lap and, brimming with excitement, joined Fox on the floor.

"Fox, look what Bewok made for me!" Oak exclaimed, holding a figurine in his hands.

Fox drew in his breath with amazement.

"Oh, it is a lion!" Fox said. "He stands on his hind legs like a man!"

Oak nodded vigorously.

"Bewok says I will be a Lion Man when I am big." Oak reached behind his father, trying to tug free something that Black Wolf apparently was sitting on.

"Have a care not to tear it," Black Wolf instructed Oak, shifting himself a bit so Oak could retrieve the article. "Your half-sister Petal went through a lot of trouble to mend the lion skin and make this cloak for you."

"Is it made from the lion skin you brought back from that mammoth hunt a few years ago?" I inquired.

"Yes," Black Wolf answered. "The one the mammoth tore in two when we tried to use the lion skin to scare it. Petal had a difficult time piecing it back together neatly, but now you can hardly tell where she mended it. The skin's torso is shorter because she trimmed off the ragged edges before stitching them together, but she did a fine job curing the hide and fixing it."

Oak had donned the heavy cloak, which was so huge it nearly overwhelmed him. It was a rather alarming sight to see the lion's skin, with the open-mouthed head still attached, enveloping Oak. Oak struggled to hold the ponderous garment around him.

"It is awfully big, but it is warm," Oak said.

"Too warm," Black Wolf chuckled. "That is why you took it off, remember? But do not worry about its being too big. You will grow into it."

Oak shed the covering but picked up his lion figurine once more, holding it close to his chest. I was intrigued by the novel carving.

"May I look at your lion figurine?" I asked Oak.

Oak held out the carving, so I took it from his hands. Morning Star and the girls leaned in to get a closer view of it as well. The figurine was indeed a lion, standing erect and wearing a hint of a smile. I had never seen such an amiable looking lion, but as this was a child's toy, it was only appropriate to make it appear friendly. Bewok had carved many playthings for the children over the years we had known him, but I believed this one to be his finest. Rather than being made of wood, it appeared to be carved of mammoth tusk. It was truly worthy of a future Head Elder. I returned the Lion Man to Oak, who smiled as he recovered his cherished toy. It was then that I noticed that Oak and the lion shared the same grin.

We ate a fine meal in relatively short order. In fact, the food was consumed so quickly I wondered if those who had spent days preparing it were at all discouraged to see the fruits of their efforts disappearing so quickly. However, it seemed nothing could dim the mood of this festive evening. Broad smiles were evident on every face.

Soon it was time for Bror's story. The fire was allowed to burn down so the temperature in the room might moderate a bit. Over the course of the evening, many of the lamps had also burned through their fuel, and now we sat in semi-darkness, fully prepared to listen to Bror with rapt attention.

Bror was silent a moment as he collected his thoughts. I had a moment to study him, this man I had known from boyhood. Like most of the men in our family's clan, Bror's face and hands were weathered a deep pink, but the skin on his torso was nearly bone-white. Bror had an exceptionally sturdy build, even for an Old One, and his left shoulder bore a large vivid scar where he had been swiped by a bear some years ago. Bror took a sip from his cup and then he started to speak.

Sometimes stories come to us through Dreams and sometimes Dreams come to us as stories. And sometimes, it happens the Dream becomes the story. A Dreamer once saw something very unusual in a Dream. The sun had gone out and we were left in blackness.

The idea of living in a land of perpetual night seemed preposterous, so he gave it little thought. But then, one day, the sun did begin to go out, and a shadow crept across the land, bathing everything in darkness. Only a circle of illumination remained to show that the sun was still there, but it was so brilliant that no one could behold it without snuffing out the light in their own eyes. Thus, we turned away from the spectacle and fervently hoped the sun would triumph over whatever force was attempting to destroy it. The sun must have been very strong that day, because it was not long before the sun threw off the evil darkness and a bright luminescence tiptoed in to replace the shadows with light.

It was said that a phenomenon such as this happens only when something of great importance was going to take place. Little did we guess it would usher in two profoundly significant events. First, we would lose one of the finest friends we would ever know, a great leader of her people. Her name was Willow Woman, daughter of Head Elder Standing Oak, and mother of future Head Elder, Black Oak.

We lament her loss and affectionately honor her memory, but tonight we also celebrate the second event, the ascension of The People's new Head Elder, Black Oak.

Oak had been listening attentively, but now he sat up straighter as he heard the names of his mother and himself mentioned. Black Wolf looked upon his young son proudly, but he also wore a deeply poignant expression on his face.

Bewok now rose to his feet.

"If it is acceptable, I would like to sing a last farewell for Willow," he said.

"Yes, do sing," Black Wolf responded eagerly.

Bewok had sung for the dead several times previously. This was quite different from the Wolfmen's typical rhythmic songs. The music simply consisted of wonderfully soaring notes, sung with such beauty that it touched my heart to hear them.

Bewok pushed his now-shoulder-length hair out of his face and closed his eyes for a moment. Then, as he opened his mouth, the truest tones came forth, so strong as to fill the entire room. I also closed my eyes to better absorb the sounds that flooded my ears. Tears began to stream down my cheeks before I realized that I had started to weep. This did indeed feel like a final farewell to Willow Woman.

When Bewok was done and I had opened my eyes again, I could see the many tear-dampened faces glittering in the low light.

"Thank you, Bewok," Black Wolf spoke, his voice strangled with emotion.

"Yes, thank you, Bewok," Morning Star added. "The song is so lovely."

Bewok smiled bashfully.

"You are most welcome," Bewok said. "It is a very old song. I suppose you do not understand the language, but it is simply the words *farewell, this is our last farewell to you, our beloved, farewell,* sung over and over again."

"Bewok, I thank you as well," Oak said solemnly. "Mother held you in high regard. She would be so pleased that you have sung for her in this way."

Bewok paused before he answered, regarding Oak with admiration for several moments.

"You are welcome, little Lion Man," he replied.

* * *

We returned home pleasantly sated. The children were happily tired from their visit with everyone and went to bed still gabbing about all the fun they had enjoyed. I was in the midst of building up the fire for the night when suddenly I noticed that all was quiet. I looked at Raena, who thumped her tail when our eyes met.

"Do you hear that?" I said to Raena. "It is silence."

"They must be exhausted," Morning Star said softly as she came into the room. "I think they were asleep moments after they set their heads down."

Morning Star began to extinguish our lamps. It was time for us to settle down for the night, as well. Our sleeping chamber was just large enough to contain our nest of bedding, and it was little more than a place to screen us off from the fire's heat and provide a little privacy. We removed our clothing and buried ourselves in the layers of blankets of various hides and pelts. We preferred to sleep in a cool room, which meant our bedding was cold until it was warmed by our body heat. I felt Morning Star shiver beside me in the darkness.

"Come closer, my sweet, I will warm you," I offered, gathering her up in my arms.

"Hmmm," Morning Star said, pressing herself against me and nuzzling her face into my neck. After a moment she said, "Tris, I love you."

Even after all our years together, those words always made my heart swell with emotion.

"As I love you," I told Morning Star. "And every day I love you more."

Later, we lay together no longer feeling the chill, and feeling wonderfully spent, but not yet sleepy. We were still embraced, waiting for sleep to overtake us.

"We are so fortunate in what we have," Morning Star whispered.

"We are, indeed," I replied, holding her tighter. "I count myself very lucky. I have the woman I have always loved; we have our children and our home, and we have all we need."

"Yes," Morning Star agreed. "I am trying to enjoy this time. Spring will be here all too soon and then you may have to go away on the spring hunts."

"I am trying to savor this time, as well," I said. "At least while we live up here, we do not have to travel far for the spring hunts. You have done a lot of traveling lately. Do you not think you might not like to try a spring hunt with us?"

"I think not," Morning Star said with a little laugh. "After that last trek home from the Gathering, I have had quite enough of travel for a while. Besides, next spring I plan to be very busy."

"*Very busy?*" I repeated. "It seems to me you are always very busy."

"I am," Morning Star concurred. "But next spring I will be even busier."

"How so?" I asked.

"Have you not noticed any changes in me?" Morning Star asked, placing my hand on her stomach.

If Morning Star meant changes to her stomach, the only time I saw it under lighted conditions, it was hidden beneath several layers of clothing.

"Do you mean . . . ?" I trailed off.

"If our good fortune holds, I will be taking care of our new baby," Morning Star said blithely.

* * *

The chamber is dark, dank, and dusty. An oddly bright light illuminates a small circle in front of me as my footsteps echo down a stone corridor. Then I see them: the ancient deer skulls with their broad spreads of antlers staring down at me from the rocky ledge above.

Author's Note

As usual, I will make the obligatory disclaimer stating that all characters depicted in this novel are completely fictional. Any resemblance to persons either living or dead is coincidental.

* * *

I would like to touch on something that I believe has been part of the human existence for almost as long as there have been humans. Our lineage is a complicated one. The Homo sapiens from which we are descended are thought to have come out of Africa. They eventually traveled much of the world, meeting various peoples along the way. Thanks to genetic research, we know they interbred with the Neanderthals and Denisovans, and possibly others, as well. There has been much speculation regarding the initial and subsequent contact between ancient peoples. Were they friendly? Were they hostile? Were they suspicious of one another, or did they welcome strangers as new-found friends?

Science weighs in with assorted hypotheses on the subject, but it's my guess that there is no one answer. Then, as now, it seems to me that the interactions would have run the gamut from quite pleasant and polite, to murderous and war-like. My portrayal of the characters' experiences is not meant to be examined under the lens of today's societal expectations. It is simply how I imagine it must have been for the people who inhabited the Earth approximately 40,000 years ago. As the Ice Age wore on and conditions worsened, I think they would have been forced to make the most of every resource, including their reliance on each other. After all, many species did not survive those extreme climate changes; humans may have only pulled it off by dint of ingenuity and by pulling together with their neighbors. Additionally, I believe humans newly arrived in a strange land would have soon recognized that the long-time inhabitants knew how best to exist in this unknown environment, which would have provided ample reason to seek out friendships and alliances with the local residents.

* * *

This book is dedicated with affection and gratitude to my dear siblings, whose ongoing love and support are so important to me, and without whom my childhood would have been very dull, indeed.

* * *

The next and final book in the series, *The Dreamer VIII ~ The Talking Stones*, is due to be released in the summer of 2023. Thank you for following along on this literary journey.

With warmest regards,
E. A. Meigs

Index of European Ice Age Animals

Antelope (Saiga Antelope) These small antelope (24 to 36 inches tall at the shoulder weighing approximately 80 to 140 pounds) ranged over a good part of the northern hemisphere. They are exceptional in appearance due to their unusual muzzles, which feature a long, flexible snout that looks much like a truncated elephant's nose.

Aurochs (Extinct) Predecessor of domesticated cattle. Size varied between 61 to 71 inches at the shoulder, with weights of 1500 to 3300 pounds. Their horns could reach up to 31 inches in length. Sometimes aurochs is spelled "auroch", but from

my readings, I am lead to believe that but the "s" is often included even when the animal is referred to in singular form because it is an alternative form of spelling "ox" and isn't intended to indicate plurality.

Boar Wild boars are the plows of the animal world. They are built for digging. Their heads and massive

shoulders make up a good part of their bodies and their large, sharp tusks, which continue to grow throughout the life of the animal, are very effective at turning over soil. The largest adult male boars can reach weights of nearly 800 pounds and attain a shoulder height of 49 inches. Sows (females) are much smaller and they lack the mane and thick shoulder/back "shield" of the boars. Their tusks are also of a more modest size. The coloring of their coats varies from anything between white and black, but most tend to run towards darker shades.

Brown Bear (Eurasian Brown Bear) Although this bear is called a "brown bear" its color can range from black to a tawny light brown. Males average 550 to 650 pounds but very large specimens can exceed

1000 pounds. Females weigh 330 to 550 pounds. During pre-history, the brown bear did consume some plant matter, but it was generally carnivorous.

Cave Bear (Extinct) This was a very large, stout bear. The average male weighed in at 880 to 1100 pounds. Females averaged a little over half that (495 to 550 pounds). Despite their size, bone analysis and other indicators suggest that cave bears were primarily herbivores.

Cave Lion (Extinct) (European Cave Lion) These efficient feline predators were some of the largest known cats in animal history. Based on skeletal

remains, it is speculated that the males may have reached 11 ½ feet in length from nose to tip of the tail, and weighed over 880 pounds.

Chamois A medium-sized goat/antelope. They are 28-31 inches tall at the shoulder and range in weight from 55-132 pounds. Besides being a fine source of meat, their hides were used to make garments.

Crow (Carrion Crow) A large black bird, approximately 18 to 21 inches in length with a large, heavy beak that is well adapted to catching and eating small prey such as mice, frogs, insects, etc., and scavenging off the kills of other animals.

Elk (Eurasian Elk) ("moose" in North America) A medium-sized elk/moose, now extinct in many parts of Europe. They average from just over 600 to just over 1000 pounds, with shoulder heights at 5.6 - 6.9 feet.

Fallow Deer A medium-sized deer, about 30 to 37 inches at shoulder height and weighing 66 pounds (small doe) to 220 pounds (large buck), although unusually large bucks may tip the scales at 330 pounds. Their winter coats are brown, but they are

freckled with white dots on their backs and sides during the summer.

Giant Deer (extinct) (Irish Elk) The giant deer was one of the largest deer ever to walk the earth. Commonly, it has mistakenly been called an Irish elk, although it was neither exclusive to Ireland nor an elk.

This huge deer averaged nearly 7 feet in height at the shoulder and carried antlers with a spread that could span 12 feet. They are estimated to have weighed nearly 1200 to just over 1300 pounds but larger individuals could have reached upwards of 1500 pounds.

Horse The Eurasian Ice Age horse came in many different varieties. They were more than likely the size of modern ponies and appeared in all colors, spots and stripes. They may have resembled the Przewalski's horse

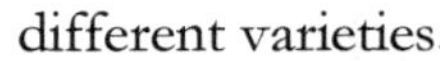

that still exist today or the now-extinct Tarpan horse.

Ibex (Alpine Ibex) A moderate-sized, dun-colored mountain goat. The bucks' horns sometimes reach 39 inches in length. The does' horns may grow to a length of nearly 14 inches. Similarly, bucks achieve a much larger body size (35 to 40 inches at the withers and weighing from 150 to over 250 pounds) than the does (29 to 33 inches at the withers and 37 to just over 70 pounds).

Lynx (Eurasian Lynx) The biggest of all species of lynx. Approximately 24 to 30 inches at the shoulder, and including its short tail, it may be 31 to 51 inches in body length. The largest males weighed nearly 100 pounds, but the typical lynx will run between 18 (very small female) and 66 pounds (good-sized male).

Marten (European Pine Marten) A small, weasel-like animal with dark brown fur, often with blond markings or a blond bib on its chest. At a little less than 3 ½ pounds and about 21 inches in length, the marten was hunted for its beautiful, silky fur.

Mink (European Mink) A small mink,

even the largest is just under 20 inches in length and only about 1¾ pounds. They have been prized for their dense, luxurious winter coats.

Porcupine (Old World Porcupine) This rodent wears an impressive coat of quills, some of which may be up to 14 inches in length (Crested Porcupine). These species of porcupines come in a variety of sizes: the smallest adults run from 11inches to 34 inches long, and may weigh between 3.3 to 60 pounds.

Red Deer (European Red Deer) Another very large species of deer. The buck weighs in at 350 to 550 pounds (48 inches at the shoulder) and does run 260 to 370 pounds (45 inches at the shoulder). These deer, unsurprisingly, are known for their

reddish coats. During autumn, the males often have a short mane on the backs of their necks.

Red Fox The biggest of the fox species, the adult ranges from 14 to 20 inches tall at the shoulder and weigh from 5 to nearly 40 pounds. These animals were often harvested for their fine fur.

Reindeer (Also known as caribou) This important game animal consists of several different subspecies and varied in size from 120 to 550 pounds. Color varied as well, but all subspecies shared many of the same basic characteristics, such as a fairly impressive set of antlers (in most reindeer, both the bucks and the does grow antlers) and a two-layered coat of fur, featuring a woolly undercoat that thickens

dramatically each winter and an overcoat of longer, coarse, hollow hairs.

Roe Deer (Western Roe Deer)

This small deer averages just over two feet to two feet, 6 inches at the withers, and a mere 33 to 77 pounds. Nonetheless, they were an important source of meat for prehistoric humans.

Sheep The actual breed(s) of ancient sheep that roamed

Ice-Age Europe are unknown, but it is recognized that sheep were hunted and eaten by early man. It is possible that the Mouflon (shown in image) is the modern day link to prehistoric sheep. The Mouflon have a shoulder height of less than 3 feet and weigh from 75 to 110 pounds.

Snow Leopard This beautiful cat is well adapted to life in a cold, mountainous habitat. It has a stout build and long, dense fur that varies in color from white to pale gray, with dark gray to black spotted markings. It is about 24 inches at the shoulder with a weight of 60 to 120  pounds, although larger males have been noted at 165 pounds. Their fur was considered to be very desirable and they have long been hunted for their pelts.

Vulture (Eurasian Griffin Vulture) This large scavenging bird may have a wingspan of over 9 feet and weigh as much as 33 pounds, although most individuals range from 14 to 25 pounds. It is known that early men consumed the meat of vultures. 

Wisent (European Bison) An impressive animal, the wisent is the heaviest land animal that still resides in modern day Europe. Fully grown specimens range from 5 to 6 ½ feet at the shoulder and weigh 660 (small female) to

more than 2000 pounds (large male). The wisent was an important source of food and hides for prehistoric humans.

Wolf (Eurasian Wolf) These are the largest of the European or Asian wolves. Their sizes vary greatly from 70 to 212 pounds. Although their coats could be black, white, or even reddish, by far the

most common color was a grey/buff and white combination of medium length, dense fur.

Wood Grouse (Western Capercaillie) This Eurasian bird is the largest of the grouse species, weighing as much as 15 pounds. The cocks have an average weight of 9 pounds and a wingspan of 36 to 48 inches. The hen is considerably more modest in size, with a weight of  approximately 4 pounds and a wingspan of 28 inches.

Woolly Mammoth (Extinct) This large mammal lived in Eurasia and North America, and was similar in size to today's African Elephants, but with considerably longer tusks, a shorter tail, and much smaller  ears. The males of this huge species could attain heights of up to 11 feet at the withers and weigh over 12,000 pounds. Females were somewhat smaller, although still impressive in size at up to 9½ feet at the shoulder and weights up to nearly 9000 pounds. Their hairy hides came in a wide range of colors that could be anything from blond to quite dark. They were protected from the extreme Ice Age weather conditions by a double fur coat that consisted of a short, dense, woolly undercoat and strands of long outer guard hairs.

Woolly Rhinoceros (Extinct) Looking much like a  modern rhinoceros in a heavy fur coat, the woolly rhinoceros sported two horns on its long snout and carried its thick body on short, stout legs. This animal averaged about 4000 to 6000 pounds, with a shoulder height of about 6½ feet. The larger front horn that grew from the woolly rhinoceros' nose could reach lengths of 24 inches.

About the Author
E.A. Meigs

I was raised on Cape Cod (Brewster, Massachusetts, USA) at a time when the Cape was still a rural area made up of woodlands, marshes, beaches, streams, and ponds. There, my life was divided between the land and sea. My father was a commercial fisherman, backyard boat builder, and an outdoorsman; so I had an early introduction to boats, working in the commercial fishing industry and spending lots of time in the local fields and forests. When I wasn't on a boat or roaming around the great outdoors, chances are I was reading or writing. I have been a compulsive writer literally since I could first put words on paper, producing my first full length novel at ten years old. Even at that age, my goal in life was to someday find a way to combine my love of nature, the outdoors, and writing.

After raising a family and embarking on a long and varied career that included many years working on and around boats and in the commercial fishing industry; a stint with Florida Fish & Wildlife in a small field office; and other jobs that actually allowed me to use my writing skills, I awoke one day with *The Dreamer* in my head. I began writing the novel with the intention of producing just one book, but as the story progressed it became apparent that the plot would require much more than one volume to tell the tale.

I have two wonderful adult daughters and nine delightful grandchildren. I am an avid camper and I strive to get out hiking as often as possible, daily, when my schedule allows.